AF265949

Also by Glenda Goertzen

The Prairie Dogs Adventures

The Prairie Dogs
City Dogs
Miracle Dogs

Lady Oak
ABROAD

GLENDA GOERTZEN

Library and Archives Canada Cataloguing in Publication

Goertzen, Glenda, author
Lady Oak abroad / Glenda Goertzen.

(Audrey O'Krane chronicles ; 1)
Issued in print and electronic formats.
ISBN 978-0-9879232-2-6 (pbk.)
ISBN 978-0-9879232-1-9 (ebook)

I. Title. II. Series: Goertzen, Glenda. Audrey O'Krane
chronicles ; 1

PS8613.O37L23 2014   C813'.6   C2014-908264-9
                                     C2014-908265-7

Published in Canada

Hazeldell Productions
Prince Albert, Saskatchewan

Printed at CreateSpace

Lady Oak

ABROAD

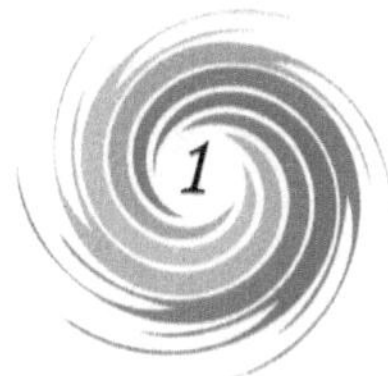

Failing Pierre Elliot Trudeau

The first winter solstice of the new millennium (the real millennium, not the fake one that had everyone freaking out the year before) fell on my seventeenth birthday. This was also the day I got expelled from Pierre Elliot Trudeau Collegiate and found three strange men living in an igloo in my front yard. No, not an igloo—a quinzhee. But that comes later. On with the expulsion.

The principal called me into her office late that afternoon. She flinched as I blew into the room and shucked my backpack. It was the last day of school before Christmas break, and I was more hyper than usual. I flopped into a wooden chair and bounced right out of it, nearly taking a header across Jersicke's desk. I had forgotten about my new birthday tattoo. I sat down again more carefully. Jersicke straightened the photo I had knocked over. Her mouth scrunched so tight, red and white lines radiated from her lips. I sighed and scowled at my hiking boots, wondering what I had done wrong this time. I used to smoke weed and get into all kinds of trouble, but that was years ago. Since I hit senior year I'd been getting completely acceptable marks and hardly ever skipped class. I was even punctual, most days. I had stopped trying to fit in with the cool-but-boring crowd, and now hung around with the weird-but-interesting crowd who got me hooked on bizarre crap like *Star Trek* and *Lord of the Rings*.

"Here at Pierre Elliot Trudeau, our motto is ROAR. Respect, Optimism, Attitude and Responsibility," Jersicke announced.

Conversations with Jersicke made you want to look over your shoulder to see if you had wandered onto the set of a TV commercial. Her office looked like an ad for a used car lot. Every vertical surface was plastered with posters advertising school achievements, with an entire wall dedicated to her own accomplishments. The photo I had knocked over showed her shaking hands with Prince Charles during his tour of Saskatchewan in April. Rumour had it she planned to run for mayor before she turned fifty.

"You, Audrey O'Krane, have displayed none of these qualities," Jersicke went on. "I'm sorry to say you have failed Pierre Elliot Trudeau, and therefore we must fail you. You are expelled."

My head snapped up. "What? Why?"

Jersicke slammed a handful of papers down on her desk. I stared at them blankly. It was a short story I had written for English class last week.

"How dare you. How dare you!" A red stain crawled up her neck. "Because of your obvious emotional difficulties, we've been willing to tolerate your behavioural challenges over the years, but this goes beyond what any school would tolerate."

Emotional difficulties? Excuse me? "I know I handed it in late, but Mr. Weldon said—"

"I'm referring to the content of the work. I am shocked that any student of mine could write something so repulsive!"

The light dawned. I'd written a story about two lesbian teachers who deny their love for one another because they think it will damage their careers. In the end they go public with their relationship, only to be shot by their deranged and bigoted principal. I'm no great writer, but I liked this one. I had even let my friend Irene post it on the school newspaper's website.

"I've been receiving enraged phone calls from parents. And the teachers are livid. They're ready to box your ears, and I don't blame them."

Box my ears. I didn't think people said this anymore. I wasn't even sure what it meant. It sounded like something the Mafia would do. I pictured Aunt Ellen receiving a mysterious package in the mail. She opens the box and faints upon finding my severed ears wrapped in a note: *Don't mess with Pierre Elliot Trudeau.*

"Because the characters are lesbians?" I said.

"Of course not. Your choice of lifestyle has nothing to do with our decision to expel you. This story—"

"*I'm* not a lesbian! I have a boyfriend. He's in university," I added, as if having a university-aged boyfriend would help my case. Going by the look on her face, it didn't. It was a lie, anyway. Lyle had dumped me in the spring. "And if I was a lesbian, so what? Did you even read the story? There's no sex in it. Well, there's *implied* sex, but no *described* sex. And no graphic violence, either, it all happens, like, off screen, or maybe I should say off page—"

Jersicke cut off my babbling with a slicing motion of her hand. "I did read it, and you know perfectly well what the problem is. This story was meant to humiliate me and the teachers you so obviously drew upon for inspiration."

"No, it wasn't like that! They're not supposed to resemble anyone real." A cowardly quiver shook my voice. I tried to swallow it down. "Look, I'll apologize to the teachers."

"It's too late for that, Audrey," Jersicke said coldly. "This time you've behaved yourself into a corner you can't talk your way out of."

Geez, how old did she think was I, ten? "I want to talk to the guidance counsellor."

"I don't think a school employee would meet your counselling requirements, Audrey, especially with your background. In September, you brought a weapon to school."

"Weapon? It was a Swiss army knife!"

I had put it in my backpack when Irene and I went camping and then forgot to take it out when I came back to school in the fall. I was showing off the tool attachments to my classmates when one of the teachers noticed it had a knife. You would have thought I was walking around with a switchblade. If I'd actually wanted to hurt someone with it, they would have had to wait around patiently while I broke a thumbnail wrestling the little blade out of the handle. After September's terrorist attacks and all the school shootings in the news, a few teachers had decided every student was a potential murderer and every backpack held potential weapons of mass destruction.

Jersicke's lips drew even tighter. "And before that, you were admitted to the psychiatric ward of the hospital for a suicide attempt."

"That's private!" I was on my feet now, shouting. "And it wasn't a suicide attempt. There was a mouse . . ." I trailed off. There was no way to explain the incident and still maintain an aura of sound mental health.

She shook her head, eyes brimming with false pity. "Audrey, you're a tragedy waiting to happen. And I will not let it happen in my school. In the best interests of both Pierre Elliot Trudeau and yourself, I am expelling you."

A shudder ran over me, and to my horror, I started to cry.

Jersicke was no stranger to students bawling in her office, but my tears had an odd effect on her. She stared at me, the red flush draining from her face. "You . . . Audrey, how old are you?"

At the moment I really did feel ten years old. I tried to pull myself together. "You can't do this. I'll tell the school board. I'll tell the newspapers."

She blinked at me, then gave her head a shake and picked up the phone. "I'm going to have some of the teachers escort you out of the school. You can tell your parents to pick up your things in the new year."

"My parents are dead," I said, and as I backed out of the room I saluted her, Trudeau style.[1]

---

[1] If this confuses you, look up the phrase "Trudeau salute."

The Quinzhee

I didn't wait for the teachers to escort me out. I ran to my car, shoving people out of my way, and drove straight home. On the way, I turned on the radio and listened to the news, hoping the world's problems would make my own seem trivial. New York firefighters had finally put out the smouldering fires of the World Trade Center wreckage. U.S. military forces were bombing caves in Afghanistan in their endless hunt for the elusive terrorist Osama Bin Laden. Wars, riots, disease, starvation, pollution, corruption, blah, blah, blah. This planet was a waste of space. I wished we could throw it away and start over.

I had been staying with Irene for a couple of days to help her paint a mural in her bedroom, and things at home had changed in my absence. A rusty old van stood in front of our house, and a pointy igloo stood in the front yard. The three middle-aged men inside the igloo welcomed me politely when I crawled through the tunnel entrance.

"Hey," I said, and carefully backed out. The strangers seemed to think there was nothing unusual about camping in my front yard, and I didn't want to disagree in case they were psychopaths.

Entering the house, I found myself confronted by an unfamiliar butt protruding from the back of the refrigerator, which had been dragged to the center of the kitchen.

"Is something wrong with the fridge?" I asked, dancing to avoid the welding sparks that skittered across the linoleum like fiery spiders.

"Compressor," the butt muttered.

I picked up a vase of red carnations from the kitchen table, struck by the urge to tuck one of the blossoms into the fuzzy buttcrack peeping over the leather tool belt. My guidance counsellor told me I could fend off these impulses by pausing to review the consequences. For example, in response to my floral assault, the butt might:

a) Strike its head on some vital component within the fridge, destroying the appliance and rendering itself unconscious.

b) Attack me with its welding torch.

c) Say "Thank you!" and continue with its work.

The butt's efforts knocked a fridge magnet to the floor. A photo went fluttering after it. I grabbed it in mid-flight. It was the picture I had taken of my aunt and Prince Charles while he visited a local attraction, the weir across from our house. She had just walked straight over to the delegation and started nattering away at the future king of England as if she had known him all her life. He graciously refrained from having her arrested, even laughed when she went all flirty. I smiled now, though I had suffered near-fatal embarrassment at the time.

A car door slammed. I rushed to the blinking answering machine and pressed PLAY.

"Good afternoon, Ms. Trini. This is Pamela Jersicke calling from Pierre Elliot Trudeau Collegiate. I regret to inform you—" I hammered the STOP button with my thumb.

"Trudeau! You can blame him for all that metric crap, God rest his soul," the butt shouted from the depths of the fridge.

"Ok," I said. I erased the message and met Aunt Ellen at the door. She downloaded a hundred pounds of groceries into my arms and gave me a refreshing winter hug.

"Happy birthday, sweetie. I thought you were spending another night at Irene's house?"

"I changed my mind. I'm staying home tonight."

"Are you? Oh dear."

Normally that "oh dear" would not have slipped past me, but today my mind dwelled on other matters. "Aunt Ellen, there are three men living in an igloo in the front yard."

"I know," Aunt Ellen chirped as she struggled to free herself of multiple layers of winter gear. "How was school?"

I put down the groceries and helped her wrestle off her boots. "Don't ask. Who are they?"

Aunt Ellen paused and scratched her fluffy copper head. "I don't know."

"You don't know the strangers camping on our property."

"They're professors from the university. I just can't remember their names. Look, I bought those little chocolate Santas you like so much, and some candy canes for the tree."

I grabbed the Safeway bags and followed her into the kitchen. "Aunt Ellen, why is there an igloo in our front yard?"

"Not an igloo—a quinzhee. This is Bernie," she introduced the grunting butt beneath the fridge. The butt twitched at the sound of its name, and a sooty, goggled face emerged for a moment before ducking back into the cave. "While I was babysitting Kelly she found an article on the Internet about Dene snow houses, so we decided to build one. A TV station ran a story on it, which inspired people all over town to drive over with truckloads of snow. In return, I invited them to spend the night in it."

Kelly Winters lived down the street. She was an amazing kid, one of those child prodigies. She was in first grade and could read like she was my age. We had bonded over our love of books and our lack of parents. Kelly's widowed mother was "abroad," according to Aunt Ellen, travelling for months at a time for some high up government job. I'd never met her. Kelly was basically being raised by her uncle. They had moved into the neighbourhood about a year ago.

"I'm not sure I like the idea of half the city sleeping in our front yard," I said.

"Oh, they'll be fine. It's quite safe. The walls are very sturdy."

When Bernie Buttcrack and the professors left, Aunt Ellen took me out to have a look. The quinzhee filled the entire yard, a giant snow cone whose peak rose higher than the eaves of the house. Inside, the ice-glazed walls glowed faintly from the early solstice sunset. Aunt Ellen lit the candles embedded in snow shelves protruding from the walls. The candles and the lingering body heat from the professors made it surprisingly warm.

"The professors ate the ice cream!" Aunt Ellen said indignantly. She had brought some of the fridge stuff out here while Bernie was working on it.

"Winter turns prickly in my nose," a muffled voice sang as we emerged from the tunnel entrance. "It burns my ears and bites my toes. Happy birthday, Audrey Oak! D'you like the quinzhee? Uncle Nick and I helped build it."

A kid perched on the peak of the snow house. I squinted at the tiny patch of face visible between toque and scarf, deep within the fuzzy cave of the kid's parka hood.

"Hi, Kelly. Yeah, the quinzhee's cool. Do you think you should be up there, kiddo? It's pretty high."

"No it's not. Look!" Kelly hurled herself backwards and landed flat on her back in the snow. I gasped arctic air into my lungs and went into a coughing fit as my bronchial tubes froze shut. By the time I recovered, Kelly had climbed the quinzhee again, a miracle of agility in clunky boots and fifty pounds of clothing.

"Get down from there, Kelly." Nicholas Winters approached our yard with a stern look for his niece and a cold one for me. "Good afternoon, Lady Trini."

My friends thought Winters was hot, with his scowling eyebrows and sulky Mick Jagger mouth. I just couldn't see it. Not only was he nearly twice our age, he was condescending, self-absorbed, and the poster boy for the Overprotective Parent. He wouldn't even let me babysit Kelly. He trusted her only with Aunt Ellen. According to Aunt Ellen he was from Switzerland, her own home country. He and Aunt Ellen spoke with an accent they classified as Swiss but which my friends described as a weird combination of Scottish and Jamaican.

"I thought you were staying elsewhere tonight," he said.

"I changed my mind," I said. Like it was any of his business.

"I see." He frowned his disapproval of my presence in my own front yard before turning back to Aunt Ellen. "Are you all set for . . . Christmas, then, Lady Trini?" He always called her "Lady." Aunt Ellen said it was a Swiss thing.

"Yes," she said with an odd intensity. "I am ready."

"I wish you'd let me join you. I don't trust—" He broke off, his frown deepening as he glanced at me.

"I know, but your presence would complicate things," Aunt Ellen said.

I looked from one to the other. This conversation was getting a little strange.

"I have something for you." He produced two copies of Kelly's school picture. "I would be grateful if you could have one delivered to her mother . . . though I can't imagine it will please her."

I grabbed the pictures from him. "What are you talking about? She's adorable."

"As always." His expression turned even more sour. God, what a jerk. Too lazy to buy himself a couple of stamps, and he can't stand his own niece's picture.

"Can we sleep in the quinzhee tonight, Uncle Nick?" Kelly asked. She had flung herself in the snow again and was flailing her arms and legs like a stranded turtle to make a snow angel.

"No. Come on home, now." Kelly groaned pathetically, but her uncle wasn't moved. She threw her arms around me and demanded a hug and a kiss, which I provided, although it took some time to find my way through all the layers around her face.

Aunt Ellen nudged me toward Winters. "Don't forget a hug for Kelly's uncle!" I turned on her, appalled.

"That won't be necessary. Best of luck to you, Lady Trini." Winters offered me a cool nod before taking his niece home for supper. I fought the urge to chuck a snowball at the back of his head. Not one word about my birthday!

"What was all that about?" I asked.

"About time you learned some manners, Audrey O'Krane," Aunt Ellen scolded. "You could show a bit of civility toward the man."

"Geez, Aunt Ellen. Why don't you just rip off my clothes and holler, 'She's all yours, Winters!'"

"Don't be crude, Audrey. I just think it would do us well to be on good terms with Nicholas Winters. He's well connected—he could help you find a job once you graduate."

I winced. "Um, Aunt Ellen . . ."

"Do you have something to tell me, Audrey?" She peered closely at me. "Have you experienced anything . . . unusual today?"

"No!" I said, taken aback by her sudden perception. "Um, no. Everything's fine." I just couldn't tell her. Aunt Ellen put a lot of emphasis on education. Back in Switzerland she'd been a history professor. She was retired now, but volunteered at Kelly's school. Mainly, I think, because Nicholas Winters wanted her to keep an eye on Kelly. Rather than spoil the holidays for us, I'd tell her after Christmas.

Aunt Ellen whipped up a fantastic birthday supper, but I had little appetite. Normally she would have questioned my lack of enthusiasm for my favourite foods, but tonight she seemed even more flighty and distracted than usual. I did manage to show enthusiasm for her gift, a digital camera to replace my old 35 mm, but my excitement faded quickly. After supper I dragged myself into the bathroom, feeling depressed and achy. I got out my toothbrush, glanced up at the mirror and screamed.

Aunt Ellen rattled the doorknob. "What's wrong, Audrey?"

"Nothing! I thought I saw a mouse." What I had seen, or imagined I saw, were facial wrinkles and grey streaks in my hair. I really, really needed sleep.

"You and your mice," Aunt Ellen muttered as her footsteps faded down the hall.

I showered myself pink, slipped into bed, and snapped wide awake. After hours of tossing and turning, I got up and headed for the kitchen, where I microwaved some cider. I took my steaming cup into the dark living room to do some serious sipping and pacing.

As I passed the front window and looked outside, I nearly dropped my cup. An intense, fluctuating light shone through the silvery walls of the quinzhee. A whisper of pale mist rose from the luminous quinzhee's vent. I noted that my brain had gone all poetical. In moments of crisis, my mind splits into a thousand chattering voices, and one of those voices thinks she's a poet. A number of voices discussed the possibility of a mental breakdown. *Jersicke was right; I'll have to go back into therapy,* one observed, while another composed a description of the phenomenon for the media. *It was beautiful. The light flickered across the walls like dancing fairies.*

And what did you see when you looked inside? the imaginary reporters inquired.

That silenced the voices. I would have to take a look, wouldn't I? That's what you do when presented with supernatural phenomena. You step into the spaceship, jump down the rabbit hole, fling open the rattling closet door. No one ever reports, ". . . but I was too scared, so I just stood there until it went away."

Impulse Control sprang into action. If I entered the quinzhee, she warned, I might:

a) Die.
b) Disappear forever.
c) Confront a situation of such incomprehensible strangeness that my sanity would be ripped away from me—but since no one would notice the difference, what the hell.

I threw a coat over my Rider jersey nightie and ran outside in my moccasins. As I did, the light went out. I dropped to my hands and knees and thrust my head into the entrance of the quinzhee, only to crack heads with someone crawling out of it. I fell back, clutching my skull.

"I thought you were in bed!" Aunt Ellen groaned, rubbing her own forehead.

"I thought *you* were in bed." I helped her to her feet. "What were you doing in there? What was that light? What are you wearing?" A bizarre patterned skirt stuck out from under her winter coat, and she had crammed a wide-brimmed straw sun hat over her red hair.

"Oh, um . . . Bernie is a little nervous of the quinzhee collapsing. He thought it might become more stable if we iced the walls, so he's having a go at them with his welding torch."

"Bernie the electrician? Aunt Ellen, why are you and Bernie welding a quinzhee in the middle of the night?" Aunt Ellen fussed with her sun hat and didn't answer. "Oh, Aunt Ellen. You didn't sneak him out here to spend the night, did you?"

Aunt Ellen gave me a pat on the cheek and a wink. "Is that hot cider I smell? Be a sweetie and bring us some, would you? And I wouldn't complain if a splash of rum found its way into the thermos."

Aunt Ellen had probably kicked butt as a university professor, but as an aunt she could drive a person completely insane.

I did eventually fall asleep, only to get caught in a nightmare about Jersicke trying to cut off my ears. I thrashed awake. The rough hand on my shoulder and the angry voice were real.

"Where is she? Where is Kelly?"

Nicholas Winters, dressed in winter boots and a purple bathrobe, stood beside my bed.

"What?" I mumbled, blinking. He had turned on my bedside lamp.

"Did your aunt have anything to do with this?" he roared. His eyes were bloodshot, and he had jaw stubble. "Where is she?"

I shoved his hand off my shoulder. "Calm down! Aunt Ellen's in the quinzhee."

"The quinzhee is empty. It's the first place I looked. I woke up five minutes ago, and Kelly was gone. Our front door was open."

I scrambled out of bed, threw on my bathrobe, and hurried to the front door. Fog had fallen over the city, wrapping the house in a pale cloud.

"Aunt Ellen?" No reply from the dark quinzhee. I ran down the steps. As I approached it, the quinzhee suddenly came alight again. I knelt and squinted into the entrance. I saw a swirl of colour that crackled around the edges like storm clouds. I eased slowly through the short tunnel until I reached the heart of the quinzhee. On hands and knees, I stared up at a ring of light that rippled and blazed and finally parted to create a ragged opening.

The voices united in one frantic cry: *Where is my aunt?*

Probably she was in the sunny forest on the other side of the opening. The summery perfume of exotic wildflowers wafted into the cool air of the quinzhee—there I go again with the poetry. To tell the truth, I didn't stop long enough to sniff the wafting of foreign scents. Before the doorway could disappear, I closed my eyes and dived into it.

Worldhopping 101

I promptly fell on my face. For a moment I just lay there, the frozen ache of my body soothed by the warm ground. A swarm of bugs buzzed around my ears, glittering like bits of tinfoil. I swatted them away and got to my feet, marvelling at the silky grass stroking my bare ankles, the sun baking my white December face. The frigid air that had followed me through the opening became a warm mist that swirled around me. I stood in a grove of trees on a hill that sloped down into a shallow river valley. It looked somewhat like Saskatchewan terrain, but this was most definitely not Saskatchewan. I was highly doubtful it was even Earth. The sky had too much violet in it, and the birds flying across it had little forelegs.

"Heia, you! Worldhopper!"

The tallest woman I had ever seen came around the perimeter of the fiery ring I had jumped through. Her head was shaved bare except for a golden braid that swung from the crown of her skull. A cluster of fangs dangled from each earlobe. She wore only a fur-trimmed leather bustier and a pair of wrap-around leather trousers. She stalked toward me on bare feet.

"It is unlawful for overlappers to enter Migrara." The woman unsheathed a glistening ivory sword. Her eyes blazed gold in the sunlight.

I snapped out of my stunned trance as she made a grab at me. Ducking under her arm, I scrambled through the opening and rammed face first into the frozen wall of the quinzhee. As I flopped onto my back in the snow, the warrior lunged through the swirling circle. The quinzhee was easily large enough to hold six men standing up, but the woman filled it all by herself. She stood for a moment in dramatic silhouette against the wild light. Then the light winked out.

The abrupt darkness was followed by incoherent shouting and frozen chopping sounds as the warrior attempted to hack her way out of the quinzhee. Chunks of snow rained on my head. Her heel struck me square in stomach, driving the last few ounces of alien air from my lungs.

"There's an exit tunnel over this way," I wheezed, curling into a ball. A moment of stillness while flakes of ice tinkled to the ground. A grunt and popping knees as the warrior crouched and located the entrance with her sword. She squirmed and cursed her way through the narrow tunnel to freedom.

"I do not like closed in places!" the warrior thundered as I emerged behind her. Her accent was strange, yet oddly familiar.

"Sorry," I apologized, like a good Canadian. I lurched to my feet, flailing my arms when my moccasins skidded off in various directions. Her own bare feet must have been freezing. It was at least minus twenty out here.

"As you should be, boy. Girl," she amended as my efforts to stay on my feet jostled my frontal protrusions. Her sword was still in her hand, and she looked ready to use it.

"My name is Audrey O'Krane," I said, trying to inject a friendly, non-violent tone into the conversation. "What's yours?"

"Latiana."[2] The woman jammed her blade savagely into its sheath. "I am Captain of the Cauldra Cats, the Queen's personal guard. My world is Migrara,[3] which means 'wheel' in the oldest tongue. I live on the mainland, the hub of the Six Circling Islands."

"Uh huh. So, what's the deal here? Time travel, parallel universe, what?"

"You mean, how is my world connected to yours?" She scowled uncertainly, like my classmates when the teacher fired a question at them to see if they'd been paying attention. "Our learned ones teach us that the universe runs in a circle. Worlds that lie years of travel in the distance might also share the same time and space as our own. The overlapping worlds do not mirror one another, but they do influence one another, especially near the fault lines."

I nodded my incomprehension.

"A fault line is a weakening of the barrier between overlapping worlds. Fault lines are at their weakest two times of the year; the longest night and the longest day. This is your longest night, yes? On my world, it is the longest day. At these times, a worldhopper—that is, anyone who was born along a fault line—may open a porthole and enter a world that overlaps her own." She looked around and rumbled, "Why would he have fled here? This has the look of an ironbound world. Not to say it's colder than an ice ape's arse."

---

[2] Lay-she-ANN-ah. I find it irritating when a narrator makes you guess how to say tricky alien names, so I will be providing word pronunciations and a few explanatory notes. Although to be fair, is it really that important? I mean, it's not like you can expect to run into these people at the mall and have to introduce them to your friends.

[3] Mih-GRAH-rah.

"I think my aunt is in your world." I was shaking, and not just from the cold. Shock pitched my voice high. "Red hair. Seventy-ish. Ditzy, but lovable. Might be with our electrician and a little girl. Have you seen them?"

"No. Have you seen Keirt Prai?"

"Carrot who?"

"Prai. He couldn't have arrived more than 1.247 hours ago. Did you let him through the porthole?"

To save time, I pretended we were having a logical conversation. "What does he look like?"

To my alarm, the fierce warrior burst into poetry. "'A face to inspire laughter or lust, but certainly not trust.'"

I shook my head. "I thought for a minute it might be Bernie Buttcrack, but that doesn't sound like him. Latiana, you need to take me back through your portal so we can look for them."

"Porthole, not portal. The first Migrarans to discover a fault line were sailors. Your companions are not my concern. Queen Teriquilla's[4] Court Mage, Keirt Prai, has stolen a powerful royal artefact—the Wakitaki. I won't return to my world before I lay my hands on him, may the Lioness devour his testicles."

The warrior flung herself face down in the snow and sniffed at the footprints leading to the house. With a satisfied grunt she leaped to her feet and stalked toward the front door, hefting her sword in a manner that boded ill for the thief.

Nicholas Winters appeared in the doorway. "I checked the rest of the house. There is no sign—"

"Traitor!" The warrior woman gave a truly terrible scream and launched herself at Winters. Was she actually *snarling*? Yes, she was. She smashed into him, knocking him back into

---

[4] Tare-ih-QUILL-ah.

the house. I heard thumps, shouts, a tremendous crash. She emerged from the house dragging Winter's limp body behind her by the collar of his bathrobe.

"Oh my God, did you kill him?" I gasped.

"The Prince lives, but only until he faces the Queen's justice." Her sword was out again, poised to maim. "You are in league with him, aren't you, worldhopper? What are you, his lover?"

"No! Yuck! I'm not in league with anybody. I'm just trying to find my aunt. Prince? I thought you said he was some kind of magician."

"Keirt Prai is the Court Mage," she said impatiently, hauling Winters toward the quinzhee. "*This* rotting carrion is Prince Nicholas, the traitor who slew our King. No wonder Keirt crossed over to your world. Do you see this scar on the Prince's chest? Keirt gave it to him the night the Prince fled Migrara. I'll have to abandon my pursuit, though I would like to know how he discovered the Prince's whereabouts. Didn't tell anyone, of course, just went haring off in pursuit of vengeance. Pixens! All whim and passion, no brains."

"No," I said. "No way. You've got the wrong guy. Nicholas Winters is an accountant or something. He barbecues hamburgers on Sundays. I mean, come on, he drives a Honda Civic!"

She shoved him headfirst into the quinzhee's entrance, cursing when he got stuck. "I would also like to know how the Prince gained access your world. He is not a worldhopper. Someone had to open a porthole for him. If you are not his accomplice, then perhaps it was this aunt of yours, or the man you call Bernie Buttcrack," her accent infusing the name with elegance, *Bahtcracke*. "Wait here. I will give the Prince over to the Cauldra Cats, then return to arrest you. Even if you and your compatriots are not involved, you are a worldhopper, and you know your way onto my world. The Queen will want to detain you for questioning."

She yanked Winters out by the ankles and wiggled herself feet first into the quinzhee, dragging him after her. The walls flared with sudden light, then went dark.

I stared at the quinzhee while the voices scolded me. An alien barbarian had kidnapped my neighbour, and I just stood there and let it happen. I hiked up my Rider jersey and scooted through the quinzhee's entrance on frozen bare knees. *Worldhopper*, she had called me. Did that mean I could open these porthole things?

I concentrated. For a brief moment, the dark interior of the quinzhee flared into a churning blizzard of colour. Then an avalanche of snow slammed down on me. I couldn't move, couldn't breath. The voices chattered frantically, grew faint, and finally fell silent.

Keirt

I woke stretched out on the thick rug in front of the fire-place. A roaring blaze threw its lovely heat all over me. *It was all a dream*, the voices soothed. *Never mind that you are wrapped in every quilt in the house. Ignore your wet hair. Overlook your nudity beneath the quilts. The man sitting on the back of Aunt Ellen's armchair, juggling flaming onions, exists only in your imagination.*

The onions must have come from the pantry. I remembered Aunt Ellen stowing a nylon sack of them when she returned from Safeway. What is it with old folks and onions? It's like an addiction with them. Six of them whirled through the man's hands, each glowing a different colour. The flickering colours fell upon a face . . . well, to quote my latest acquaintance, a face to inspire laughter or lust, but certainly not trust. His hair was pure white, but not from age. He was a few years older than me. He wore leather breeches, a tunic, and a vest with many patches and pockets. A small snake lay draped over his shoulder, white with scarlet rings and eyes like rubies. A pair of frog-like arms sprouted just below its head. It flicked its tongue at me and scratched its jaw with a long claw.

Kelly sat on the couch, clad in a parka, pink boots, and Winnie-the-Pooh pyjamas. She had wrapped one of Aunt Ellen's crocheted afghans around her and was sucking on a candy cane from the Christmas tree. "Faster," she challenged, laughing, her face lit by the onion glow.

The airborne onions gained velocity, became a ring of streaming colour, and then a circle of white light. The man's face glowed golden in the center, smiling and wild.

I heaved all but one of the quilts off me and wobbled to my feet. The loop of light disintegrated as the onions flew free of their orbit and bounced to the floor. Papery bits of onion peel drifted across the kayak I had last seen stored in the basement. What was it doing in the middle of the living room?

Kelly ran to me, the afghan streaming out behind her like a cape, and thrust a fistful of bedraggled wildflowers at me. "These are for you, Audrey Oak. I picked them while I was waiting for Keirt. He's who saved you out of the quinzhee. It was so cool, his hands were all crackly like lightning." She wiggled her sticky fingers at me to pantomime lightning. "He just put them on the snow and it all melted, it was like a lake and you floating in the middle. I thought you were drowned, but Keirt said no, you weren't, but we had to take your nightie off and you were *absolutely bare-butt naked*. It's okay; I made him close his eyes. Keirt wrecked the power," she added as I reached for the floor lamp. I twisted the switch a few times to no effect. "He wrecked the TV, too."

I turned to the juggler, still perched on the armchair. The last two onions remained balanced on the tips of his index fingers, spinning like tops. His snake curled lazily around his neck.

"Yes, I wrecked it most thoroughly. My apologies." Carrot's voice was deep for such a youthful face. He spoke with the same odd accent as Latiana—and Nicholas Winters, I realized with a shock. And Aunt Ellen! "I should never have interfered with your roots."

"My what?"

"The roots through which so many of your tools draw their strength," he explained. "Perikelli[5] was showing me the Visions of Tellah. I sensed power flowing into the Tellah through the black roots embedded in the wall, and when I put my hands on them—"

"Zap!" Kelly put in, obviously impressed by this mishap. "All the lights went out."

"So you're the missing mage," I said. "I was expecting someone more Gandalfish."

"Gandalf?" He juggled the pair of onions one-handed. "He was Court Mage before me. I took over when he was called away to deal with all that ring foolishness."

"Ah," I said.

He burst out laughing, nearly falling off the chair. "You should see your face! That's what I love about species with no knowledge of overlapping worlds. You believe anything you're told."

"I need some answers from you, Carrot. My aunt—"

"Keirt."

"What?"

"You say my name wrong. It's Keirt."[6]

"Keirt," I said through clenched teeth. "Where is my Aunt Ellen?"

"I was hoping you could tell me. She said she would meet me here. I promised to arrive at midnight, but eluding the Cauldra Cats delayed me. Lady Trini and her companion must have gone on to Migrara without me."

"To Migrara? Why? Why would she and Bernie Buttcrack step into a place like that, where anything could happen to them?"

---

[5] Pare-ih-KEL-lee.

[6] Kairt. I know, it sounds exactly like "carrot," but apparently there's a difference.

He grinned. "Perhaps because anything could happen to them?"

"This isn't funny! That crazy warrior woman kidnapped my neighbour and probably Aunt Ellen too." My voice squeaked and trembled like a violin string. Overlapping worlds, Aunt Ellen disappearing—it was all too much. And this juggling lunatic sat there treating it like a joke.

He sprang off the armchair and stepped close to me in one smooth motion. I could feel the heat of his body and smell the dust of unpaved Migraran roads on his skin. He wasn't as tall as Latiana, but taller than me. I took a step back, burrowing deeper into my quilt.

"I will help you get her back, but you must help me return to Migrara."

"How? Won't Latiana and these Cats be waiting for us on the other side of that porthole?"

"The river." He pointed at the kayak, loaded up with the wetsuits and other gear Lyle and I had planned to go diving with this past summer. We had broken up before we had a chance to use it. "Your weir was built along the fault line that passes through this house. As the water carries us over the weir, we can open another porthole onto Migrara. The river in my world flows swiftly and will carry us out of the reach of the Cauldra Cats when we emerge."

I stepped to the living room window, expecting the view to be blocked by the quinzhee, but all that remained of that giant snow cone was a slushy crater. The fog had cleared enough to let a quarter moon glimmer on the dark stretch of the South Saskatchewan River. Steam rose from the smooth curve of water spilling over the weir. At the base of the weir, the water churned into a deadly mixture of ice and froth.

"You can't be serious. The undertow would kill us. Why don't we just open a porthole on the other side of the river? How long is this fault line?"

"About 1.064 kilometres."

I raised my eyebrows. "Are your guesses always this precise?"

"Passing through a porthole translates my unit of measurement into yours, as it translates our languages. Whatever the way, I can't travel through a city crisscrossed by lines of iron. They disrupt the magic in my blood. This world is a nightmare for a pixen."

"He's allergic to train tracks," Kelly translated.

I turned to her. "Your uncle was looking for you, Kelly. Where have you been?"

She plucked the candy cane from her mouth. "Waiting for Keirt. I remember he came on your last birthday, so I went over to Migrara and let him in. We couldn't find Granny Ellen *anywhere*. We went into your bedroom and had a whole big argument because I didn't want to go back home and you never even woke up. Then Uncle Nick came and Latiana pounced all over him, but Keirt said that was okay because they were playing hide and seek. I don't think Latiana knows how to play. You're not supposed to knock people down when you find them."

I looked at Keirt. "You were in my *bedroom?*"

"Don't be frightened, Audrey Oak. I mean no harm to either of you, I promise you."

"But you mean harm to Nicholas Winters, don't you? That's what Latiana said. That Winters was some kind of fugitive from your world, and you're hunting him."

"On my world, it is commonly believed the Prince murdered his brother, our King, in a fit of jealous rage."

"Like in *The Lion King*," Kelly interjected.

"Exactly," Keirt said, as if he watched Disney movies all the time. "Why don't you hop into the kitchen and find yourself a bite to eat, Pea Frog. You've had a busy night and your tummy must be turning inside out with hunger."

Kelly was eyeing a small leather backpack beside the kayak. "Did you bring me a present, Keirt?"

Keirt dug into the backpack and produced a small box wrapped in red paper. Kelly tore into it and pulled out a wooden carving of an animal with long legs and a strangely curved neck. The creature swished its tail and tossed its head. So that's where those came from! Kelly had a whole collection of them and often brought them over to play with. The weird wooden animals flapped, hopped, and galloped, and I could never for the life of me figure out how they did it.

"Thank you, Keirt. Did you bring a present for Audrey Oak? It's her birthday, you know."

"I will give her a present later. To the kitchen with you, my little lady."

"Granny Ellen always has Pop-Tarts. Can I have a Pop-Tart?"

Keirt rolled his eyes. "As many Pop-Tarts as you wish."

Kelly shot into the kitchen. We heard her rummaging through the cupboards, and then the ratchety snap of our old toaster grudgingly accepting a pair of Pop-Tarts. I wondered how long it would take her to realize the toaster wouldn't work without power.

"She will have to come with us," Keirt said. "There's space in the front of your vessel. She could lie between your feet."

"So let me get this straight. Kelly is—"

"Princess Perikelli, and her father was the King of Migrara. But no more questions, Audrey Oak. Do you want to find your aunt or not?"

"When we do find her, you and I are going to have a long talk. Stay here while I get dressed." As my quilt and I left the living room, I threw over my shoulder, "By the way, you say my name wrong. It's O'Krane."

5

Not-So-Intelligent Life Forms

I changed into fresh underwear, jeans, a fleece sweater and an undershirt made from a material the guy at the sports store promised would "wick moisture away from your skin." I never liked the idea of my clothes wicking me—not in public, anyway—but this was no time to be picky.

I rejoined Keirt in the living room, and we pulled the wetsuits over our clothes. Keirt found the Velcro straps fascinating. He ripped them apart over and over again until I handed him his paddle and showed him how to use it. We carried the kayak out the front door. I stepped into the street and fell smack on my new tattoo, thanks to all that ice from the melted quinzhee. I took the kayak down with me, and Keirt went sprawling across it.

"You said a swear, Audrey. You too, Keirt." Kelly skated around us in her thick pink boots, giggling. The kid was all cranked up on sugar.

"Keirt's the one who turned the street into a skating rink," I defended myself as we uprighted ourselves. And why was I being so belligerent about that? I wondered. He had done it to save my life, after all. For some reason, I couldn't bring myself to thank him for it.

Gingerly we portaged the kayak past the new "Prince of Wales Promenade," a landscaped stretch of riverbank overlooking the weir. We would have to launch the kayak upstream of the weir and paddle to the middle of the river before the current swept us over it.

"So, can all of you Migrarans do magic?" I asked.

"Not all, no. The gift originates with the inhabitants of the island of Tuoaue.[7] Tuoaueans cross paths only rarely with other Migrarans, but sometimes one of them will walk away from these crossings with a pixen in her belly."

"So a pixen is a half Toe—Tawoo—whatever. You must have very interesting parents."

"My mother is dead," he said. "And I've never met my Tuoauean father."

"Oh," I murmured. I would have liked to know more, but didn't think he would appreciate my curiosity any more than I would welcome questions about my own parents' deaths. Instead I said, "Tell me more about Migrara."

"It's a world very similar to your own. In fact, the Queen refers to them as sister planets. Migrara is slower paced, perhaps, and not so populated. Our people are not nearly as adept as yours at harnessing the world's natural forces. Our world's leaders are more concerned with harnessing the powers of the mind."

I assumed he was talking about magic and not intelligence. I had yet to see signs of vast intellect among these people. "Who are your world leaders?"

"Politically, the most powerful person on Migrara is Queen Teriquilla. Magically, the Alphan of Tuoaue." He took on a more formal tone, for the first time sounding like a man employed by royalty. "At present Tuoaue is strongly allied with the Queen, thanks to King Glaem's founding of the Mage Hall, a school for Migrarans of Tuoauean ancestry."

"Is Earth the only world Migrara's in contact with?"

---

[7] Too-WOE-ah-way.

"Oh, no. Countless worlds overlap Migrara. It has more fault lines than any world we've come across. We like to call it the capital of the worldhopping universe."

"Geez, you guys must be overrun with aliens."

"Not at all. Since the Eshkian invasion thirty years ago, overlappers are no longer welcome on Migrara. Unauthorized visits seldom end well. But of course you'll be under my protection," he hastened to reassure me. I wasn't reassured.

We came to a rough walking path that wound through the frosty trees lining the bank. The wind blew twisty little snakes of ice crystals through a dark hollow from which I expected Ichabod Crane to emerge screaming at any moment. The elms that arched their green limbs so gracefully over the trail on a summer afternoon now clawed at each other with ghostly hands.

"Oh, here, I almost forgot." I handed Keirt a pair of rubber gloves. "Wear these under your other gloves; they'll protect your hands from the ice water. Are you listening to me?"

He was looking over his shoulder at the train bridge. I wondered what all that iron would do to him if the river carried us past the weir and under the trestle.

"You were born in that house, weren't you?" he asked.

"Yeah," I said, surprised by the change of subject. "It was Grandpa Trini's idea. He told my parents it was a Swiss tradition."

"We should be all right, then. What time were you born?"

"Around midnight. Why do you ask? Are you into astrology?"

"Midnight on a solstice," he muttered. "Incredible."

"Not really. When you're born this close to Christmas, people skip your birthday."

He took the rubber gloves and my hand along with them, pulling me into his arms in one quick movement. Ice crackled in my damp hair as he kissed me. His lips were warm against mine in spite of the cold, and they tingled.

"Happy birthday, Audrey O'Krane," he said.

I pushed him away and punched him on the shoulder. "Keep your hand out of my suit!" *This* was why I wasn't in a hurry to thank him for pulling me out of the quinzhee.

He looked down. "That wasn't my hand."

I followed his gaze and saw a red and white tail disappearing down the front of my wetsuit.

"Hold still." Keirt started to pull off a glove.

"No! I'll get it!" I plunged my own icy hand into my suit and rummaged around. Kelly was in danger of wetting herself due to hysterical laughter.

Keirt drew in his breath. A blazing hole had opened in the center of my front yard. Through it poured half a dozen . . . I didn't know what to call them. Life forms, I guess, to quote Mr. Spock. They carried swords and spears, and there was just enough light to make it obvious that they were female, and more feline than human. The weapon clatter and growling voices faded as they caught sight of us standing at the head of the trail.

"Oh, hell," Keirt groaned. "The Cauldra Cats. Run!"

Kelly raced ahead as Keirt and I launched the kayak down the path. We towed it through the snow at a gallop, stumbling and sliding along the winding trail which did its best to tip us into the sharp embrace of the trees. Twirling seeds skittered off our heads as we fishtailed through a snowdrift and slammed the kayak into a tree trunk. Behind us we heard the enthusiastic roar of creatures who are about to get violent and enjoy it.

"Here, Audrey!" Kelly called from a gap in the trees. We hauled the kayak over to her, yanked her out of her parka, and stuffed her feet first into bow. We gave the kayak a shove and fell across it. It tobogganed down the snowy bank and onto the shelf of ice that stretched partway across the river. The river would have been completely frozen over if not for the heat produced by the power plant upstream.

We drove the kayak toward the open water, our shoes skidding on the rough ice, until an ominous creak stopped us.

"Get in. We'll have to push ourselves the rest of the way with our paddles." I jumped into the kayak and secured the sprayskirt that snugged over my waist and the opening of the cockpit, twisting around to make sure Keirt did the same. We dug into the ice with our paddles, hoisting the kayak forward with the breathtaking velocity of a crippled snail. The Cauldra Cats hesitated at the river's edge, tapping the ice shelf distrustfully with their spears.

The kayak lurched, the ice creaked and cracked beneath us, and the kayak settled into the river with a splash. The current washed against the side, pinning it against the thick jumble of broken ice at my elbow. I chopped helplessly at the slushy water. Only three meters of ice stood between us and open water, but it might as well have been thirty.

I looked back at the cat women. They were no longer women, but fully feline, clawing their way across the ice on their furry bellies. Keirt flicked a ball of blue flame from his fingers. It sizzled across the ice, spread out, and struck the cats. They screamed in rage but kept coming.

"If we can't go over the ice, we'll just have to go under it," I said, clenching my jaw.

"If you say so," Keirt consented unsteadily. It was satisfying to rattle *him* for a change.

I knocked on the bow. "Kelly, we're going to be upside down for a little while."

"Okay," came the muffled reply.

We pulled our diving goggles into place. They covered the ears as well as the eyes to prevent eardrums from bursting under pressure. "On the count of three, we tip right. One . . ."

"What?" he shouted. "I can't hear you."

I tilted sideways, and the kayak went over. My face burned in the icy water. My skull seemed to contract until my brains threatened to squirt out my ears.

The kayak didn't move.

I had counted on Kelly's weight in the bow to pull the kayak's nose beneath the ice, but it wasn't working. The capsized kayak remained stubbornly afloat as the current swirled around it, jostling against the ice that held it in place.

A heavy thump jolted the kayak. It dipped beneath the surface, its belly scraping noisily along the underside of the ice as the water dragged it sideways. I felt a large life form thrashing near me in the murky black water. One of the cats had jumped on the kayak and slipped off. I suspected the Cauldra Cats were recruited more for muscle power than brains.

I thrust my paddle at the ice shelf. The blade caught on the uneven surface. We grated forward until at last we bobbed up into open water. It took three tries, but I managed to flip us upright and turn the kayak's nose downstream.

"All right, Keirt?" I coughed. A frozen sputter in reply. "Lie flat and hold your paddle tight against the side. Here we go!" I yelled as we shot toward the weir.

"Open the porthole now, Audrey," Keirt shouted.

"Me?" I shrieked, twisting around to stare at him. "I thought you were going to open it!"

"I'm not the worldhopper here. You are."

"But I don't think I know how!"

"Then you'd better learn quickly!"

The current thrust us over the steep curve of water, the kayak's nose diving straight into the churn. The roiling white water clenched around us like a fist and dragged us into the depths of an icy hell.

What a bummer that here I was about to die, and my final thoughts were bad poetry.

Migrara

A paddle prodded me in the back. "Wake, Audrey O'Krane. You're missing the sights of my world."

I opened an eye. My cheek rested on top of the kayak. The sun beat down on my cold, aching shoulders. A paddle flickered through my peripheral vision.

"Where we going, Lyle?" I muttered.

"Zantallion City. Who is Lyle?"

Oh, right. Migrara. Keirt. Cauldra Cats. I raised my head, which throbbed from being bounced around the bottom of the weir. I had a watery memory of tumbling over and over. The muffled sound of fibreglass scraping against stones and concrete. A flash of light. The kayak lunging for the surface, its nose breaking into warm air and sunlight and churning rapids. Now it skimmed quietly through more tranquil waters, racing ahead of a gentle current.

I glanced over my shoulder at Keirt. He had looked mysterious in firelight and fog, but in sunlight he looked positively alien. His white hair flared out in all directions, and his green eyes were startlingly bright in his tanned face. But he wasn't the alien here, I was. This was his home.

I pulled off my goggles and tapped on the bow. "Kelly? Are you all right?"

"It's stinky in here. Can I get out?"

Keirt handed me the paddle I must have dropped. "By the way, may I have Tist back? I'm starting to worry about him."

"Tist?"

"My viper."

I couldn't believe I had forgotten there was a snake nestled between my boobs. I yanked it out of my wetsuit and thrust it at Keirt. He tapped it sternly on the nose and slung it across his shoulder, where it lay basking in the sun.

We disembarked and liberated Kelly. She raced up and down the sandy bank, pointing out fascinating aspects of the alien flora and chasing after tiny peeping frogs.

"Your aunt and her companion went to the city of Zantallion," Keirt said as we stripped off our wetsuits. "See their footprints along the bank? No sign of the Cauldra Cats—good. If we head downriver, we should meet Lady Trini on her way back."

"What about Kelly's uncle? We can't just abandon him to those cat women. They'll eat him or something."

"The Cauldra Cats rarely devour prisoners unless ordered to do so," he assured me cheerfully. "They might be having a bit of sport with him, though. You know how cats are."

Keirt wore an earring, a simple gold hoop just big enough for me to hook my little finger into.

"'The time has come,' the Walrus said, 'to talk of many things. Of shoes and ships and sealing wax, of cabbages and kings.' And queens. I want to hear the whole story, including why you came to my world and how you know about Tolkien. Talk."

I gave the earring a little twist, and yelped as a jolt of energy shot up my arm. I gritted my teeth and hung on. We glared at one another, our faces inches apart. Then he smiled, and the current running between us faded to a faint tingle that felt kind of nice. *Too* nice. I let go and hastily stepped away.

"If Lady Trini has told you nothing of Migrara, neither will I," he said firmly. "She can explain herself when we find her."

I heard a heavy crackling in the trees behind me, and a snarling beast knocked me to the ground as it launched itself at Keirt.

I sputtered sand out of my mouth and looked up. It was no beast; it was Latiana, her long, golden braid whipping out behind her like a cat's tail. She ploughed into Keirt and had him down on the ground before he knew what hit him. Tist went flying into the river and calmly wiggled his way to shore. Latiana straddled Keirt and wrenched his arms behind his back so she could slap a set of manacles on his wrists. He arched his back and cried out in pain.

"Latiana, don't! He's allergic to iron. Stop, you're hurting him!" I grabbed her arm, and when that had no effect I grabbed her braid. Something, a fist or possibly a foot, found its way into my stomach. As I writhed in the sand, begging my lungs to function again, I decided Keirt was perfectly capable of looking after himself. He was probably just faking those groans of agony.

Thud. The sounds of the struggle ceased. Kelly had run up behind Latiana and with a piece of driftwood added a lump to the warrior's skull.

"She's always *pouncing* on people," Kelly said indignantly. "It's no fair. She's bigger than everybody."

She snatched a key from Latiana's belt and opened the manacles. Keirt staggered to his feet and disappeared. I don't mean he ran away; I mean he actually vanished before our eyes. I gave a yelp of surprise.

Latiana heaved herself up from the ground, her golden eyes narrowed in anger, and loomed Godzilla-like over us. Kelly looked up at her and wisely burst into tears.

"Did you see that?" I asked, throwing Latiana a diversion. "Did he teleport, or what?"

"He has gone nowhere. He bends the light around himself so we can't see him." Latiana drew her ivory sword and hacked vigorously in all directions, impressing Kelly right out of her tears.

"I'm sorry about the hair pulling, Latiana," I said. She was more than a little scary, and she scratched herself in rude places, but when she wasn't trying to maim people I found her strangely likeable.

"And I'm sorry if I injured you just now, Audrey, but it was foolish to engage me in battle. I am a trained warrior and you're but a clumsy little gawkling who has yet to grow a full bosom."

Okay, maybe *likable* was too strong a word. "Where is Nicholas Winters?"

Latiana sheathed her sword and searched the kayak until she found Keirt's backpack. "If you mean the Prince, my Cats are taking him to Mount Cauldra. Ah!" She pulled a cloth-wrapped object from Keirt's pack. Reverently she drew aside the crimson velvet.

"My old walkie-talkie!" I exclaimed.

Latiana's expression of triumph turned to one of indignation. "How dare you claim ownership of the Wakitaki!"

"But it's my old walkie-talkie. Look, my initials are scratched on the back. When I was little, Aunt Ellen and I pretended they were CB radios. She had a thing about trucker movies. We still have the matching one in the house somewhere. I always wondered where this one went."

Latiana held the walkie-talkie before her if it was a holy relic. "This device provides communication between the Queen and one of her oldest friends."

"No way. Its range is no more than a kilometre. And after all these years the battery would have died." I took it from her and popped open the battery case. Instead of a battery, it contained a large green gem. I flipped the *on* switch and listened to the familiar crackle of static. I pressed the *talk* button and raised it to my mouth. "Breaker one-nine, breaker one-nine, anybody got their ears on?"

Latiana snatched it back and fumbled furiously to close the battery case. "It's not enough that crazy pixen steals it—you must desecrate it as well!"

The walkie-talkie crackled to life. "Audrey? Was that you, sweetie?"

Latiana dropped it as if it had bitten her. I scooped it up and pressed the button. "Aunt Ellen! Aunt Ellen, it's me! Where are you? Are you all right?"

"Don't shout, dear, there are a lot of people around. Bernie and I are passing through the livestock at the Rainbow Bazaar and everyone thinks I'm having a conversation with the talking yammer birds. Where are you? Is Keirt with you?"

The walkie-talkie was suddenly plucked from my hand, and Keirt popped back into existence. "We're just north of Zantallion City, Lady Trini. Could you meet us along the river?"

Latiana, who had made a move to grab him, froze at the words "Lady Trini."

"Audrey is on Migrara?" Aunt Ellen's astonishment crackled through the radio. "Keirt, where have you been? I waited hours for you. You weren't answering the walkie-talkie."

"I'm sorry, Lady Trini. The Queen sent the Cauldra Cats after me. I disabled the Wakitaki so it wouldn't give away my position, and then it seemed to stop working."

"That's because I turned my own off when we reached the city. Teriquilla sent the Cauldra Cats? What for?"

"Well . . . remember when I told you the Queen allowed me to *borrow* the Wakitaki?"

Aunt Ellen groaned. "Oh, Keirt. But even so, I don't see why she would—Watch out Bernie, they bite! Oh, lord, I've got to go. Don't move, Keirt; I'll be there as quick as I can.

See you soon, Audrey. Oh dear, I have some explaining to do, don't I? That's a big ten-four from Aunt Ellen. I'm gone."

The radio went dead. Latiana stared at it, then at me. "Lady Ellen Trini is your aunt?"

"Great aunt. You know her?"

"Lady Trini taught Universal History at the Mage Hall for many years, and more recently served as Overlap Advisor to Queen Teriquilla. She left Migrara to care for an orphaned relative on an overlap world, but she remains one of the Queen's most trusted advisors. The inventions of our world's scientists and engineers advance like wildfire, thanks to the wisdom Lady Trini sends through this wondrous device."

Aunt Ellen was passing our world's modern technology on to the medieval Migrarans! Damn right she had some explaining to do!

Latiana glared at Keirt. "You can't imagine the Queen's rage when she discovered her own Court Mage had stolen it. Give it over, Prai!"

Her hand shot out and clamped on Keirt's throat. Instantly a storm of blue lightning crackled all around her body. She bellowed and released him.

"Cut it out!" I yelled. "You're scaring Kelly!" Actually Kelly was too busy chasing frogs to be frightened, but they were scaring the crap out of me.

Latiana whipped around and stared at her. "Kelly? Do you mean to say this is Princess Perikelli? But she's—bloody pixen!" She growled in exasperation as Keirt flickered out of sight again. She stalked over to Kelly and sniffed her. "It really is her, isn't it?"

I shook my head. "I have no idea. I don't even know who I am anymore."

She studied me curiously. "You would be the granddaughter of Lady Trini's brother, Lord Trini. He left Migrara over sixty years ago. Like Lady Trini, he was a worldhopper."

In June of 1939, a Saskatoon city crew had been working on the construction of the weir when they discovered a half-drowned young man sprawled across the concrete. The crew brought him into my great-grandparents' house, where he met my grandmother. He claimed to have amnesia. He knew his name, but he had no idea where he had come from. This hadn't bothered my grandmother. A year later they were married.

I barely remembered Grandpa Trini. He had died when I was four. That was when Aunt Ellen made her first appearance in my life. She had come to the funeral and told my surprised parents she was from Switzerland. But she wasn't Swiss. Heck, she probably wasn't even human. What did that make me?

It made me freaking angry. Why had no one told me all this? Our whole family was based on a lie.

Latiana was pacing and growling to herself. "But this is terrible. It means Lady Trini is in league with Prince Nicholas. I cannot believe it. Perhaps it is a trick. I know at least one pixen who can disguise faces and voices."

Latiana handed me her sword, then removed her clothes and handed them to me as well. She sank into a crouch, sprouted fur and pointed ears. Her face stretched into a fanged muzzle. Now an enormous golden leopard with black diamond spots stood on the riverbank. She was still wearing the fang cluster earrings. I learned later that the number of fangs determined a Cauldra Cat's rank. She crisscrossed the bank, sniffing at the sand. With a final decisive snort, she rose to her hind legs and became a woman again.

"No, it is definitely her," she sighed, taking back her sword and clothes.

"Is this common on Migrara, people changing into cats?" I asked.

"Only Migrarans from the island of Quampu shift into cat form. Our island overlaps a world of felines. Female children born on the fault line are not only worldhoppers, but shapechangers as well. The fiercest of them train to be warriors of the Queen's personal guard. Keirt's mother was Quampuish."

"Does he turn into a cat too?" He did have a feline air about him. It was the way he moved, and his intense gaze.

"Only women take the change, according to our cycle."

"What cycle?" I asked. She gave me a look, and I blushed. "Oh."

"Three days of our cycle we remain in cat form, and three days we can't be other than human. At other times, we take the change as we wish."

Kelly let out a piercing scream. Latiana had scooped her up over her shoulder.

"Let me go!" she yelled.

"Don't be afraid, Princess. I am taking you back to Cauldra Castle and your mother. That will be nice, won't it?"

"No!" Kelly shrieked. "I want Granny Ellen!"

"Hey, put her down!" I started toward them, only to be grabbed from behind by strong, invisible arms.

"No, Audrey," Keirt's voice said in my ear. "Let them go."

"Don't interfere, pixen!" Latiana called. "That girl is under arrest for conspiring to harbour an assassin."

"Audrey Oak!" Kelly cried. "Where are you? Help me!"

Keirt clapped a hand over my mouth before I could answer. He wrestled me over to the kayak and dumped me into the front cockpit. Latiana seemed to see none of this. She wasn't even looking in the right direction.

"I've hidden us from their eyes," Keirt whispered, grabbing his snake, which was snatching up frogs with its little forelegs and stuffing them into its mouth. "I'm sorry, Audrey, but you must let her go. She'll be perfectly safe with the Cauldra

Cats, which is more than I can say for your aunt and her companion if we don't find them quickly. Besides, it will be good for Perikelli to return to her mother. It might sort out her malady."

"What malady?"

He shoved the kayak into the water. "Isn't it obvious? Look at her!"

I twisted around and stared at Latiana and Kelly as the river carried us away from them. "What do you mean? She looks like a perfectly normal kid."

"She refuses to grow up."

"Well give her a break. She's only six."

Keirt shook his head. "She is sixteen. She hasn't aged a day since she left Migrara."

The Explanation

"How can Kelly not have aged in ten years?" I asked.

"On Migrara, aging is a selective process," Keirt panted, paddling furiously. "You are as old as you feel. You do have a paddle of your own, you know. Don't be afraid to use it."

I thought of all the times I'd woken to find Aunt Ellen's hair had gone from silver back to its original copper overnight. "Oh, I couldn't sleep last night, so I decided to dye my hair," she'd say brightly, and change the subject. And it might explain why my own face had been acting strangely. I recalled the wrinkles in the bathroom mirror, and Jersicke's stunned expression when I burst into childish tears in her office. Had my face suddenly lost a few years?

"It would be best if we don't mention the Cauldra Cats are escorting Prince Nicholas and Perikelli to Mount Cauldra," Keirt said. "Your aunt would want to pursue them, which would leave her trapped here until the next solstice."

"Won't she realize something's wrong when we get back to my world and they're missing?"

"You can tell her after sunset. Sunrise, on your world. The fault line will be sealed then, and she will be unable to return to Migrara."

"This invisibility stuff—why didn't you use it when we were running from the Cauldra Cats on my world?"

"There was no point. They would have followed our trail through the snow. Ah, there they are."

I nearly overturned the kayak in alarm, but it was Aunt Ellen and Bernie he was pointing at, not pursuing cat women. They waved to us from the bank as we rounded a bend in the river. Bernie had replaced his tool belt with a pair of snappy, buttcrack-resistant suspenders. I could see his face for the first time. It was a nice face, though somewhat stunned. I'm not sure if it was a reaction to finding himself on an alien world, or if it was his usual expression.

"Audrey!" Aunt Ellen threw her arms around me as we came ashore, and unexpected tears flooded my eyes. "Oh, sweetie, look at your nose! Didn't you bring any sunscreen? Here, use mine." She rummaged through the enormous woven bag that hung from her arm, pulling out a collection of bizarre goods and a half-empty box of melting chocolate Santas. "They don't have chocolate on Migrara—they'll trade anything for it—of course, trading overlap world goods is illegal, but some merchants turn a blind eye. How did you two meet, by the way?"

"Audrey brought me onto your world," Keirt said as I started to answer. "You were right. She has become a world-hopper."

"Of course she has." Aunt Ellen beamed at me. "Since she was born on a fault line, it was only a matter of time before her power manifested itself. I'm surprised Kelly hasn't shown signs. I suppose she's been delayed by her arrested growth."

"Actually, I think she is—" I began, but Keirt interrupted again.

"Lady Trini, was your visit to Zantallion City successful?"

Aunt Ellen seemed to wilt. "No, it was not. Years ago I had a bad fall, and the Saskatoon doctors put a metal plate in my leg. It disrupted the magic of the pixen healer. As for Bernie, the healer recognized him as an overlapper and wouldn't even touch him. It was all I could do to talk him out of having us arrested."

"What healer?" I asked. "Why do you need a healer?"

Aunt Ellen hesitated. "I'll tell you once we return to—"

"Oh, no you don't." I planted my feet and folded my arms across my chest. "I'm tired of feeling like Alice in Wonderland chasing white rabbits. I am not moving another step until you explain everything to me."

"Audrey—"

"Not another step!"

"Oh, all right." Clearing her throat as if gearing up for a class lecture, Aunt Ellen presented The Explanation.

Her narrative, helpfully expanded upon by Keirt, was long-winded, meandering, and involved centuries of convoluted Migraran history. I'll be merciful and condense the confusing mass of information into a few comprehensible highlights, which is more than anyone did for me at the time.

Aunt Ellen was born on Migrara and lived there until I was five, when my parents died. She gave up a successful career at the royal court to cross over to my world and raise me, the only grandchild of her Migraran brother. Over the years she had remained in contact with the royal family, continuing to serve as one of their Overlap Advisors via the walkie-talkie. She was like a consultant for communications between Migrara and its overlapping worlds.

"Then came an unpleasant surprise. A few months ago I was diagnosed with cancer."

"Oh my God, Aunt Ellen!" I grabbed her hands, then let go, afraid of hurting her. For the first time, I noticed the pallor of her face, the dark circles under her eyes. How could I have been so wrapped up in my own problems I didn't even notice my own aunt was dying?

"Bernie too. We met at the clinic. Both of us are at the untreatable stage. On Earth, at least. Diseases are a snap of the fingers for pixen healers. Unfortunately, it's forbidden to bring overlappers onto Migrara. I asked the Queen to make an exception for Bernie, but she pointed out that sharing Migrara's healers would bring on a flood of sick overlappers. So I called upon my other ally at court. Keirt had taken it upon himself to deliver various goods between me and the Queen on solstices. I asked him to take it a step further, and deliver me and Bernie to Zantallion City. Oh, don't blame yourself, Keirt. Even if you had escorted us, it wouldn't have done any good. The healer was ridiculously paranoid about 'consorting with overlappers.'"

"What will you do now, Lady Trini?" Keirt asked.

She thrust her jaw forward. "I'm taking Bernie to the island of Delene. I know a healer there, a full-blooded Tuo-auean, who is immune to the effects of iron and cares nothing for rules."

Keirt winced. "Yinkara Belderkin. Are you sure that's wise?"

"No, but we have no choice. Time is running out."

Bernie raised his hand hesitantly, as if we were in a classroom.

"It's all right, Bernie. You can speak now," Aunt Ellen said. "I told him not to talk to anyone. His accent gives him away as an overlapper."

"I just wanted to say, don't put yourself in danger over my account, Ellen," Bernie said gruffly. "If the doctors here can help you, don't drag me along."

"Don't be an ass, Bernie. There's no reason you should throw your life away over my world's foolish politics. Will you come with us to Delene, Keirt?"

"I'll do better than that," he said. "I will go in your place. The journey would be too dangerous, even if you were well. I will bring the healer to you."

"That's impossible, Keirt. Delenes never leave the island."

"I will make it possible. Take Bernie to your nephew's vineyard. It's a short walk from here. I will meet you there when I return."

She hugged him. "Thank you, Keirt. You're a dear, no matter what they say at Mount Cauldra. Before you go, could you return Audrey to the fault line?"

"Aunt Ellen. Do you honestly believe I would go home and leave you here?" I said.

"Audrey, you have school to attend. You'll be graduating in June—"

"Nope. Jersicke expelled me yesterday. Didn't like the short story Irene and I posted on the school website."

"Audrey! Why didn't you say anything?"

"Why didn't you say anything about Migrara? Or about the fact that you're dying? Why didn't you trust me?"

I was shouting. It wasn't fair to lash out at her like that, but it was all too much. Suddenly my aunt didn't exist anymore, just an alien who had been wearing her face all these years.

Aunt Ellen tried to pat my arm, but I pulled childishly away, swiping at tears. "Audrey, I'm sorry. I was planning to tell you on your next birthday. When you were growing up, I couldn't take the chance that you would find your way onto Migrara. About thirty years ago, Migrara was invaded by a hostile overlap world. In the years that followed, anyone even suspected of being an overlapper would have been imprisoned, even killed."

I could get that. Since the terrorist attacks in September, I'd seen a similar attitude toward anyone who resembled an Arab.

"May I borrow your boat, Audrey?" Keirt was already preparing the kayak for departure, taking my response for granted.

"Sure. When will you be back?" I was reluctant to see him go. He was the only one who seemed to have all the answers I was looking for. Not that he was willing to share them.

"Within 7.041 days, if all goes well." Keirt offered a formal bow to our electrician. "We'll have you fixed up before you know it, Bernie Bahtcracke."

"Er—thank you," Bernie said.

"It's too bad I can't send a message to Nicholas," Aunt Ellen fretted as she led me and Bernie up a path that would take us out of the river valley. "He'll worry when I don't return. I suppose Keirt explained to you about Nicholas Winters being a political refugee?"

"Sort of. What's that all about?"

"It would be presumptuous of me to tell his story. I'll let Nicholas explain it to you."

"That will be six months from now," I said, wondering if I should tell her about his arrest before she heard it from someone else.

"Six months," Bernie said with a worried frown. "Who will shovel the sidewalk? Bring in my mail?"

"We might be able to return sooner than that," Aunt Ellen said. "You have the potential to be a very powerful world-hopper, Audrey, one who is not limited by the cycles of our worlds."

"Really?" I felt a flash of excitement at the thought of exploring an entire universe of worlds.

"But you're not to open portholes without the permission of local authorities, especially on Migrara," she warned. "You'll have to attend the Worldhopping Studies Branch of the Mage Hall. As the granddaughter of a Migraran emigrant, the Queen will probably agree to waive your overlapper status. In two years, you'll be granted a license and—"

"Two years!" I said in dismay. "I can't use my worldhopping power until then?"

"Of course you can, but only under professional supervision."

"But I want to check out all these other worlds. Can't I just—"

"I'm sorry, Audrey, but this is for your own safety. Ah, here's the road to my nephew's vineyard." She handed me a cloth bag. "This is a Migraran outfit I had meant to give you for Christmas. You don't want to stand out. Change quickly, dear. I'd like to arrive before dark."

In a daze, I took the cloth bag into the trees. The bag contained a Migraran tunic, vest, trousers, knee-high leather boots, and a cloak. As I went to pull my T-shirt over my head, I heard rustling in the trees. I looked up and screamed. A disembodied grin floated among the tree branches above me.

"You asked me about my knowledge of Tolkien." The rest of Keirt flickered into sight, still grinning down at me from his perch halfway up a tree. "I have read the story of the rings. I've also read about Narnia, Oz, and Camelot. For years, your grandfather, and then your aunt, sent books from your world to the Royal Library at Mount Cauldra. One of my favourites is *Alice in Wonderland*. I've always been fond of the Cheesy Cat."

"Cheshire Cat.[8] What are you *doing* here? Why aren't you on the river?"

"Audrey?" Aunt Ellen called. "Are you all right?"

"I'm fine!" I yelled. "A mouse ran over my foot."

A snort of exasperation. "You and your mice . . ."

"I want you to accompany me to the island of Delene," Keirt said softly. "I have heard much about you over the years

---

[8] My grandfather O'Krane told me the original Cheshire Cats were these grinning cat-shaped cheeses sold in Cheshire County, Ireland, where he was born. This has nothing to do with anything. I just thought it was cool and worth a mention.

from your aunt. If even half the stories about you are true, you would be a useful—or at least entertaining—travelling companion."

"You can't seriously think I would abandon my dying aunt to go running around with a thief who zaps people."

"No zapping, I promise."

"Look, I'm grateful for what you're doing for Aunt Ellen and Bernie, but I still don't quite trust you. So forget it." I grabbed my shopping bag and walked away.

"You'd rather attend school for two years and see nothing of the universe that lies at your fingertips?"

I stopped and slowly turned around. "Aunt Ellen says it's dangerous to learn worldhopping on your own."

"You won't be on your own. I'll help you, and your talents, not constrained by the laws of my world, will help me get our pixen healer away from Delene."

"All right," I said.

I'll never understand the way my brain works. I fuss and dither over the simplest decisions, like whether to buy the navy sandals or the black, yet when it comes to plunging into alien worlds or volunteering for a risky adventure, I'm in there like a dirty shirt. But aside from saving Aunt Ellen and Bernie's lives, how could I pass up the chance to explore new worlds? Especially when my own world was such a freaking mess.

"I'll let her know I'm going," I said, turning away.

"And you think she'll just let you go?" He shook his head at my naiveté.

I hesitated. "I can't just sneak away without telling her. She'll go ballistic."

Keirt dug into one of the deep pockets of his vest and held out the walkie-talkie. "You can talk to her when we're safely away."

I stared at it the way Eve might stare at an apple offered by a smooth talking serpent. Impulse Control launched into a long list of potential consequences, none of them beneficial to my physical and mental health. I reminded Impulse Control that for years I'd been struggling to please people—trying to be a good girlfriend, a good student, a good niece. What had it gotten me? Dumped, expelled, deceived and manipulated by my own aunt.

I grabbed the walkie-talkie. "Okay. Let's do this."

Full Moons and Tattoos

Our strokes fell into perfect sync, the kayak gliding gracefully through calm water or darting quick as a minnow through short bursts of rapids. Keirt had done something funky to the kayak, stroked its sides until they glowed to provide light to steer by. Golden moths with luminous wings trailed after us, drawn by the light.

While I admired a sunset sky of lavender and peach, Keirt presented a lecture on the Six Circling Islands. "The islands fall under the protection of Queen Teriquilla, but they are self-governed—those that are inhabited, that is. Jring hosts a fast-growing population of industrious builders and scientists. The 'technology' your aunt gives us is put to good use there. Little is known about the island of Tuoaue, except that it is dangerous and visitors are unwelcome. I tried to visit my father shortly after King Glaem's death, but the Alphan of Tuoaue forbade me to set foot on the island. Tuoaueans prefer not to acknowledge the existence of pixens."

"That's hardly fair."

"Oh, pardon me. I hadn't realized the Queen had decreed a new law stating that life must be fair."

I flicked a paddleful of river water at him. "Don't be snarky. What about this island we're going to, Delene?"

"Delene is a prison for the worst of Migraran, Jringian, and Tuoauean criminals. Unauthorized visits are forbidden, so if anyone asks, we're going to Jring. Wake up, Audrey. You're steering us into the bank."

"Freaking right I am. I have no intention of visiting Migrara's Most Wanted or putting Aunt Ellen in the hands of a dangerous felon."

"The healer won't harm her, I promise. We'll be perfectly safe on Delene. I'll conceal us from their eyes."

At this point, we passed the city of Zantallion. I couldn't see much except for wooden docks and tall stone buildings lit with glowing globes suspended from ropes. Distant music and laughter floated on the air. Keirt paddled harder to take us past the lights. So much for spending the night in a comfy Migraran hotel.

We paddled until Migrara's three full moons had risen high into the sky, throwing silver sparkles on the water. Keirt directed me to the bank, where he jumped out and got a fire going. I helped him gather grass and leaves to stuff into the sack he used as a mattress.

"Hey, what happened to your arm?" His sleeve had fallen back. Blood, black in the moonlight, stained a clumsy bandage he had wrapped around his upper arm.

"A spear skimmed a little too close when the Cauldra Cats first caught up to me. It's nothing."

"Let me see this nothing."

I removed the ragged bandage while he summoned a sphere of light in the palm of his hand for me to see by. "It's not too bad, but you shouldn't ignore it. Wash it in the river, then pour this on it to disinfect it." I handed him a bottle of Migraran booze I'd found at the bottom of the bag containing my Migraran clothes. Aunt Ellen must have gotten her bags mixed up while she was shopping. When he returned, the bottle was empty, and he was whistling. I suspected he had disinfected the lining of his stomach as well. I rummaged through my backpack. It held food, water, odds and ends from my camping gear, my new digital camera, a change of underwear, various feminine supplies, ointment for my new tattoo, and a little first-aid kit, but no large bandages. I would have to improvise.

"Nice dressing," he approved as I pressed it against his arm and bound it with a strip of gauze. "Very soft."

"With quick-absorbing pores and re-adjustable wings," I added.

"Are you going to contact your aunt?"

"Yeah, no use putting it off any longer," I sighed, and switched on the walkie-talkie. "Breaker-one-nine, this is the Little Ant calling the Big Ant, you got your ears on?"

"Audrey!" Aunt Ellen answered immediately. "Where are you?"

I took a deep breath. "Sorry about running off like that Aunt Ellen but Keirt needs my help to get this healer away from Delene so I'm going with him and then we'll meet you at your brother's vineyard. See you then!" I turned off the walkie-talkie and stuffed it into my backpack.

"Very reassuring," Keirt said.

My jaw crackled with yawns as I opened cans of ham and creamed corn from my backpack. Keirt refused to touch food that came out of a can, but made do with fruit and strips of dried meat from his own backpack.

"What's that?" he asked. I had finally figured out how to work my camera and was snapping pictures of our surroundings. I showed him the results on the tiny screen and invited him to take a picture of me posing against Migrara's moons.

"Like this?" he said, fumbling with the buttons. "Oh, sorry."

"You did that on purpose!" I wailed, staring at the trickle of smoke emerging from the ruined device.

"I did not. I can't help it if my pixen magic doesn't agree with the delicate instruments of your world."

Yeah, right. He probably didn't want me recording evidence that would alert my world to the existence of Migrara. I hurled the camera into the middle of the river, wincing as pain shot through my shoulder.

"Stiff already?" he said. "You'll be in sad shape come morning."

"A bus hit me this past spring. The muscles in my shoulder still tighten up once in a while and make my arm fall asleep." I flexed and twisted the arm, trying to work some feeling back into it. I jumped when a pair of hands fell on my shoulders. "What are you . . . oh. Oh wow, that feels great."

Tingling warmth seeped from his fingers into my muscles, untying the knots and chasing away the soreness. I let him work his magic across my shoulders and back, and I was just on the verge of nodding off when he said, "Your hair was much shorter when I last saw you."

I jerked wide awake. "What do you mean? Have we met before?"

"Not exactly. I've been visiting your aunt every solstice for years. Usually she arranged for you to be away from home on those days, but one afternoon you stormed into the house and ranted at Lady Trini about a party you were forbidden to attend."

"I assume you turned yourself invisible?"

"I certainly did hide myself from your eyes. You scared the wits out of me. You were dressed all in black, with spiky hair, and had black paint on your face."

I laughed. "It wasn't paint, it was makeup. I was going through this phase. Can all of you with Tuoauean blood go invisible?"

"Actually, it's a rare ability among pixens, though common among full-blooded Tuoaueans. Shragon Bratch, Headmaster of the Mage Hall, uses it frequently to keep staff and students in line." He traced the lines of the tattoo on my shoulder. "You didn't have this back then. What is it?"

"A dragon." Aunt Ellen and my Grandpa O'Krane, the coolest geezers on earth, had taken me to a classy tattoo parlour for my sixteenth birthday present, shortly before Grandpa had died. "Don't you have them in Migrara?"

"I've never seen such a beast."

"What about unicorns?"

"No."

"Elves? Dwarves? Hobbits?"

"No, no, and no. Now your other tattoo, the black and pink circle, what is that?"

"How could you know about—?" Oh, right. I had forgotten he had seen me absolutely bare-butt naked. "It's a yin yang. It's supposed to be white, not pink. I just got it yesterday. It symbolizes balance between opposing forces. Light and dark. Good and evil. Male and female. The two smaller circles remind us that nothing is ever totally black and white. In every good person, there is a bit of evil, and vice versa."

"Then in every female, there is a bit of male?"

"And vice versa. And if you think you're going to slip a bit of male into this female, forget it." I slapped away the hand that was pursuing my yin yang. I had seen this coming a mile away. Practically since we'd met he'd been studying me like I was a giant Pop-Tart.

"May I ask why?" he inquired politely.

"Pregnancy. AIDS. Brad Pitt in *Thelma and Louise*. Seriously, if we're going to travel together I've got to know you won't grope me every time I turn around."

"No zapping, no groping," he murmured sadly. "You have so many rules, Audrey O'Krane. I think you've been talking to Latiana. I don't know what she told you, but those days are behind me. I was . . . going through this phase, as you say."

"Yeah, right. Look, you're cute, but not my type."

"What is your 'type'?"

He wasn't taking me seriously. It was time to get brutally dishonest. "Prince Nicholas is my type."

He narrowed his eyes at me. "When Latiana asked if you were his lover, you said, 'Yuck.' That did not sound like an expression of enthusiasm."

"How did you know what I said?" I sputtered. "You weren't there."

"I was, but with both Latiana and Prince Nicholas raging about, I thought it best to conceal myself and the Princess. We were in your bedroom when Prince Nicholas barged in. For a lover, he was remarkably rude toward you."

"We have to be careful to hide our relationship from Aunt Ellen," I said. "She wouldn't approve because of the age difference. But trust me, sexual tension has been smouldering between us for months."

He gave a mocking little bow. "I congratulate you on your high standards."

I refused to feel guilty about lying. Maybe I had taken the flirting too seriously, but with Aunt Ellen's life on the line, I needed to stay focussed on our mission.

Keirt stretched out on his cloak, stroking Tist, humming to himself. I lay down on the bedsack and looked up at the night sky. My familiar stars were gone. I didn't recognize a single constellation. I had no idea where I was in relation to my world. I had asked Keirt during our kayak ride, and he had shrugged. Distance was meaningless when it came to world-hopping, he said. Meaningless to him, maybe. It meant a great deal to someone who had never even been out of her own country before.

Keirt looked over at me. "Are you all right?"

"I'm so far from h-home." I jumped to my feet, shaking, my heart galloping. "At least astronauts can look out the window and get used to the distance gradually. They don't just suddenly—"

Keirt held my shoulders to steady me as I hyperventilated. "This is normal. Terror often takes overlappers shortly after they leave their world for the first time. It will pass."

He kept his arm around me until the threat of fainting had passed. That was ok. I would do the same for him if he had a panic attack. It didn't mean anything.

"It's not that I'm homesick," I said, suddenly afraid he'd try to send me back. "I mean, how could anyone miss a planet as screwed up as mine? It's just a big adjustment, that's all."

"I don't think your world is 'screwed up.' I've studied your world's history, and I find it much more interesting than mine."

"Are you serious? Your world has *magic*."

"That's what I mean. You Earthish have accomplished so much more than we have, all *without* the aid of magic."

Earthish? Oh well, it was better than Earthlings, which would make me think of Marvin the Martian. "We've accomplished wars, world hunger and pollution."

"And Vell-crow," he pointed out, as if that made up for everything. "Trust me. Once you've visited other worlds, you will learn to appreciate your own."

More likely, I thought, I would never want to go back.

9

Impulse Control Triumphant

I woke feeling rested, which threw me into a panic. It could only mean one thing—I had overslept and was late for school. I fumbled for the alarm clock, and my hand came down on Keirt's snake. I yelped and sat up, wiping my hand furiously on my jeans.

Sunlight spilled all over us, and it felt great. Everything around me looked fresh and gorgeous—including Keirt. All right, I admit it. I thought he was hot. Especially asleep, looking all peaceful and harmless instead of unpredictable and intimidating. I took the opportunity to examine him head to toe. He had the slender, athletic body of a runner, or maybe a gymnast. I leaned close to see if that silvery white mane had dark roots. Nope, it was natural. The hair on his arms was pale too, catching the sunlight in a way that cast a silver sheen across his tanned skin. His eyebrows were dark, and so were his eyelashes where they lay across his cheek-bones. No doubt about it, he was a total Pop-Tart. I leaned closer, noticing his jaw had no sign of morning stubble, and was struck by an urge to stick my tongue in his ear to see how he'd react.

Sex? my hormones piped up hopefully.

Impulse Control, still grappling with the tongue-in-ear thing, groaned in dismay. *Give me a break.*

Sex, Hormones insisted. *Sex NOW.*

No, Impulse Control said sternly. *Not with a guy we can't trust.*

Don't want trust, Hormones said sulkily. *Want sex.*

In desperation, Impulse Control flashed forward to pre-school registration day, several years in the future.

REGISTRAR: Does your daughter have any allergies?

ME: Just iron.

REGISTRAR: Anything else we should know?

ME: Don't upset her. She'll either throw lightning around or turn into a cat. And if she goes invisible on you, just ignore her.

Sex, Hormones chanted obstinately. *Sex sex sex SEX!*

"Leave me alone!" I snapped. Keirt's eyes flew open. He bounced to his feet, cupping a blue lightning ball in one hand like a pitcher preparing to throw to second.

"Mosquitoes," I explained.

He sent his lightning ball sizzling through the trees. It struck a life form peering at us from a clump of dazzling wildflowers. It resembled a small kangaroo with enormous, bat-like ears. I gave a shriek of protest and scrambled after him as he bounded over to collect the stunned creature. He turned it upside down and pulled open its bulging pouch. I quickly cupped my hands beneath it, but instead of a baby kangabat, a stream of nuts and berries tumbled out.

Keirt thrust the creature at me. "Breakfast."

"No!" I snatched it away from him, cradling it protectively in my arms. "There's no reason to slay God's innocent creatures when I have a backpack full of perfectly good canned ham."

With a snort, the kangabat came to life and drove a powerful hind leg into my face. Moments later it was bouncing away from us, using its giant ears to catch the breeze and sail over logs and bushes with great long leaps.

Keirt produced a hanky from one of his many vest pockets and helped me mop up my bloody nose. "How about fish, then?" he suggested. I nodded. One of God's innocent creatures would look pretty good in a frying pan.

I followed him down to the river to wash my face, then took a look at Keirt's own injury, which looked better this morning. After I changed his pad—uh, dressing—I went into the trees to try on the Migraran clothes Aunt Ellen had given me. The tunic was cream linen embroidered with gold thread. The trousers were the wrap-around style worn by Latiana, except made of soft red cloth instead of leather. The pant legs flared out when I pranced and twirled. A leather vest went over the tunic. In one of the trouser pockets I found seashell earrings and a pendant necklace. The pendant was a colourful spiral that reminded me of the swirl of light around an open porthole.

As I admired my new look, I had an attack of conscience about my hasty message to Aunt Ellen last night. I turned on the walkie-talkie and hailed her once more. Her response nearly blasted my new earrings off.

"Speaking of poor judgment," I interrupted her tirade, "what about you teaching Earth technology to the Migrarans? Don't you know bad things happen to good people when you dump modern advancements on an undeveloped culture? Have you never watched *Star Trek*?"

Aunt Ellen snorted. "No civilization ever collapsed for having achieved advancements in education and communication. My goal is to see a computer in every Migraran school and a telephone in every Migraran home."

I had a mental image of a Migraran kid with a cell phone tucked under his ear as he played video games on his new PC. Instead of fantasy games he would become addicted to Earth-based games. "The Quest for Environmental Sustainability." "You Be the President." "Where in the World is Osama Bin Laden?"

"Queen Teriquilla is also keenly interested in equipment worldhoppers can make use of, such as oxygen tanks for airless worlds," Aunt Ellen said. "In fact, she recently installed a facility for Worldhopping Technology Development on the island of Jring."

"Aunt Ellen, did Mom and Dad know about this world-hopping stuff? About Migrara?"

I barely remembered my parents. My strongest memories were of Dad's goofy sense of humour. I had confusing memories of Mom, with her long, deep silences interspersed with sudden whirlwinds of playfulness and laughter.

"Oh, no. My brother told no one, not even your grandmother, that he wasn't from Earth. He was a fugitive, guilty of unlawful worldhopping. He had accidentally revealed himself to the inhabitants of a hostile world, and they invaded Migrara."

"Oh my God! What happened?"

"Well, the Jaddats were only a few inches tall and armed with little slingshots, so their reign of terror was brief. Even so, King Glaem was furious. He sent the Cauldra Cats to arrest him. Your grandfather jumped into the river in the middle of winter and nearly drowned. He opened his eyes and found himself in your grandmother's arms in the summer of your world. Meanwhile, everyone back home thought he was dead. I knew the truth, but kept quiet. I was tutoring little Pilla—Glaem's mother—and didn't want to jeopardize my position."

"Wait a minute. You tutored Kelly's *grandmother* when she was a little girl? How old are you, Aunt Ellen?"

"Older than I look, but not as old as you fear."

For the first time, I wondered how my own Migraran heritage would affect my aging process. Would I become one of those women who claim the age of twenty-nine year after year—and get away with it?

"You might think it's a fine thing to regain your youth from time to time, but it can be quite aggravating," Aunt Ellen said, reading my mind. "I once had a meeting with your seventh grade teacher, who turned out to be unexpectedly young and well-formed. All at once a good thirty years dropped off my face and figure. It nearly sent the poor man to an asylum."

"Mr. Shellbrook was well-formed," I agreed, "and he acted weird around me after that meeting. So, did anyone ever figure out where Grandpa had gone?"

"Yes, Awnvale Worallan, a worldhopper employed by the royal family, caught me sneaking over to your world to visit my brother. Fortunately, your grandfather's misadventure had long since been forgiven. But the King liked to keep an eye on Migraran emigrants, so Awnvale was a frequent visitor to your world. It was he who informed me your parents had died."

We concluded negotiations with the agreement that if Aunt Ellen could corrupt innocent Migrarans with Earth's technology, I could help Keirt spring this healer from the prison island.

"I'll keep you posted," I said. "Say, Aunt Ellen, how long is this battery good for?"

"Battery?"

"The walkie-talkie battery."

"Batteries don't work on Migrara. The walkie-talkies have been spelled to draw the power they need from the air."

"Then why does mine have a gemstone in the battery case?"

"Maybe the Queen upgraded it." She sounded distracted. I heard voices in the background. "I have to go now, but first let me talk to Keirt. And Audrey—be careful of him."

"Why? Do you think he's dangerous?"

"Not exactly. He's wilful and capricious, like most pixens, but he has a good heart. It's *your* heart I'm worried about. Those with magic in their blood don't take the rest of us seriously. I've seen so many young people give their hearts to pixens and receive only heartache in return."

"Don't worry. My heart will remain firmly within my rib-cage. How old is Keirt, do you know?" I asked, suddenly afraid I'd been kissed by an old geezer who imagined himself much younger.

"Hm . . . about 22.156 years," she said, and I realized she was speaking Migraran. She had reverted back to her native language. If I concentrated, I could almost hear the Migraran words underlying the English translation. That, and the fact that she kept referring to Earth as *my* world, not hers, gave me a strange, lonely feeling.

Keirt, stripped down to his underwear, was stretched out along a tree trunk that slanted over the river. As I approached, he shot a bolt of energy into the water, then jumped right in after it. He surfaced after a few moments and wrestled a breakfast-sized fish out of the river.

"That's cheating!" I said. "And probably bad for the river ecology. You should have used a line. What in God's name is wrong with that fish?"

"It's supposed to look like that. It's a spinlet. You should have been here earlier. A whole school of them came spiralling through the water." He looked me over appreciatively. "Very nice. But you've put the trousers on backwards."

I was trying not to look him over appreciatively. I focussed instead on the corkscrewy fish, wondering if Aunt Ellen's information sharing policy had led to the creation of a nuclear power plant in the area. "Is it safe to eat?"

"Yes, but a challenge to clean. Care to give it a try?"

"On my planet, we have a law: you catch it, you clean it. Here, Aunt Ellen wants to talk to you."

He took the walkie-talkie from me and carried it into the forest. I could just barely hear his voice—at first confident and soothing, but gradually becoming more defensive. I'd seen Lyle receive one of Aunt Ellen's lectures when he brought me home two hours late, and I didn't envy Keirt. When he returned from his conversation, his face was flushed with ire. He threw on his clothes and set about cleaning the twisty fish with such vigour, scales flew in all directions.

"I didn't *know* you were only seventeen." He glared accusingly at me.

"I guess my life experiences have matured me." A total lie. While my classmates studied university calendars and plotted the course of their lives, I immersed myself in sci-fi and fantasy, imagining myself wielding a sword against supernatural foes. Well, here I was in the land of swords and magic, and it was time to take advantage of it.

"When can I go worldhopping?" I asked.

He set the fish to cook and pulled a leather packet out of one of his vest pockets. He unfolded a square of faded white silk covered with splotches of dye. It showed a large blob surrounded by six smaller blobs. Lines of varied colours and lengths marked the silk. Fault lines. This was a map of Migrara's fault lines.

"We'll cross a fault line tomorrow," Keirt said. "The day after that we'll reach Port Everywind. Since it's midsummer, Delene will just have passed the Port. The island should cross this cluster of ocean fault lines while we're there."

I studied the arrows that curved around the islands and the continent of Migrara. "Wait a minute. You mean these Six Circling Islands actually circle around the mainland?"

"As the moons orbit the planet. What, do you expect them to defy the ocean currents and sit in one place year round?"

"Of course not. That would be silly. Where is your mother's island?"

"There. Quampu." He pointed to a small blob far to the south. "It doesn't circle," he added apologetically, as if embarrassed by the island's lack of ambition.

Tist dropped from Keirt's shoulder and undulated across the old silk, his tongue flicking at various fault lines. My hand shook with excitement as I traced the snake's path with my finger. So many worlds, and I had the power to reach them. Maybe. I didn't know if I could still open portholes now that the solstice was a day behind us.

Our second day on the river wasn't quite as eventful as the first. In fact, it was rather dull. Paddle, eat, paddle, eat, pee, paddle . . . Even the exotic Migraran landscape failed to thrill me after a while.

The monotony of our journey didn't bother Keirt. "I've missed being on the river," he said. "As a boy I longed to go rafting, like Blueberry Finn and his friend Tom."

"It's Huckleberry Finn, and it wasn't Tom Sawyer who went down the river with him, it was Jim the slave." I had to laugh. He was a magical creature from a fantastic land, yet he imagined himself in the stories of *my* world.

"What do you long for, Audrey?" he asked.

I longed for many things, most of which were out of my reach. An exciting career, for one. There weren't many of those available to someone who'd been kicked out of high school. And I'd always wanted to be part of a large family. I envied my friends their noisy, chaotic homes, their sibling battles and their gatherings of cousins at Christmas.

"I've always had a longing to travel," I said. "I'd say it's most certainly being fulfilled."

At first I waved and called out to the Migrarans we saw on the riverbank, but they ignored me. When I commented on their rudeness, Keirt said, "Oh, I forgot to tell you. I've hidden us from their eyes. Your boat and your small stature, among other things, would quickly give you away as an overlapper. Most Migrarans wouldn't interfere with us, but some might feel compelled to report your presence."

He was right about the small stature. The men looked normal sized to me, but most of the women topped six feet. Kelly had been the tallest kid in her grade, and Aunt Ellen towered over the other old fogies she hung around with. Sadly, I hadn't inherited the height gene. I was going to feel like an elf on Migrara.

"What other things give me away?" I asked. "My accent, I suppose."

"And your bald legs. They're very nice legs," he assured me as I peered at my carefully shaven knee. "Just a little odd-looking."

I had another look at his map when we stopped for lunch. "Why are the fault lines different colours?" I asked.

"They're coded according to how great a threat the overlapping world might pose to Migrara. Here's the fault line that overlaps your world." Keirt pointed to a short purple mark that slashed across the blue squiggle of a river. Purple probably meant *mostly harmless*.

"What are all these little circles?"

"Those are fault lines that have been locked to protect our world from overlap invasion or contamination. Only the Queen's spies are allowed to visit those worlds."

"Locked how?"

"The Queen once had in her service a powerful worldhopper, Awnvale Worallan. Don't ask me how he locked them—I only know that he did. His greatest regret was that he didn't do so before the assassination. Of course, that wouldn't have stopped the assassin. He seemed to have the ability to world-hop wherever he chose, regardless of fault lines. He opened a porthole into the castle and summoned lightning from a storm-wracked overlap world to kill the King."

"A worldhopper? I thought you said the assassin was Winters—Prince Nicholas."

Keirt took the map back from me and tucked it into his pocket. "It is commonly believed Prince Nicholas hired the assassin. Are you ready to go?"

I frowned at him. "This is too weird. Prince Nicholas had your King murdered and kidnapped his daughter, but you've been visiting them regularly with presents and stuff. Why were you and Aunt Ellen helping him? Is he a friend of yours?"

"Hell, no. I can't stand the man. He's as irresponsible and arrogant a prince as I've ever met. But I never said he killed the King. I said it's *commonly believed* he did so."

"Well, did he or didn't he?"

"No, actually," he said grudgingly. "But so many Migrarans believed he did, he had to flee our world. Taking Princess Perikelli with him was the only unselfish act he has ever committed, to my knowledge. The royal family had an enemy who could walk into Migrara's most heavily guarded fortress. Perikelli would never be safe on Migrara until it was discovered who had really commissioned the assassination."

My head was spinning. "But the Cauldra Cats arrested Nicholas. Don't they know he's innocent?"

"Very few people know. It's safer that way."

"And you just let them take him away!" My voice was climbing into the violin range. "God, I can't believe I was actually starting to trust you. What about Kelly? There's still a killer running around loose. She could be in danger!"

"I know, and that is another reason I'm anxious to visit Delene. The prisoners are a wealth of information. I have been searching for this assassin for ten years. With you to help me, I might at last find the missing pieces of the puzzle."

"Well, thanks for finally letting me in on the plan. What else haven't you told me?"

"Let's pace ourselves, shall we? One shocking revelation at a time." He stepped over to the kayak and offered me my paddle. I didn't move. "I can't leave you here, Audrey. Without my protection, you'll be caught and sent to Mount Cauldra."

With much stomping and muttering, I got into the kayak. For the rest of the day, I made sure to flip river water over him at every opportunity.

Maybe to make amends, Keirt paid for a comfortable room at the inn of a riverside town imaginatively named Riverside. In the tavern he taught me to play a game called toc. It resembled snooker, except the balls and pockets floated in mid-air and if you hit the cue ball too hard it exploded and covered you with green powder. He let us become visible to the other customers, but other than a few curious stares, no one bothered us.

"Perhaps you would like to share some shocking revelations of your own," he said as he carefully lined up a shot. "You said your life experiences have matured you. What life experiences would those be?"

I shrugged and sipped my drink. "Family stuff. School stuff. Loser boyfriend stuff."

"Your parents died when you were a child," he said. "That was why Lady Trini left Migrara."

I opened my mouth to tell him I didn't want to discuss it, and out came, "Their car was hit by a train, which some people think was not an accident, because my mother suffered from depression and might have been suicidal. We'll never know for sure, and that's the part I can't get over." And then I found myself telling him about the mouse.

I had met Lyle on campus for lunch that day and was waiting for the bus home. I watched the mouse travel all the way across College Drive without getting flattened. A few feet short of journey's end, it discovered a sunflower seed . . . right in the path of the bus I was waiting for.

"I just wanted to give the poor little guy a few extra moments to realize his danger," I explained. "Besides, the bus was moving slowly. It had plenty of time to stop."

The downfall of my heroic plan was the bus driver, who happened to be talking over his shoulder to a passenger. By the time he noticed me standing in the bus lane, it was too late.

I was too embarrassed to tell the paramedics why I had stepped in front of a moving bus. I was too embarrassed to tell the emergency room staff at the hospital. I did tell the psych ward staff who placed me on suicide watch, but they still whisked me into counselling.

The therapist wanted to discuss my parents' death, but I instead ranted about Lyle dumping me when he found out about the "suicide attempt." He had spoken at great length about "giving me space to heal," but what he actually meant was, "You're as crazy as your mother and not worth the extra maintenance."

"And no, I have no idea if the stupid mouse survived," I concluded.

"Lyle is an imbecile," Keirt announced.

"Tell me about it. This one party we went to, he passed out drunk. I wrote PROPERTY OF AUDREY O'KRANE across his butt with a permanent marker. He didn't discover it until the next day in the locker room with his soccer buddies. He totally freaked out on me about it. No sense of humour whatsoever."

"He should have been honoured to wear such a label," Keirt said, and ended the game by pocketing three balls with one shot.

When we went up to our room, I expected him to make another try at my yin yang, but he stretched out on the floor and went straight to sleep. Impulse Control was annoyed. She'd been all set to do battle, and now she had nothing to fight.

Maybe he's using reverse psychology in an effort to make you *pursue* him, Paranoia suggested.

Aha! Impulse Control exclaimed, and ordered me to ignore his insidious ploy.

Oh, just get it over with, Hormones pleaded. *You know you're gonna cave eventually*.

While Keirt snored peacefully on the floor, I tossed and turned in the soft bed, praying he'd do something incredibly obnoxious tomorrow.

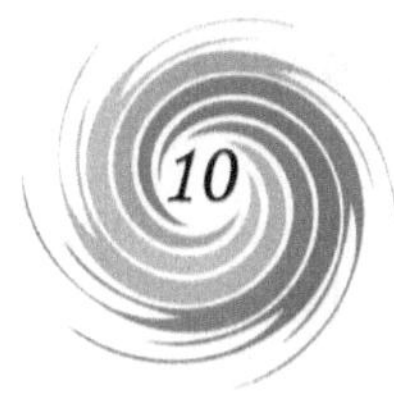

Worldhopping 201

"What do you say we visit the Swinahé?"[9] Keirt asked the following afternoon.

"The who?"

"Swinahé. Friends of mine. Their world lies across the fault line we'll be passing shortly."

My heart pounded wildly. "Okay."

The fault line lay at the outskirts of a small village. It was marked by a stone statue of a wild boar. I vibrated with anxiety as we approached it. If I failed to open a porthole, my dream of independent universal travel would end. I'd have to go to Mount Cauldra and give myself up to professional supervision.

"Wait!" Keirt said. "Never stand directly in front of a porthole as you open it."

I stepped back. "There's so much I don't know about worldhopping. Is there a way to tell if there's anything dangerous on the other side of a fault line before you open a porthole? Does all that swirly stuff around an open porthole cause cancer in rats?"

"Powerful worldhoppers often have a sense of what lies on the other side of a fault line, but I don't know how it's done. The 'swirly stuff' is called rimfire, and most of the time it's harmless. You wouldn't want to touch it, though, as it can give you a jolt."

---

[9] Swee-NAW-hey.

"If you're not a worldhopper, how do you know so much about it?"

"I often travelled with Awnvale Worallan, the powerful worldhopper who served the royal family and taught at the Mage Hall. You could have learned much from him. Unfortunately, he died in a worldhopping accident several years ago."

I felt my face turn pale. "Worldhopping . . . accident?"

"Very rare," he assured me. "He was showing a group of students how to combine their powers to open a porthole on an off-solstice day. One of the students lost concentration and . . . well, never mind. It would never happen with a porthole opened by a solitary worldhopper."

Great. As if I wasn't nervous enough. I focused on the fault line, and of course nothing happened. My shoulders slumped.

"You have to think about the other side," Keirt said. "Think about what you want that's over there."

Other than the chance to meet a new species, what did I want over there?

Freedom! the voices cried fiercely. Freedom to go where I pleased, to pursue dreams and adventures the people of my world couldn't even imagine. Freedom to create memories that would overwhelm every crappy thing that had ever happened to me.

The porthole whooshed open. I whooped and did a happy dance around that amazing, sparkling hole in the air. Smiling, Keirt grabbed my hand and pulled me onto a vast, rolling plain under an orange sky. He led me toward a collection of houses dug into the sides of a ravine. They reminded me of the sod houses from *On the Banks of Plum Creek*.

The Swinahé were a bit of a disappointment. For one thing, they were butt ugly. I try not to judge, but my God, they had tusks. And snouts. Long ones, with a double row of fluttering nostrils down the sides. Keirt said they were the best trackers in the universe. Those multiple nostrils could detect a range of scents beyond any creature he knew of. I found this hard to believe, because the Swinahé smelled even less attractive than they looked.

My wariness was quickly overcome by the Swinahé's friendly nature. One of the young men threw his bristly arms around Keirt, making delighted snorking sounds. His fellow villagers offered us food and drink, lit bonfires, and got some excellent music going. Keirt flirted with the snouty women, made the even snoutier men roar with laughter at witty stories, and entertained the kids with a handcrafted fireworks display. At the conclusion of the fireworks, the whole community burst out dancing, their hooves thundering on the ground. Yes, hooves. I avoided the dancing out of concern for my crushable feet. Declining offers of ale, I sipped juice and smirked at the drunken revellers, feeling morally superior in my sobriety.

I noticed Keirt showing the walkie-talkie to the young man who had hugged him. The Swinahé sniffed it carefully. He said something to Keirt, who gave the device a puzzled frown.

I went over and joined them. "What are you two talking about?"

"Shwenn here tells me the Wakitaki carries the scents of many overlapping worlds. I don't see how that can be. The Queen keeps it always in her possession, and she rarely leaves Migrara."

I wondered if the walkie-talkie would work on this world. While Keirt joined one of the wild stomping dances, I hailed Aunt Ellen.

"Hey, Big Ant. Just checking in."

"Audrey?" came the soft reply.

"Who else? Why are you whispering? Is everyone asleep?"

"These bloody women never sleep. But they haven't found the walkie-talkie yet, and I hope to keep it that way."

"What bloody women? Are you not getting along with your relatives?"

"I'm with the Cauldra Cats. I've sort of been arrested."

I stiffened in shock. "Arrested? What for?"

"Harbouring an assassin and aiding in the kidnapping of the Princess. But Bernie is fine. We hid him in one of the wine cellars, and they never found him."

"Bernie is the least of my worries. What's the penalty for harbouring and aiding?"

"Oh, it will all get sorted out once we reach the castle," she said cheerfully. "You and Keirt stick to the original plan and bring the healer to Bernie at my brother's vineyard. One way or another, I'll find my way back there. If I don't—oh, damn!"

There came sounds of a scuffle, a snarl, and then the walkie-talkie went dead.

"Aunt Ellen? Aunt Ellen!" I cried. "Will you leave me *alone?*"

Throughout the evening I had been receiving numerous romantic invitations from the young men, which Impulse Control had no difficulty convincing me to decline. While I was talking to Aunt Ellen, a persistent young man had been literally pawing at me to get my attention. I smacked his hand. He scuttled back, seeking the security of his friends. They wrinkled their snouts at me, revealing the full length of their sharp tusks. All at once, the Swinahé didn't look so friendly.

Keirt was suddenly at my side, breathless and dishevelled from the dancing. He bid everyone a gracious good night and escorted me back to the fault line. The sulky young Swinahé men trailed after us, but didn't interfere.

"They aren't as dangerous as they'd like to appear," he assured me as we returned to the relative safety of Migrara. "In the past, the Swinahé have been a great help to me. My friend Shwenn and I explored many overlapping worlds together when I became a—" He hesitated, then grinned at me. "Audrey, do you realize you opened a fault line locked by Awnvale Worallan? I can think of no more than three worldhoppers who are that powerful. And I can't think of *any* who could do it on an off-solstice day."

"Never mind that. Aunt Ellen's been arrested!" I brought him up to date on the walkie-talkie conversation.

He groaned. "Bloody Latiana! She's so depressingly efficient." He took the walkie-talkie from me and tried to hail Aunt Ellen, but there was no reply. "Don't worry for your aunt's safety. She is a friend of the Queen, after all. They won't harm her."

"We have to go to the castle," I said. "We have to get her out of there."

"Easily done. Look." He took out his fault line map and pointed out Cauldra Castle. A multitude of fault lines webbed the mountain that formed the base of the castle. It was a nexus for overlapping worlds. Probably its location had been chosen for that reason. "You can worldhop her onto an overlapping world. But first we go to Delene. We need that healer."

I would have liked to stay awake talking about Aunt Ellen and the Swinahé and worldhopping, but the excitement of the day had wiped me out. I threw my bedsack onto the riverbank, not even bothering to stuff it with grass. I didn't protest when Keirt lay down next to me. I found that if I stayed close to him, the Migraran bugs left me alone.

I woke several hours later to discover the moons had turned green. I frowned at this phenomenon and sat up. My face smacked into something soft and flexible that left a coating of slime on my cheeks. I jerked back and reached out cautious hands. We were enclosed in a wobbly green bubble. The walls of the bubble flinched at my touch and let out a sound suspiciously like a belch.

I said, "Keirt, wake up. We've been eaten."

He opened his eyes and examined our living prison. "Don't worry; it's just a bloart. They're harmless river creatures. Our body heat drew it out of the water."

"Harmless? It swallowed us alive!"

"It's just absorbing the air from our lungs."

"Oh, so it won't digest us, just suffocate us."

"We won't suffocate. It gives us its own brand of air in return, rich in healthy vapours. When I attended the Mage Hall, I did a study on bloarts. They—"

"Never mind the nature lesson. Get rid of it, now!"

"How?"

"Stab it, zap it—I don't care!"

"And have it collapse on us? Just lie still. It will return to the river when the sun rises."

He put a small flute to his lips and tootled what was no doubt meant to be a soothing melody. I was not soothed. I scrunched into a ball, pulling my arms and legs as far as possible from the gently undulating green dome that covered us. The rubbery walls seemed to draw closer. I was on the verge of leaping to my feet and thrashing my way free of the creature when the flute music stopped and a multicoloured glow flickered beside me. Its source was a ball of energy cupped in Keirt's hands. He drew his hands apart, creating a web of light that transformed into a red bird with fluttering wings. With a twitch of his fingers, the bird became a galloping horse with a flowing mane and tail, then a ship tossed on a stormy sea, then my face, with sparks shooting out of my blue eyes and my hair whipping wildly around my head.

Impulsively, I stretched my hand toward it, then drew it back.

"Go ahead," he invited. "It won't hurt."

I slipped my fingers into the writhing web of energy. My palm sprouted an electric rose surrounded by sparkling butterflies. It prickled, but it didn't hurt.

"So what does a court mage do?" I asked. "Perform magic shows for the royal family? Grow fantastic gardens? Zap royal enemies?"

"I sometimes perform skyplays," he said. "No gardens, though. My magic is limited to the elements of fire, light and lightning. Mostly I act as a liaison between the court and the Mage Hall, though not a very effective one. I've never gotten on with the Mage Hall Headmaster. I am also supposedly the ambassador to Tuoaue, but Alphan Oureil[10] has never invited me to the island. The Headmaster took on the role of ambassador when the Queen assigned me my new duties."

"What new duties?" He hesitated. I tried to read his face, but he had clapped his hands together to banish the light. "All right, what aren't you telling me?"

"Nothing you need to know," he said. "Yet."

The bloart let out a squelching sound, and I began to hyperventilate again. "Okay, that's it. We have to get out of here or I'm going to have a panic attack of epic proportions."

He sighed, then leaned over and kissed my forehead. "Go to sleep, Audrey."

It seemed only a moment later I opened my eyes to sunlight. The bloart was gone. Keirt stood with a ragged group of men from a travelling caravan, sharing bad jokes and a pot of porridge steaming over a fire. The caravan had arrived in the night, and I hadn't even noticed.

---

[10] Oo-RAY-il.

I joined the men, took Keirt's bowl from him, and up-ended it over his head.

"You promised no zapping!" I shouted.

"That wasn't zapping," he said, wiping porridge out of his eyes. "That was—"

"Just keep your freaking magic lips off me!" I shouted.

As I stomped away, the men from the caravan gathered around him, offering sympathetic advice on how to cope with a dissatisfied lover. I paced the riverbank, fuming. Okay, maybe I had overreacted, but you don't just go around kissing people unconscious without their permission.

"My aunt was right about you," I said as he waded into the river to wash the porridge from his hair. "You have no re-spect for anyone without magic. You think you can just do whatever you want to me and get away with it because—" I waited impatiently for him to finish swishing his head around under the water— "because you're more powerful than I am."

He waded back to shore, shaking the water from his hair. "I wish you would stop listening to tales others tell about me. They are greatly exaggerated. As for being more powerful than you, that might not—" He broke off and turned his head sharply, listening. Then he popped out of sight.

"Get back here, you coward!" I flung blobs of wet sand in all directions, hoping for a lucky hit. As I bent over to collect a second round, something tackled me from behind.

I shrieked in outrage and struggled to look over my shoul-der. It wasn't Keirt who sat on me. It was Latiana in leopard form, sword strapped to her back, her paws pinning my arms to the ground.

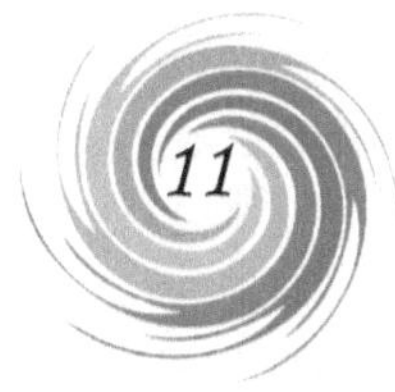

More Revelations

The men from the caravan dropped their porridge and scrambled for the safety of their painted wagons. Oh, don't worry about me, I'll be fine, thanks.

"Get off!" I yelled.

"I would have expected some small thanks for rescuing you from your kidnapper," Latiana said, shifting to human form. Now I had a naked woman sitting on me. I was not comfortable with this.

"I haven't been kidnapped." I struggled to break free of her. "I'm here of my own free will."

"A foolish will, if you agreed to travel with Keirt Prai. Where was he taking you?"

"The island of—" I hesitated. "Jring. I want to tour that Worldhopping Technology place."

"Out of the question," Latiana snapped, finally letting me up. "An untrained worldhopper running loose on Migrara?" She sniffed at me in sudden horror. "By the Lioness, you've been among the Swinahé! I'll tear the ears off Keirt Prai!"

I shook the wet sand out of my clothes and hair. "Oh, don't make such a big deal of it. We just partied with them a little. I didn't even have anything to drink. Who is this lioness you keep talking about?"

"*The* Lioness, She who watches over us, She who provides for us, She who suckles us at Her—"

"Okay, okay, I get the picture. Look, shouldn't you get dressed? Those men from the caravan are going to sprain their eyeballs."

"Keirt has far too much confidence in himself." She yanked at the bundle of clothing tied around her neck. "When we last travelled to Swina together, he got into a fight with a hot-headed Swinahé youth. It was only my quick intervention that prevented us from being apprehended, or worse."

"You've travelled together? The way you talk, I thought you and Keirt were enemies."

"Actually we were lovers, for a time," she said casually.

"You're kidding," I said, uncasually. "Isn't he, well, a little young for you?"

"Years don't mean as much to Migrarans as to people from worlds like yours, where everyone ages at an even pace. But it's difficult to share a bed with a man who lives for vengeance," Latiana said, apparently feeling the need to explain their break up. "Also, I found it restrictive to limit my bounces to only one man's bed, as he insisted. A surprising trait in a man who is half Quampuish."

That *was* surprising. I would have expected Keirt to be the wandering one in that relationship.

"What do you mean, he lives for vengeance?" I asked. "Are you talking about the King's assassination?"

"And the death of his mother, of course," she said. "Did he not tell you? Drandima, Captain of the Cauldra Cats, was the first to reach the Prince's bedchamber the night the world-hopper assassin invaded the castle. She was too late to save the King from the bolt of lightning that killed him, but her courageous intervention allowed the Queen to escape. A second bolt of lightning struck Drandima down."

I shook my head in shock. "No, he didn't tell me."

"He had been watching over Perikelli that night. The Princess had been suffering nightmares and would not sleep unless Keirt sat with her. He heard his mother cry out and came running. She and the King lay on the floor of the Prince's bedchamber, dead. Prince Nicholas stood over them with a drawn sword. Naturally the lad tried to kill the man. Would have succeeded, too, if the Prince hadn't struck him unconscious."

I recalled the burn scar Latiana had pointed out on Nicholas' chest, and shivered. "What were the King and Queen doing in the Prince's bedchamber?"

"The King was there because he had discovered the Queen was there, and the Queen was there because . . . well." She shrugged.

"Holy crap. The Queen was messing around with the Prince!" I tried to imagine boring, sour faced Nicholas Winters in a torrid affair with a queen. My brain recoiled in horror.

"A ploy on the Prince's part to draw the Queen and her husband away from their protectors," Latiana assured me. "Once he had them where he wanted, he summoned the worldhopper assassin, snatched the little Princess and was never again seen on Migrara. I suppose he hoped to use Perikelli to wrest the throne from the Queen, but the Princess foiled his plot by refusing to grow up. Clever girl! The Queen will be well pleased to have her back."

"I've heard rumours," I said carefully, "that Prince Nicholas is innocent. That someone else hired the assassin."

"You are a gullible child to listen to the lies of a traitor, and it is high time you were taken in hand. Gather your belongings. I am bringing you back to Mount Cauldra with me. Your aunt is already halfway there."

My protest died in my throat as Latiana hoisted a foot onto a fallen tree, cocked her hips, and gave the log a good soaking, much to the outrage of the colony of blue ants who inhabited it.

"My God, I had no idea we could pee standing up," I said. "This changes everything."

"Are there no warriors on your world?" Latiana retied the cord of her wrap-around trousers. "A warrior never squats to squirt."

"We have too many warriors, actually, but most of them are men."

Latiana threw back her head and laughed. "Male warriors! Of course, you see the odd male warrior here and there on Migrara, but most are too small, too emotional, and they lack the protective instinct that makes women so fierce in battle. Fighting is no job for a man. Although in Port Everywind, there lies a fault line to a world with a most impressive male army. That world is a feast of the most delicious men you would ever lay eyes on." Latiana's own eyes closed as she savoured yummy memories.

"Port Everywind? That's where Keirt and I are going. Why don't you come with us? I'll open the porthole, and you can chase all the tasty guys you want," I suggested, hoping we were talking about romance and not cannibalism.

Latiana's eyes flew wide. "That is forbidden! You are untrained and unlicensed, and you would never manage it whatever the way. That fault line is locked."

"Not for me. I opened the porthole to Swina, remember? Come on. No one would know."

"The Queen would strip me of command for dereliction of duty."

"Well, suppose I escaped you, and you had to follow me to Port Everywind, and I just happened to come across the fault line to this world, and decided to visit it, and you had to come and get me?" I edged toward the river.

She grabbed me by the collar of my tunic. "So you can trap me there? How foolish do you think I am?"

"I'd come with you. I'd like to meet these men."

"Latiana. I must speak with you." Keirt appeared beside us. For a moment, Latiana tensed into pounce mode, then relaxed and let him lead her further into the trees. "Stay here," he said rudely as I made to follow. We exchanged angry frowns. Did he think I was serious about joining Latiana on a worldhopping sex romp? I didn't know whether to be insulted or amused.

They spoke intently for several minutes, throwing occasional glances back at me. The roar of the river drowned out their voices, but I caught a few words here and there. From Keirt I heard, "—won't care once she meets Audrey—" and "—incredible potential—" and "What exactly did you tell her about me?" From Latiana I heard unflattering comments regarding his intelligence, but judging by her thoughtful expression, he seemed to be winning her over.

Impatient at being left out, I walked toward them.

"Well, on your head be it," Latiana was saying as I joined them. "Though the Queen will certainly send you to Delene if you fail."

"Oh, you told her about Delene?" I said to Keirt. "I thought we were keeping that a secret."

Latiana stared at me, and Keirt closed his eyes in dismay.

"I was joking about Delene. I meant the Queen would imprison you if you do not succeed in this venture." Latiana turned back to Keirt. "You are actually taking this girl to Delene, Keirt Prai? For a moment, you had me convinced you were sane, but I see I was mistaken. That settles it. I am placing you both under arrest for violating Migraran worldhopping laws."

"I'm sorry, Latiana," Keirt said, and zapped her. She hit the ground like a WWF wrestler, all flailing arms and legs, and went still.

"Latiana!" I knelt at her side. She had hit her head on the way down. Now she had two lumps on her partially shaved skull. You'd think the woman would invest in a helmet.

"We'll have to move swiftly if we want to reach Port Everywind before her," Keirt said.

"We can't just leave her here, at the mercy of . . . whatever!" Blue ants marched toward her, intent on revenge.

While we had been arguing, the caravanners had packed up their camp and set off down the riverbank with all possible speed. Keirt hoisted Latiana over his shoulder, staggered after the departing caravan, and heaved her into the back of the last wagon.

"That should slow her down," he said cheerfully. I went to climb into the rear cockpit of the kayak, but Keirt steered me firmly into the forward one. "I don't want you at my back while you're angry with me."

"I'm not pissed off anymore. Latiana told me about your mother. I'm sorry." When he didn't reply, I said, "Where did this worldhopper assassin come from, anyway?"

"It was easy enough to find the world he emerged from, but he was likely not native to it. He would have used it as a bridge. It's a common trick among outlaw worldhoppers, to travel from world to world to hide their trail. The Queen sent spies across many fault lines, and they found nothing. I will waste no more time searching for the assassin's home world. What would any overlapper gain by murdering the Migraran royal family? It had to have been a politically or personally motivated Migraran who commissioned the assassination."

"Well, if it's politicians we're looking for, a prison is a good place to start."

"How cynical you are, Audrey O'Krane."

"Spend a few years on my world and you'll understand why." I looked over my shoulder. "Speaking of naughty politicians, did you know Queen Teriquilla was having an affair with Prince Nicholas?"

His nodded grimly. "I grew up in the castle, and I was not a lad to keep secrets from. Although it did take me some time to discover the truth of the Prince's innocence. I hunted the Prince for years . . . years while the real killer walked free."

The tight anger in his voice worried me. I wondered what would happen if our efforts to bring this healer back to Mount Cauldra threatened to interfere with his search for his mother's killer.

Late in the morning—the final hours of Christmas Eve, back home—I detected the distant odour of rotting fish. We had reached the Southbowl Ocean. By sunset, Keirt said, we would be on Delene.

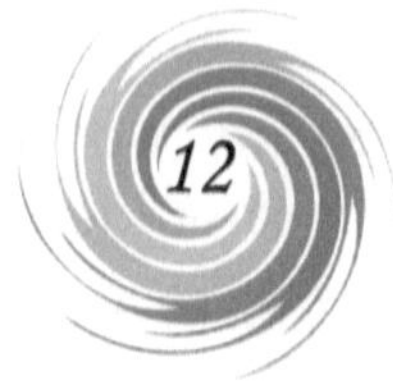

The Prisoners of Delene

"Let's visit the world that overlaps this city," I said as Keirt led me to the waterfront of Port Everywind. "It comes highly recommended."

Keirt was counting the coins a merchant had given him for the kayak. The trading of overlapper merchandise was strictly regulated by the Migraran government, so of course there was a huge black market for it. He scowled without looking up. "We don't have time. I want to reach Delene before sunset."

"Geez, I was joking. Don't bite my head off. So how do we get to this island? By boat?"

"Not exactly." Keirt pointed to a giant life form perched on a cliff that rose up behind the docks.

I gasped in awe. Its slender, powerful body glittered a metallic red in the sun. A sunburst mane of red and gold feathers framed a raven-shaped head perched on a swanlike neck. It spread its glossy wings, flared its silky golden tail and gave a haunting cry that rang across the ocean.

"We're riding that gorgeous creature to Delene?" I whispered.

"Not that one. The one behind it."

The one behind it stood in danger of losing the remainder of its ragged plumage to the next strong breeze. A bedraggled mane of greasy grey feathers framed a turkey-shaped head that hung precariously from a thin, drooping neck. It was blind in one eye.

"No, seriously," I said, but Keirt was already climbing the steep path up the cliff. At the top, he hailed the bird's rider, a balding man who bore a remarkable resemblance to his steed.

"Heia,[11] Keirt!" the man bawled, waving a bottle at us. He heaved himself out of a wicker chair propped against a shabby hut in the shadow of the giant bird. He and Keirt thumped each other on the back and traded a few friendly insults. "So, what's new in the life of Keirt Prai?" he inquired, thrusting his eyebrows in my direction.

Keirt introduced me as Lady Audrey Oak, a worldhopper in training travelling under Keirt's protection. "Are you making a flight to Delene today, Baub?"[12]

"Within the hour." He nodded at a man and woman making their way toward us through the crowds on the docks. The Migrarans parted to give them a wide berth. The man's hands were tied behind his back. The woman led him with a rope looped through a leather collar around his neck.

"If you want your old job back, you'll have to take it up with *her*," Baub continued. "I'd just as soon have you back. Half the time *she* doesn't even bother to sedate them for the Embedding. Wretched gruesome thing to watch when they're wide awake for it."

"I'm not looking for work, just a ride." Keirt ignored my frantic attempts to pull him aside for a private conference. "We have business on Delene. Can Dusty carry the five of us?"

---

[11] What he actually said was "hey," which is a common greeting on Migrara, but it was so unsettling to hear these medieval people saying hey! to one another that for my own peace of mind, I've assigned the word an exotic spelling.

[12] Rhymes with "Bob."

"We'll have to harness the prisoner to her chest strap, but if the Blue Hag has no objection, it's all right with me."

We waited for Baub's other two passengers to arrive. The prisoner was a sullen man with stringy hair, and the woman gripping his leash looked about as friendly as a Nazi with a hangover.

"It matters not to me if you wish to ride along, so long as you share the price of passage," shrugged the Blue Hag, who also went by the name of Chalissa Nake. The "Blue" came from her skin colour, a sign of Tuoauean heritage. Like Keirt, she was a pixen. She looked me over and grunted as if to say she was just too busy to report the presence of an overlapper today.

Baub rigged four saddles and helped the warden stuff her prisoner into a harness attached to Dusty's chest strap. It didn't look very comfortable, but at least he'd have a good view. The man was a cook, I found out later, and his crime was deliberately using iron utensils to prepare and serve food to a pixen customer, who consequently died. That might explain Chalissa Nake's lack of warmth toward him.

The other three climbed aboard the bird and waited for me to join them. Dusty swung her moulting head around and blinked her good eye piteously, begging us not to do this to her. I sighed, apologized to poor Dusty, and climbed up behind Keirt. Dusty groaned.

Once we were strapped in, the giant bird lurched toward the edge of the cliff, spread her creaky wings, and miraculously rose into the air. At this point, the theme of *The Flintstones* started up in my head. It would be stuck there for days and would drive everyone around me crazy as I hummed it ceaselessly in an attempt to shake it loose from my brain.

"The island lies southwest of us," Keirt shouted. "Why do we fly southeast?"

"Easier on Dusty," Baub shouted back. "Ever since that run-in with the frost eagles over the Island of Agneld, she tends to list to starboard. Have to compensate for it."

Dusty moved more gracefully through the air than on the ground. It was smooth sailing until about an hour out from the mainland. With nothing to see from horizon to horizon but choppy water, she stalled, let out a hiss, and went into a nosedive. I clutched the saddle bar in front of me and closed my eyes against the tearing wind. The leather straps around my waist creaked with tension. The wind deafened me as it screamed past my ears—oh wait, that was me screaming.

Seconds before slamming into the ocean, Dusty levelled off, stabbed something out of the water with her beak, and swooped toward the clouds again. With a brisk snap of her head, she swallowed a giant, shark-like life form.

"Sorry about that," Baub yelled. "She's absolutely mad for gribbets. Once she sets her eye on one, there's nothing for it but to hold on."

Fortunately, the Southbowl Ocean only contained about ten million gribbets. By the time the fifth flapping tail slid down Dusty's throat, I was begging the others to let me jump off and swim the rest of the way. I imagine the prisoner strapped to her chest felt the same. Once in a while he would shout something at us, but we couldn't make out the words, which was probably fortunate.

On the plus side, the extra protein gave Dusty a burst of energy. The Island of Delene rose on the horizon and slipped toward us until we were gliding over the coastline. The Delenes on the docks barely glanced up when Dusty's vast shadow slid over them.

We flew over a small coastal town and then over rugged mountains wrapped in a tangled tropical forest. Dusty pumped her wings to clear a thick wall of trees, and I do mean *wall*. They stretched hundreds of meters into the air.

Their twisting trunks and branches wove so tightly together, I doubted a bird could slip through them, let alone a human. I expected sentries, guard dogs, and barbed wire, but the wall of trees contained nothing more than a sparse forest with occasional clusters of wooden huts. Apparently Delene had no security. The Delenes just threw the prisoners in here and left them to their own devices.

"What's to keep people like us from grabbing prisoners and flying off with them?" I asked.

"You'll see," Keirt said shortly.

Dusty flapped toward a low mountaintop, where a large crater formed a natural arena. Thousands of prisoners sat on benches of stone lining the sides of the crater, watching a battle between two life forms that resembled badgers. These badgers were the size of locomotives. With their grunts and snarls and the encouraging roars of the spectators, it sounded like a Grey Cup game. Dusty veered away and drifted toward the base of the mountain. No one appeared to notice her.

Baub landed Dusty on the crumbling wall of the ruins of an old temple. Below us lay a rubble-strewn courtyard overgrown with a thick tangle of vines. Chalissa Nake jumped down to free the prisoner from his harness. As Keirt and I dismounted, she released the man's wrists from their bonds with one swift stroke of her knife, then shoved him off the wall. He landed on a heap of vines. The vines came to life, wrapping their strong, sticky stems around the prisoner's arms and legs. His cries for help escalated to terrified screams as the vines writhed toward his face.

Keirt grabbed Nake's arm. "You're supposed to sedate him for this!"

She shrugged, a small smile curling her lips as she watched the prisoner's ordeal. "I forgot."

"Dusty, gribbet him!" Baub said. Dusty stretched out her long neck and made a grab for the man, but when the vines tried to wrap around her beak she tore free with a shudder and backed off.

The man's screams rose in volume. A vine had wound around his head, pinning it to the ground. Another frond curled around and thrust itself into his screaming mouth. Blood erupted from his nostrils. I screamed, Baub took a long pull from his bottle, and Keirt leaped off the wall.

He dodged through the flailing vines, flinging lightning in all directions to keep them from overwhelming him. They had already pulled back from the prisoner, who thrashed around on the ground, clutching his head in agony. Keirt reached for him, and I wondered if he was going to zap him—or kiss him?—unconscious, but I never found out. The man lashed out with a booted foot, catching Keirt in the chest and throwing him onto his back. A churning mass of leaves pounced gleefully on him.

"Help him!" I screamed at Nake.

She settled comfortably against Dusty's leg. "He'll manage."

I snatched the long knife from her belt and scrambled down the side of the crumbling wall. I had almost reached Keirt when the vines caught up to me. They whipped around my waist and ankles and yanked me to the ground. I started to scream as a thick vine curled toward my face, then remembered how ineffective a defence that had been for the prisoner. I clamped my mouth shut and the vine smacked me in the face a few times while I hacked grimly at it with the knife. Finally it drew back, thought for a moment, and went for my nose. A burst of light exploded behind my eyes.

I woke to an upside-down view of Keirt's backside, and a fine view it was, but I was in no shape to enjoy it.

"Put me down, I'm going to throw up."

Keirt stopped and pulled me off his shoulder, holding me while I coaxed my legs to stay up and my stomach to stay down. Oddly, I was covered in white powder.

"Your aunt was right about you. What did you think you were doing?" He looked sweaty and irritated, but unharmed.

"I don't exactly remember, but I'm sure I had a good reason for it. What do you mean, she was right about me?"

He ignored the question. "I had to stun you along with the vines to free you. Did you really think a few unruly weeds could get the better of me? I am no mouse. I don't need saving."

I knew it had been a mistake to tell him about the mouse. "Is this what you used to do for a living? Dump prisoners off and let the local plants torture them?"

"It's called the Embedding. The vines have implanted a seed in the prisoner's skull. That's how they propagate. The seeds remain dormant unless they come within range of the Treewall we flew over. The vines thrive on a chemical thrown into the soil by the leaves of those trees. The trees send out a constant vibration that causes the seeds to burst and take root. So, if an Embedded prisoner approaches the Treewall, or tries to fly over it—"

"His head explodes. Kind of like the botanical version of *Aliens*."

"I did fly prisoners out with Baub years ago, back when I was still searching for Prince Nicholas, but I quickly lost the stomach for the job."

I looked down at myself. "Keirt, why am I covered in flour?"

"It made it easier to pull the sticky vines off you."

"You just happened to have a bag of flour on you?"

"To trade for information. The prisoners have little use for currency. It's all right; I still have the cheese and sausage."

I looked around. We stood on a path halfway up the mountain where we had seen the animals fighting. "Where is Baub?"

"He flew Nake back to the docks. We'll meet them there at dawn."

"I see. So we're trapped on an island inhabited by several thousand violent criminals, many of whom you yourself helped to incarcerate."

"They probably won't remember me," he said modestly. "Can you walk now?"

I put a hand to my forehead, probing for a headache. "Those vines didn't shove a seed up my brain, did they?"

"I suppose we'll find out when we leave the island, won't we?" he said unkindly. "Come on, we should try to reach the mountain top before nightfall."

Night doesn't fall in the forest, it rises. Shadows pool in gullies and hollows. Darkness crawls up the tree trunks and gathers among the branches to press against the sky. There I was going all stressed out and poetical again. Things got even more poetical when we came around a bend in the path and found ourselves face to face with a giant, badgerish life form covered in blood.

The creature hissed and lashed at us with claws like swords as Keirt yanked me off the path. It thrust its narrow snout through the trees and snapped at us.

"Make us invisible!" I shouted.

"I can't! It's wearing an iron ring in its nose. Iron makes it immune to my magic."

A wicked swipe of a paw sent us both tumbling through the underbrush. A claw hooked the hem of my cloak and hauled me back through the trees. I screamed for Keirt, but he had been thrown hard against a tree trunk and was having trouble getting to his feet. A second furry form flew over me and smashed into the giant life form, knocking me loose. It savaged the beast's shoulder and sprang back before the claws could rip it apart. A whistle pierced the air, and the larger beast hesitated. I hadn't noticed the woman accompanying it. She called to it, and it limped back to her, grunting crankily.

She patted its leg. "I know, darling, I know. Save it for the next battle. Come, let's see what poor wretch our benevolent caretakers have dropped among the ruins. If he hasn't survived, he's all yours."

They continued down the mountain. I stood and looked around for the creature that had saved me. It was gone, and Latiana, her form halfway between cat and human, stood in its place.

"How did you get here?" I gasped.

She grabbed my shoulders and turned me this way and that, inspecting me for injuries. I wasn't hurt, but I was perspiring so hard the flour on my skin had turned to a sticky paste.

"I caught up to you as your megornith took wing. I took the cat form and clung to the harness," she said. No wonder the prisoner kept shouting at us during the flight. "I leaped clear before you landed. What was all that screaming about at the old temple?"

Keirt, who had joined us and was conducting his own damage inspection of my body, briefly explained. Latiana shook her head. "You two are a pair. I'm amazed you survived this far."

She seemed surprisingly forgiving, considering we had resisted arrest, knocked her out, and abandoned her unconscious body among a caravan of strangers. Encouraged, I said, "You aren't going to arrest us, are you?"

"Not before I learn what you are doing here."

"Lady Trini needs a healer," Keirt said.

"I thought she looked unwell. But why send you to Delene?"

"She specifically requested Yinkara Belderkin."

Latiana shuddered. "By the Lioness, what for? The woman is beyond insane. She killed a man by turning him inside out!"

"He was a very bad man," Keirt assured me as I turned to him incredulously.

Latiana grunted. "This is the height of foolishness, but as you've come this far you might as well continue—so long as I accompany you, and we travel straight to Cauldra Castle from here. How will you convince the Delenes to part with their only healer?"

"With Audrey's help, I think we can slip her off the island before anyone notices." Keirt outlined a complicated strategy where we would open a porthole on one of the fault lines currently passing over the island, wait on the overlap world until the island had moved on, and then worldhop back onto Migrara. I saw many flaws with this plan, starting with the fact that this would dump us in the ocean. "But if anyone asks, we have come looking for Bwelmar Ivandel," he concluded, ignoring my protests.

"The spy turned thief?" Latiana said.

"He was an excellent information seeker before the temptation of overlap wealth corrupted him. The Delenes will readily believe a Court Mage would come all this way to speak to him."

We came upon no more prisoners until we reached the mountaintop. We climbed the stone steps leading up to the edge of the crater and looked down at the arena.

"Oh, man," I said faintly. The battle had obviously been a fight to the death, and the spectators were now butchering the loser. The giant animal's keeper stood nearby, sobbing like a baby. While the local entertainment committee supervised preparations for a massive barbecue, everyone else had fallen into party mode. Music, dancing and fights had broken out. Several victims lay on the ground, drunk or dead. It looked like a mosh pit.

Keirt gave me a playful nudge. "Don't look so worried, Audrey. They can't see us. You, Latiana, must stay here. When you're in this state, you have a bad habit of bolting out of my magic's range without warning." She looked sulky, but didn't argue.

"This state?" I echoed.

"I approach the point of my cycle when I retain the cat form," Latiana said, gesturing at her half-cat, half-woman body. "I will not be fully human for several days. Such a shame. There are many fine samples of the male species on this island. But in this form I would surely injure them."

I silently ordered myself not to have a mental image based on that statement. Crap, too late.

We walked down into the ancient amphitheatre now used as an arena. A wonderfully industrious civilization had once thrived on this island, long before the Delenes had turned it into a prison.

"What about pixens?" I asked as a wave of noise and body odour washed over us. "Does your invisibility magic work on them?"

"It does. Just stay close to me."

I tried to pretend I was at one of the university mixers Lyle had taken me to. It wasn't hard. These people were no scarier than some of the students I had seen at an Engineering Department bash. The lone exception was the man who sat on a stone bench at the edge of the arena, alone and ignored. He was huge, wrapped in an enormous tattered cloak, and possibly dead. He didn't move once as Keirt and I made a circuit around the arena, just sat there gazing at his feet. I guess if I had feet that big, I'd stare at them in horrified fascination too.

We worked our way back and forth across the arena, trying to avoid the rivers of blood that ran from the slaughtered animal. Keirt climbed onto a bench now and then to see over the heads of the increasingly rowdy crowd. I suddenly realized I had no idea what this healer looked like. What if she was that enormous bald woman with all the tattoos and piercings? No way Dusty could ever haul her to Mount Cauldra.

Our route took us past the giant sitting at the edge of the arena. I stepped carefully around the enormous bare toes, fighting the impulse to bend down and tickle them to see if he'd react.

Maybe he read my mind, because a massive hand shot out and grabbed me by the throat.

Lady Oak

"Keirt!" I screamed, twisting and flailing like a trapped squirrel. The giant's thumb and forefinger completely encircled my neck—not squeezing, just holding me there. Keirt rushed at us, lightning crackling at his fingertips.

"Don't waste your energy, son. Your pixen sparks will have no more effect on me than your tricks of concealment." The giant shrugged his cloak aside, revealing that he was wrapped all around with iron chains. The other prisoners shot nervous glances at him. As far as they could see, he was holding onto nothing and talking to the air.

"Let her go, Thamb Opi," Keirt said.

"Come closer," the giant invited, nuzzling my hair in a manner designed to irritate Keirt. I slapped him, and winced. It was like slapping a brick wall, and about as effective. Keirt stepped forward, fists clenched white at his sides. "Closer," the giant coaxed.

Another step. Keirt flinched as the toxic vibes of the iron chains struck him. Surprise rippled through the prisoners. We had just become visible to them.

"Keirt Prai." They passed the name around, and not with the fondness of fans meeting their favourite celebrity. A crowd of thousands gathered around us in a menacing circle. I prayed Latiana wouldn't do anything stupid, like charge down and try to rescue us.

"You are the last outsider I would expect to see among us, Keirt Prai," Thamb Opi said. "To what honour do we owe this visit?"

"I've come to speak with Bwelmar Ivandel."

"Ivandel is no longer with us. Royal spies are not popular in our community. Too many of us are here because of the efforts of his kind." The giant shot Keirt a scary smile. "But he served us well, in the end."

"Rather, he was served *to* us." A prisoner licked his lips. "Fresh meat is a rare treat on Delene."

Keirt made an incoherent noise deep in his throat. I decided it was all right if Latiana chose to rescue us. The sooner the better.

"What was Ivandel to you that you would walk into our midst to seek him out?" Thamb Opi finally removed his hand from my neck. I stepped to Keirt's side and glanced at him to see if he had any escape strategies in the works that I should know about. He returned a look that said, "Sorry—we're screwed."

He offered an edited version of the truth; the King's assassination, his mother's death, his quest for revenge, his suspicions that the assassin was hired by politically motivated Migrarans. Many of the prisoners showed no surprise at his revelations. I suppose even on a prison island, news of world events gets around.

"And where does the little lady come into this?" Thamb Opi asked.

I opened my mouth to protest this derogatory reference to myself, then realized that, compared to the women around me, I was a lady, and little.

"I work for the Migraran court. The Queen ordered me to help him," I said.

"Migraran, my left testicle. You're an overlapper, or I'll eat my chains."

Everyone pushed closer to get a better look at me. I tried to look tough and unappetizing, which isn't easy to do when you're covered in gravy.

"They come not for the whispering bones of Ivandel, they come for me!" A tiny, spidery woman with green hair flying off in all directions scrambled onto Thamb Opi's shoulder. She was a Tuoauean, but the chains didn't seem to bother her. "They seek healing for the wise lady and her gentleman. They would take me from you, husband!"

I stared at her, open-mouthed. This tiny creature was married to the giant? Keirt looked ill. I took a wild guess that this new development was not part of his plan. It had never occurred to us that our target inmate might not *want* to leave prison.

"What is that?" Yinkara Belderkin cried, pointing suddenly downward.

"What? Where?" I leaped in several directions at once, scanning the ground for malicious life forms. But it was me she was pointing at. She sprang to the ground and pulled open my tunic.

"Ah!" she said, staring intently.

I snapped my tunic shut. "Do you mind? It's called a bra. You could use one yourself, lady."

"Great power will pierce this breast, and blossom there," she hissed. "Worlds upon worlds hang in the balance, their fates determined by how you will wield it."

I didn't know what to say. I'd heard of reading palms, but reading boobs?

"I am less concerned with the balancing of worlds than with why Keirt Prai wishes to take my wife, and our island's only healer, away from Delene," Thamb Opi said.

"It's my aunt," I burst out. "She's dying, and no one will heal her because she brought an overlapper to Migrara, and he's sick too."

"Who is your aunt?" Thamb asked. "Who are you, for that matter?"

"This is the Lady Audrey Oak," Keirt said. "She who found and returned the lost Princess Perikelli to Migrara."

"Keirt!" I yelled. Now every wretched criminal on the planet would know Kelly was on her way back to her mother.

"The Lost Princess is found?" The delight in several voices surprised me.

Keirt stood up on the stone bench and went all Shakespearean. "She is a beautiful young lady now, brave and bold as ever a royal princess could be," he shouted at the crowd, the amphitheatre carrying his words across the mountain top. He stepped away from the giant and thrust his hands into the air. From his fingertips, streaks of lightning shot into the sky to dance among the stars. Knives appeared in the prisoners' hands. I put my back to Keirt's, trying to recall moves from a karate class I took last year.

Ignoring the rising weapons, Keirt wove the strands of energy together until they formed a crackling outline of a teenage Kelly. Good ploy. If anyone went after her, they would be looking for a sixteen-year-old, not a little girl.

"Lady Oak befriended her and returned her to our world," he continued, and an electric version of myself danced across the sky to join Kelly. "Soon the young Princess will be reunited with her mother." Lightning Audrey took Lightning Kelly's hand, and they skipped and twirled over to a woman with outstretched arms.

"Why are we all dancing?" I whispered.

"I usually perform skyplays to music," Keirt whispered back. He was tense with concentration, but a smile flickered across his face as his eyes followed his airborne creations. I'd seen the same expression on my friend Irene's face when she painted murals. Keirt was enjoying this.

The lightning women faded away. A scattering of prisoners burst into applause.

"Very noble, but you ask a great deal of us," Thamb Opi said, unmoved. "What would you give us in return?"

"We have cheese and sausage," I offered.

"Give us Keirt Prai," snarled a man who had been neglecting his oral hygiene. "We know what you really are, Prai, and it's not just a favourite pet of the royal court."

"We won't kill him," promised a bald, heavily pierced and scarred woman who easily topped four hundred pounds. She gave Keirt a cheerful slap on the butt. "Some of us can think of better uses for him than that."

"You can have what's left of him," someone shouted, and our tenuous hold over the crowd abruptly snapped. Knife-wielding prisoners surged forward while others tried to beat them back. Keirt thrust me behind him and raised his hands against the roiling mass of violence, but no lightning emerged from his fingers. He was too close to Thamb Opi and his chains.

"What if we could break you out of this prison?" I shouted.

Silence fell. The prisoners exchanged startled glances. It hadn't even occurred to them to suggest it.

"Are you aware of what would happen to us if we approached the Treewall?" Thamb Opi's hand was around my neck again.

"I know, the exploding seeds. But what if you never actually left the prison? What if I worldhopped you onto an overlapping world?"

"There are no fault lines on Delene," Thamb said.

"Sure there are. I saw at least five of them on Keirt's map."

Now it was Keirt's turn to yell. "Audrey!"

The circle of prisoners tightened around us. Thamb held out a hand to Keirt. We'd left our belongings with Baub, but Keirt always kept the fault line map in his vest pocket. He handed it over, glaring at me. The prisoners gazed upon the map with wonder.

"What a master thief and a worldhopper couldn't do with this!" one breathed.

"The fault lines actually lie in the oceans, not on the islands themselves," Thamb murmured, tracing the lines on the map. "But the islands pass over them as they circle Migrara. We just have to find one."

"In six months, you mean," I said. I didn't want them to know just how powerful I was. "That's what I meant, that we could come back on the next solstice."

"Now," Thamb said.

"But fault lines open only on solstices. Isn't that right, Keirt?"

"A powerful worldhopper such as yourself could open a porthole any day of the year," he said. "You could even sense a fault line, if you drew near enough." Apparently we were competing to see who could betray the other in the most spectacular fashion.

Rattling and clanking like Marley's Ghost, Thamb pushed me through the crowd. "Saddle the mounts and ready the children. When we find the fault line, we'll return for those who wish to leave."

"You keep children here?" I said incredulously.

"The children born among us are free to leave, but most choose to remain with their families."

Thamb lifted me onto a shaggy life form the size of an elephant. It had a long, graceful neck and a cluster of curly horns sprouting from its head. Thamb settled behind me, nearly knocking me to the ground with all those swinging chains. Keirt shared a mount with the enormous bald woman. It was hard to say whom I felt sorrier for, Keirt or the creature that carried them.

We rode for hours in search of the fault line, but all I sensed were eyes watching us from the shadows. I hoped one pair of those eyes belonged to Latiana.

"Outcast prisoners," Thamb explained. "They do not abide by our Code. Dangerously mad, some of them. I would be among them if not for the iron that binds me. I was one of the most powerful citizens of Tuoaue, until I challenged our Alphan for leadership of our people. He thrust a spell of madness upon me and sent me to the mainland. I devastated entire towns with violent magic before the Cauldra Cats brought me to bay and wrapped me in chains. I've not removed them since."

Why are you telling me this, I thought, too tired to say it out loud. He had already shaken me awake several times.

"The Alphan of Tuoaue is a ruthless creature, fiercely protective of his people. He will do anything to keep them safe."

I forced my eyes open. "What kind of things? Does he see the royal family as a threat to his people?"

"His relations with the Queen of Migrara have always been amicable. He once gave her and her mate a gift of great power. It was this gift that prompted me to challenge the Alphan. Such power should never have left Tuoaue."

"What was it?"

"Ask the Queen to show it to you. She keeps it a secret, but I think she would make an exception for you. If you could convince her to return it to Tuoaue, I would sleep easier."

"Stop," I said. "Stop, I felt something."

Our little entourage halted and dismounted. I walked back to the rotting old bridge we had just crossed, wondering if I had imagined it.

"There's definitely something here," I said. "It's like walking through a spider web, only the web passes through me instead of sticking to my skin."

"Open it," Thamb suggested calmly.

A soft, hissing voice rose from beneath the bridge as I stepped onto it. "You can't do this, Audrey. In over a hundred years, not one prisoner has escaped Delene. To release the entire population would throw all of Migrara into a state of panic!"

Ignoring Latiana, I paced back and forth across the spider webby area. Nothing happened. To make matters worse, the fault line was moving, or rather, the island was slipping past it. It had already passed the bridge and was making its merry way through the forest, forcing me to chase after it.

"This is a waste of time," one of the men said in disgust. "I say we kill them both and sell the map to our jailers in return for our freedom."

I leapfrogged desperately back and forth across the fault line. No luck. It was so easy last time. I just thought about what was on the other side. Freedom. But not my freedom, in this case. No, freedom for the prisoners. If this overlapping world was inhabited, I was about to unleash a mass of criminals upon an unsuspecting population. No wonder the porthole wouldn't open.

"They have children here, Audrey," Keirt said quietly. "Young ones who have committed no crime and have never known a day of true freedom."

Light flared and a burning circle illuminated the forest. The center of the circle peeled apart to reveal a series of windblown sand dunes. Keirt's new girlfriend gasped, then coughed and spat as sand blew into her mouth.

"It's a desert," I said, peering dejectedly into the burning wasteland. The fault line moved on, but the porthole stayed in place. "You can't live there."

"Deserts have borders. Jinthel, gather our people." Without hesitation, Thamb walked through the opening, which I widened to accommodate his enormous size. He shuffled through the hot sand, smiling. The others hurried through, swearing in amazement.

Latiana emerged from concealment. She was down on all fours now, though still human enough for speech. "That was well done, Audrey," she said, apparently resigned to a mass prison outbreak.

"They'll fry out there," I said.

"Not if they use the desert world as a bridge. Cast about for a second fault line."

She slipped back into the shadows. Delenes hauling luggage and children were approaching the porthole. Keirt and I followed them onto the desert world. A bridge, Latiana had said. We walked into the wind, closing our eyes against the grit.

Keirt swiped his wrist across his damp forehead. "We're losing sight of the porthole."

I kept walking, letting my senses guide me. That invisible spider web feeling passed through me again. I turned around, and another porthole opened in front of me. I saw a grassy plain in summer with a few stands of trees here and there, a lake in the distance. No signs of civilization. It could have been the Canadian prairie, except for the mauve sky, and the two moons that hung over the horizon.

And so I became the hero of Delene. My bones ached from hundreds of hugs from grateful prisoners, most of them parents.

"Where is she?" I said anxiously as the last stragglers of the exodus trickled through the two portholes. "Where's the healer? She'll come with us, won't she?"

I jumped as a spidery hand closed on my shoulder. "I cannot attend your aunt and her gentleman, but I can offer you this gift." Yinkara Belderkin handed me two small vials of scarlet liquid. "One for each, to reverse their ills. They will enjoy long lives, should the fates allow."

"Thank you," I said, choking up as I clutched the precious vials to me. "Oh, thank you."

She peered into my face as if it was the most amazing thing she had ever seen, then darted away through the porthole, giggling like a little kid. Close behind her came the four hundred pound bald woman. She leaned down from her mount, lifted Keirt by the front of his vest and planted her lips across half his face. Hard to tell if she was kissing him or eating him.

"I'll fight you for him," she offered when she came up for air.

I shook my head. "Consider him a gift."

"It makes no sense," he muttered as she dropped him with a laugh and rode through the porthole. "They dine on poor scrawny Ivandel, yet allow a feast like that to walk free."

"Aren't they going?" I asked Thamb, pointing to a handful of prisoners with no luggage.

"Not all of them want to leave. Some have lived here for generations. This is their home."

I found that incredibly sad, but Keirt had no time for sympathy. "You have your freedom, Thamb Opi. I think we have earned some information in return. What do you know of the assassination?"

"I have told you everything you need to know."

Only the iron chains kept Keirt from going for his throat. "You told us nothing!"

"I have told you what you need to know," he repeated. "My people will take you safely to the Treewall. Lady Oak, you have my eternal gratitude. You are always welcome here." He kissed my hands, handed Keirt the fault line map, and rode through the porthole, chains chiming at every step.

"Merry Christmas, Thamb Opi," I called, and let the porthole close behind him.

Latiana joined us as the Delenes led us to the Treewall. From a safe distance, the prisoners pointed out the unofficial visitor's entrance, a concealed tunnel that wound through the thick roots. Some desperate prisoners had attempted to escape through it. Their bones were scattered among the trees. We travelled through the tunnel for hours, encountering rats and other disgusting life forms, some of which would have had us for breakfast if not for Latiana's claws and Keirt's electric fingers.

"I'm sorry, Audrey," Keirt said as we finally emerged on the seaward side of the Treewall.

"For what?"

"For my idiotic overconfidence. For failing to protect you as I promised I would. For jeopardizing your chance to save your aunt."

Isn't that just like a guy to humble himself and take all the fun out of being mad at him. I didn't say anything, but squeezed his hand. He held mine for a moment, smiling at me.

Latiana cuffed him across the head, growling. "To the docks. I'm hungry."

The sun had risen high by the time we reached the docks. Baub was beside himself with worry. He'd had to visit the local tavern to calm his nerves. He was so calm we had to wait several more hours until he regained enough consciousness to climb into Dusty's saddle under his own power. Chalissa Nake and Latiana had a ferocious argument about which of them would ride back to the mainland with us. When Latiana took the cat form and roared at her, Nake decided to catch the next flight out.

Keirt was still fuming over Thamb Opi's final words to him. "Did he say anything to *you* about the assassination?" he asked as we struggled to fasten Baub's safety harness for him.

I described the sequence of events that had brought the giant to Delene. "I asked him if he thought the Alphan had arranged the King's death. He said the Alphan's relations with the King and Queen were 'amicable,' and that the Alphan had given the Queen a powerful gift. We're supposed to ask her to show it to us. Thamb Opi thinks it should be returned to Tuoaue."

"Do you know anything of this?" Keirt asked Latiana. Now fully locked in cat form, she lashed her tail and made no reply.

Baub recovered somewhat as we got our own safety gear done up, at least enough to get Dusty airborne.

"Home, Dusty!" he bellowed, and slumped back unconscious against Keirt. Dusty winged across the ocean, presumably back toward the mainland.

I felt a thrill of apprehension. "What do you think will happen to us when we get to Mount Cauldra?"

"I don't know, but I'm fairly certain the Queen, no matter how angry, will not have us slain on sight. In fact, I'm anxious for her to meet you."

I thought that was an odd way to put it. Why would he want *her* to meet *me*, instead of the other way around?

Cauldra Castle

It took Dusty three days to fly us across Migrara. She could have done it in two, but each time we landed it took forever to coax her to allow the fully feline Latiana to climb onto her back.

Upon landing in Cauldroot, the city at the base of Mount Cauldra, we found everyone celebrating the return of the Lost Princess. The streets overflowed with singing, dancing Migrarans. Vendors sold statues and sketches of Kelly while amateur street performers enacted the story of her disappearance. I saw pixens scattered among the crowds, and was surprised the festival didn't include magic shows. I guess when magic is a part of your everyday life, there's no call to make a show of it.

I was eager to get back to Aunt Ellen, but also disappointed. Keirt had promised me all kinds of worldhopping opportunities on our journey. Now it was nearly over, and I had barely glimpsed the universe of overlapping worlds.

"Once we've spoken to the Queen, you will have all the worldhopping adventures you can manage," he assured me mysteriously.

When Keirt and I reached Cauldra Castle, everyone we ran into reacted to Keirt's presence with horrified sympathy, as if they didn't expect him to survive his return. By "everyone" I meant the guards, castle staff, residents, and visitors who crowded around us as we crossed the castle grounds.

Keirt shouldered them aside impatiently and didn't stop until we reached the huge bronze doors of the castle. A pair of Cauldra Cats guarded the doors. One of women clapped Keirt on the back and called him a few shocking yet affectionate names.

"How fares the Queen, Oyanli?" asked Latiana, now mostly human again.

"Plenty furious with Keirt Prai." She narrowed her feline eyes at me, and I edged closer to Latiana.

"Not for long," Keirt said confidently.

"What about Aunt Ellen?" I asked. "Is she all right? And Prince Nicholas?"

Oyanli frowned. "Very odd, that. I'm not sure quite what to make of it. But we're not to speak of it outside the castle."

Latiana led us into the castle and installed us in a small, sparsely decorated chamber before departing to inform the Queen of our arrival. We waited over an hour, no doubt to allow her time to sharpen her axe. Keirt looked calm, but he had been humming the theme to *The Flintstones* and juggling his collection of coloured balls non-stop since we had entered the room. Where most people would have smoked or paced, Keirt juggled. The balls contained doohickeys that made them chirp like birds as they spun through the air, and the noise combined with the humming was slowly driving me insane. For the hundredth time, I pulled out one of the vials Yinkara Belderkin had given me. I examined the scarlet liquid, wondering if it would really save Aunt Ellen—or perhaps poison her, considering its source was more than a little insane herself.

"I can't believe I'm about to meet a queen. Latiana should have let us have a bath first." I sniffed cautiously at the Pits of Doom, wishing I had brought deodorant.

"I think our cleanliness, or lack of it, will be of no great concern to the Queen," Keirt said.

"Canada has a queen too. When I was a kid, I thought she controlled the weather because at school we sang a song about how she rained over us."

He laughed so hard his juggling balls flew out of his hands and bounced all over the room. I watched him scramble after them and felt a surge of affection.

"You know, when you give up being all charming and mysterious and let the real Keirt come out to play, you're a lot of fun," I said. He paused in the act of reaching under my chair and looked up at me in surprise, a smile tugging at his mouth. He had amazing lips, full and expressive, with nice firm edges. I had a sudden urge to lean down and—

Impulse Control gave me a mental boot in the rear. *Don't let your guard down! You thought you knew the real Lyle, too.*

The door flew open. We sprang to our feet. A girl a little younger than me stood in the doorway, smiling at us and chewing on her thumbnail. At her side stood a red tiger.

"Yes?" I said finally.

"Audrey Oak," the girl said, and flew across the room to throw her arms around me.

"Kelly? Oh my God!" I hugged her back, stunned. She was taller than me.

"My Lady Pea Frog," Keirt said with a solemn bow. She giggled and hugged him too.

The tiger pounced on one of Keirt's chirping balls and batted it across the room. Kelly shot the beast a look of annoyance. "That's Sarline. She follows me everywhere. I'm supposed to bring you to meet the Queen." The Queen, not "my mother." I wondered what she'd been told.

"Well, let's get it over with," I said. We waited for her to show us the way, but she just stood there, fidgeting. A tear trickled down her cheek.

"What's wrong, Kelly?"

"I can't do it," she sobbed. "Everybody wants me to be a grownup, but I'm scared. It's too fast."

I put my arms around her. "Of course it is. No one should have to turn into an adult overnight. You just grow at your own pace. When you're ready, it will happen by itself."

"Is that how it was when you grew up?" she sniffled into my shoulder. She was growing smaller, the young woman becoming a little girl again.

"I'll let you know when it happens."

The tiger growled impatiently. Kelly bounced out of my arms. "Oh, all *right!* Geez!"

I wiped her eyes and made her blow her nose, and then she took us to the castle library.

I love libraries, and this one was no exception. A new addition to Mount Cauldra, it was a giant frosted glass dome surrounded by fruit trees. I guess they didn't have hail on Migrara. The interior looked more like a greenhouse than a library. Flowers and vines trailed down the marble shelves, which were laid out exactly like an Earth library, probably because Aunt Ellen had designed it. I'm guessing she also donated the CD collection and CD player I saw displayed.

At the far end of the library, an elderly librarian was playing a tune on a small whistle. One of the books glowed on its shelf and echoed the tune back to him. He pulled the glowing book off the shelf and brought it to a woman seated at a long wooden table, studying a collection of silk maps. Several Cauldra Cats stood around the table, pointing to various locations on the maps. They were giving reports on fault line activity from the recent solstice. When the library staff saw Keirt approaching the table, they dropped what they were doing and evacuated the area.

Queen Teriquilla was a slender woman of approximately forty—although you never know with Migrarans. The carefully sculpted wings of her crisp blond hair were held in place by a silver tiara. Other than the tiara, her appearance was disappointingly casual. She wore a sleeveless white tunic and swishy trousers that fell to her knees. I tried not to stare at her hairy legs. I still wasn't used to Migraran women's aversion to shaving.

The Queen looked up as we approached, and her face went stern. "Perikelli."

There are plenty of mothers who would love to turn their teenage daughters back into little girls again. The Queen was not one of them.

"Audrey Oak says I don't *have* to grow up. And my name is *Kelly*." Hoisting her oversized gown above her knees, she stomped defiantly out of the library, barely missing Sarline's toes. Huffing wearily, the tiger trotted after her. The Cauldra Cats stepped back and formed a semicircle around the Queen, watching us closely. The Cats were no longer cat women, they were just women. Without fur and fangs they weren't nearly so scary, but they still had that pounceable air about them.

"Well, Keirt," the Queen said, rising from the table. I recognized that look. I had seen it on Jersicke's face just before she expelled me.

I stepped forward. "Pleased to meet you, your Majesty. I'm Audrey O'Krane." Not knowing whether to bow or curtsy, I tried to do both at once and nearly fell over.

"I am pleased to meet the niece of Lady Ellen Trini," she said as I struggled to regain my balance, "although I must question your taste in companions." She returned her icy gaze to Keirt.

A man came to her side from behind the bookshelves. My jaw dropped. The last time I had seen Nicholas Winters, he'd been wearing boots and a bathrobe. Now he was decked out head to toe in princely raiment. Nicholas Winters of Saskatoon was no more. Prince Nicholas of Migrara was here to stay.

"I thought you were a prisoner," I said.

"Only until my arrival at the castle," he said. Behind him, the Cauldra Cats twitched uncomfortably. Keirt had been right when he'd guessed the Cats would have some "sport" with their captive. He looked like he'd been chewed up and spit out.

Keirt offered the Prince a slight bow. "My apologies, Prince Nicholas. It seems I've caused you some inconvenience."

"Arrest him," Nicholas said. Swords and claws came unsheathed as the Cauldra Cats leaped forward to do his bidding.

"Not just yet." The Queen held up a hand. The women fell back into formation in the blink of an eye. "I believe you have something for me, Court Mage?"

Keirt handed over my walkie-talkie. The Queen examined it, checked the gem in the battery case, and slipped it into her pocket. Some of the tension left her face, but her voice remained grim.

"Did you use it?" She shot the question at me, taking me by surprise.

"Only to call Aunt Ellen a couple times," I stammered. "Sorry." She studied me with narrowed eyes. I felt a flash of annoyance. Those were *my* initials scratched on the back, after all, not hers.

She turned back to Keirt. "Have you an explanation for your behaviour?"

"I thought Lady Trini would have provided it."

"I would like to hear it from you. I would like to know why my trusted friend would betray me and endanger my family. For ten years, Nicholas has been living the life of an exile, allowing the people of his world to believe him a traitor, because I asked him to keep my daughter safe. For ten years, I have been parted from my own child, because I wished to see her live to adulthood."

The *Queen* had sent them away? Oh, man.

"Ten years of moving from city to city, tearing her away from friends and familiar surroundings when the local Earthish began to question her unchanging face," Keirt said. "That was no life for a child. She needed her mother. She needed to come home."

"That was not your decision to make!" Nicholas shouted. His hand was on the hilt of a sword at his belt.

"Perhaps you should take it up with Teriquilla. It was her decision to send the Cauldra Cats after me, her decision to withhold from them the knowledge that you were innocent. If *innocent* could be used to describe a man who would take a king's wife to his bed."

The Cats hissed, and I looked for a place to hide. Keirt had been mistaken when he told Latiana the Queen wouldn't remain pissed off at him for long. There was a lifetime of pissed off in the Queen's expression.

"Keirt and I have been trying to find out who killed the King," I blurted, and then winced at my lack of tact.

The Queen took it calmly. "What did you discover?"

"We discovered Audrey is a worldhopper," Keirt said, with the air of a gambler laying down a royal flush. "The most powerful worldhopper I have ever seen, perhaps even stronger than Awnvale Worallan. She can open a porthole at any point along a fault line on any day of the year."

A spark of excitement warmed the Queen's cold face. "Were you born on a fault line, Audrey?"

"Yes, and at midnight on a winter solstice," Keirt said.

"The power you must have absorbed!" she breathed. I was alarmed by the way she was staring at me, like I was a Christmas present she was about to unwrap.

"Do you suppose we could find a use for her?" I could tell Keirt was pleased with her reaction, but trying to appear casual.

The Queen abandoned the iron lady routine. Smiling, she shook her head and held out her hands for Keirt to take in his own. "I delve my heart for rage, but find only forgiveness. Such is ever the way with you, Keirt Prai, and you know it well, damn you. Come, Audrey, we will reunite you with your aunt. You will tell us of your adventures while Keirt Prai reflects upon his transgressions and decides what form his atonement will take."

Something about the way she looked at him as she said that reminded me of the way Latiana spoke about him in her less angry moments. Geez, was there any woman in Cauldra Castle he hadn't been involved with? The Prince's eyebrows crashed down, his mouth and nostrils going into spasms of disapproval.

Queen Teriquilla took my arm as we left the room. "We have much in common, Audrey. I too am a worldhopper, though not nearly as powerful as you. I too lost my parents at a young age. They were killed in an overlap invasion of Migrara."

"Not the Jaddats!" I blurted in dismay.

She laughed. "No, this was years after your grandfather's little misadventure. These invaders were poachers. They hunted species with head hair. They believed it held spiritual qualities and would bestow power upon the wearer if woven into jewellery and garments."

I stared at her in disbelief. "They killed people for their hair?"

"Conservationists among them urged the cultivation of hair producing species rather than indiscriminate slaughter, but the hunters couldn't justify the expense. Besides, it was sport for them. They had already hunted several world populations to extinction when they came across Migrara. I tell you this to warn you of the dangers of worldhopping. Even the most harmless-seeming overlap worlds can prove deadly. I do hope you plan to stay with us, Audrey. You would learn much by attending the Worldhopping Studies Branch of our Mage Hall. With your skills, you would not need to wait two years to earn a license."

Trailing behind us, Keirt asked, "Teriquilla, may we see the gift you received from the Alphan of Tuoaue?"

It was as if he had zapped her with one of his electric shocks. She stiffened and spun around, her eyes wide. "Where did you hear of that?"

"From a Tuoauean. A friend of their Alphan." Needless to say, we had decided to omit the whole prison break episode from our story. As far as we knew, Migrara was not yet aware that the majority of the incarcerated Delenes had vanished. We'd convinced Latiana not to tell.

"What do you know of it?"

"That it is very powerful." He studied her pale face. "And dangerous."

She looked from him to me. "This is not the place to speak of it." And that was her last word on the subject.

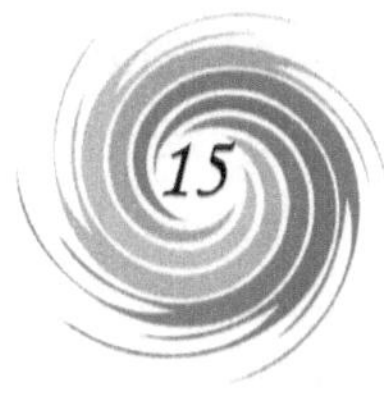

A Queen and Her Cats

The Queen had us escorted to private rooms where we could change our clothes and, thank God, bathe. An hour later we all met in a large dining chamber. I almost didn't recognize Aunt Ellen. Since her return to Migrara, years had been dropping away from her. She could easily pass for fifty. She wore a beautiful gown and had her hair done up in the latest Migraran fashion; a true lady of the court. Youth and stylishness aside, she looked awful. The cancer had taken a deeper hold on her in the days we'd been apart.

"Aunt Ellen!" I rushed at her and thrust one of my two glass vials at her. "Here, drink this."

She took it from me. "Is it from Yinkara Belderkin?"

"Yes. I have one for Bernie, too, though I don't know how we're going to get it to him."

"Audrey, you fantastic girl. Don't worry about Bernie. Teriquilla has given permission for him to join us here. She's making a special exception for him, as she is for you."

She gave me a hug, then pulled the stopper from the vial and downed the contents of the tiny bottle. I was disappointed to see no immediate and dramatic change.

"These potions usually need a day or two to take effect," she said. "Now, I want to hear all about your journey. Try not to tell me anything that will force me to ground you."

While I endured a gruelling interrogation by Aunt Ellen, Prince Nicholas and Keirt stood at opposite ends of the chamber and glared at one another. Keirt had exchanged his plain travelling clothes for a pair of polished boots, tailored trousers, and a red cape over a white shirt. This must be his court mage formal wear. He looked respectable, powerful, and uncomfortably attractive. He caught me looking and winked at me. That comment about being a lot of fun had obviously gone to his head. Remembering that I had boasted of a relationship with the Prince, I tried to fling a few smouldering glances at Nicholas when Keirt was looking and the Prince wasn't, but my timing was off and Nicholas caught one of them. His eyes widened. Oh my God, how embarrassing.

The Queen arrived and with her came a royal feast of roast beast with a load of yummy side dishes. Obviously Aunt Ellen had convinced her to create a belated Christmas dinner in my honour. There was gravy, mashed veggies, and something that resembled cranberries.

Queen Teriquilla had an air of suppressed excitement, which I thought at first was inspired by her daughter's return. But her manner toward Kelly was oddly formal. Maybe this was how Migraran royal families behaved toward their children. Kelly's own behaviour was anything but formal.

"By my sword, our Lost Princess is not half rude to the Queen, isn't she?" Latiana muttered to me following an attempt on Kelly's part to fling a blob of mashed veggies in Her Majesty's direction. Prince Nicholas wrestled the fork from her and whispered fiercely in her ear.

"I am a stranger to her," said Queen Teriquilla. Latiana was going to have to work on her muttering skills. "She would not remember me, after so many years. I am certain that after dwelling in Cauldra Castle for a time, her memories—and her manners—will return to her."

"Kelly!" Nicholas snapped, and Kelly quickly reeled in her protruding tongue. Keirt lowered his head to hide a smirk while I gulped some wine to drown a fit of giggles. Nicholas glared, clearly blaming us for both her poor manners and her regression back to childhood.

"What happens now?" I asked. "With Kelly and Prince Nicholas, I mean."

"In the morning, I will formally announce the news of my daughter's return," Teriquilla said. "I will tell my people that Prince Nicholas returned my daughter with the aid of Lady Ellen Trini. They may not believe he is innocent of the crimes attached to his name. For that reason, Prince Nicholas will leave Cauldra Castle. He will not return until I have convinced the people of Migrara that he is not a traitor."

"You mean he's going to leave Kelly here?" I looked at Nicholas. His mouth was tight. Kelly turned pale, then clutched at his arm and began to cry.

Aunt Ellen stroked Kelly's hair. "Teriquilla, are you certain about this? You know how she reacted to being separated from you. To be parted now from her uncle—"

"It is a difficult but necessary decision for all concerned," the Queen said calmly. "Perikelli needs to grow up, and I don't believe that will happen as long as she is with the Prince. I think it would ease the strain if you agreed to remain at Cauldra Castle to act as Perikelli's governess, Ellen. She has a great fondness for you, for which I am grateful. She clearly needs more guidance than I can provide."

"She has a great fondness for Keirt, too," I said, thinking now was the time to put in a good word for him, in case she meant to banish him as well.

Too late. Without looking at him, Teriquilla said, "Keirt Prai will accompany Prince Nicholas, as will Captain Latiana."

Keirt and Latiana exchanged a startled glance. "With all respect, my Queen," Keirt said, "I would rather—"

"There are no two people I trust more to protect him," she said. "You will leave tonight. I have arranged for the castle megornith to carry you to Bisgaun, where you will remain until I send for you." Bisgaun, I found out later, was a heavily guarded vacation island owned by the royal family. "As for you, Audrey, I would be pleased to have you remain with us at Cauldra Castle. I have a great favour to ask of you, but we will speak of that later. It has been a long day, and we are all weary."

Kelly jumped up from the table and fled the room, sobbing. Prince Nicholas sighed and followed her. Keirt frowned at the Queen, his fingers drumming on the table. Sparks shot out of his fingertips where they struck the wood, but he didn't seem to notice.

Latiana also looked troubled. "My Queen," she said, "why did you not warn me about Prince Nicholas when you set me on Keirt's trail? When I first encountered the Prince, I nearly slew him."

"I apologize for not confiding in you, Captain. You see, at that point I did not know whom I could trust. Remember, there may still be a traitor on the loose."

"My attempts to find this traitor produced more questions than answers," Keirt spoke up. "Some of those answers seem to lie here within Cauldra Castle. For example, I discovered an interesting fact about your Wakitaki; in recent years it has travelled to many overlap worlds. Which leads to the question—"

The Queen slapped the table, making the wine glasses jump, and me along with them. "Enough! I will not have my every decision questioned by those who are pledged to obey me. Trust that all will be made clear to you in time. The more swiftly you follow my orders, the more swiftly you will receive your answers."

Keirt murmured an apology and excused himself from the table. He exited the chamber, presumably to pack for the trip to Bisgaun. I tried to catch his eye, expecting at least a word of farewell, but he didn't even look at me. The Queen rose as well, bidding us a gracious goodnight before following Keirt. I stared listlessly at my dessert.

Aunt Ellen was watching me. "Do you want some chocolate Santas?" she asked. "I've been saving them for you."

"No thanks."

"I can't wait to show you around Mount Cauldra. We can start with the Overlap Museum in the morning, then ride to the Mage Hall in the afternoon. Did you see the arena on your way in? Next month Mount Cauldra hosts the annual tumbleball tournament. I have good money riding on the Cauldra Cats against the Jring Giants."

"Aunt Ellen, how long will we stay here? I can worldhop us back to Earth any time we want, you know. We don't have to wait six months."

"Do you want to leave?"

"Only if you want to."

"I think we should stay a while. For Kelly's sake, if for no other reason. What do you think of Queen Teriquilla, now that you've met her?"

I shrugged. "She could use some parenting lessons, but otherwise she's okay. Did you know she had been cheating on her husband?"

"Oh, certainly. It was the worst kept secret in the castle."

"Were they not getting along?"

"Whatever her reasons, she paid dearly for it," she said firmly, cutting short my attempt to fish for gossip. "What does strike me as odd is sending Prince Nicholas away yet again. In the past, she would have discussed such a decision with me. She's changed in the years I've been away."

"Did you miss Migrara very much, Aunt Ellen?" A lump formed in my throat. "You gave up an awful lot to come to Saskatoon and look after me."

"But I gained so much more," she said gently. "I'd never been a mother. After decades of teaching other people's children, the opportunity to finally raise one of my own was a great gift. I've never for a moment regretted it."

"Neither have I." The lump in my throat expanded, forcing a few tears out of my eyes. All the resentment about the lies she had told me evaporated.

Aunt Ellen went to help Prince Nicholas get Kelly settled for the night. I was too wired to go to bed, so Latiana took me on a tour. The castle architect had obviously never heard of a straight line. Rooms were circular or oval. Stairways spiralled. Walls undulated. It gave the place a disorganized look, though I suspected if you peeled the roof off the castle and looked down from a height the halls would form a pattern, like a Celtic knot. Migrara's moons shone through stained glass windows featuring the faces of Kelly's ancestors. The ceilings blazed with murals laid out in luminous paint. Older paintings depicted knights battling scary Migraran beasts and bizarre beings who might have been Tuoaueans. More recent works had mages and Cauldra Cats hurling lightning and spears at hostile overlappers emerging from portholes.

One of the painted lightning bolts suddenly broke free and hurtled down at me. I shrieked and threw myself to the floor, but the lightning passed harmlessly through me. It was just an illusion to impress tourists.

"She didn't know if she could trust me," Latiana muttered, waiting for me to pick myself up. "I, who have been trained from childhood to serve her! And now she sends me away. But she does trust me to guard the Prince. That's something, at least. Odd that she would send Keirt as well. Does the Queen know you are a worldhopper, Audrey?"

"Keirt told her. She seems to like worldhoppers."

"She certainly finds many uses for them." She looked me over carefully. "You are young and lack experience, but time will mend that. Keirt could certainly do worse, if he intends to take you on as his partner."

"Partner?" I stumbled and nearly fell again. "What do you mean, partner?"

"Has he not told you of his years at court? Of his service to the Queen?"

"Not much, but I can guess the nature of his 'service' to the Queen."

"And how you blush! It was no trick to read your thoughts as Queen Teriquilla pursued Keirt out of the dining chamber. If you hurry, you can catch up to him before she does and whisk him safely into your own bed for a farewell bounce before we leave. I'll try to delay our departure if you feel you need more time. With Keirt, one usually does."

"I have no interest in having Keirt Prai in my bed!" I bellowed, and the stone walls grabbed my words and echoed them all over the castle. I said, more quietly, "It sounds like he's been bouncing around enough beds as it is."

Latiana waved a dismissive hand. "Oh, that was years ago. These days he's quite selective. And no, he has not selected the Queen. It's no secret that she is on the hunt, but so far Keirt has managed to evade capture."

"How do you know?"

"I have a keen sense of smell," she said, which explained nothing to me.

I made another attempt to reel in some castle gossip. "Do you think the Queen and Prince Nicholas will get it on again now that he's back?"

"Who can say? When they stand together, I smell desire on the Prince, but not the Queen. In fact, his presence seems to anger her."

I decided to drop the subject before she started describing the scents Keirt and I gave off when we stood together.

She stopped next to a wall of relief sculptures done in coloured marble and gemstones. The nearest sculpture featured Latiana, in her leopard form as well as human. She pointed to the one next to it, a striking woman with dusky skin and long white hair that sparkled with tiny diamonds. Her feline form was a white tiger with emerald eyes.

"Drandima was a great warrior, Captain of the Cauldra Cats before me. My mother accompanied her on her famous tour of the Six Circling Islands. They sailed to every island, even Tuoaue. There she met Keirt's father, and returned to Migrara with Keirt under her belt."

"His father didn't come with her?"

"Tuoaueans rarely leave the island, and they make poor mates. They're ruled by whim and passion rather than reason and love. Keirt was raised collectively by the Cauldra Cats, who spoiled him shamefully. What a wildling that boy was! He settled down when Drandima sent him to the Mage Hall, but when she died, he left the Hall and went wandering. He returned several years later to complete his education, and the Queen appointed him Court Mage. I can't say he's been good at it—he's too young, and not nearly diplomatic enough—but of course it was just a cover for his true service."

"What *is* his true service?"

"That he must tell you himself."

I sighed irritably. I was getting fed up with mysterious references and condescending responses to my questions. It was like being a kid again, trying to piece together the mysteries of sex.

The hall with the sculptures led to a large barracks for the Cauldra Cats. Most of the women inside were getting ready for bed. Some of the women were already curled up in their enormous wooden bunks, which were a good distance from the floor. The Cats liked to sleep up high. Two women in cat form crouched in one corner, tearing at a wad of bloody raw meat. The cleaning staff must dread doing this room.

While Latiana packed for her upcoming journey to Bisgaun and gave instructions to her second-in-command, Ranarsha, I studied a chart on one wall. It looked like a calendar with the Cats' names scattered across the dates. "What's that, a duty roster?" I asked.

"Of a sort," Latiana said. "It's a schedule of each woman's cycle. I need to know when my Cats will be forced to take the change."

A chart like that would be useful in any workplace. You would know when to avoid asking your boss for a raise, and when to have extra chocolate on hand in the staff room.

Latiana pulled me to the center of the room. "I command you to watch over Lady Audrey Oak while I'm gone," she told the Cauldra Cats. "Also find her a selection of healthy young men to warm her bed, for she is heart-wounded by Keirt Prai and requires distraction."

The Cats made sympathetic noises and promised to do their best, and one pretty young warrior offered to warm my bed herself, never mind the young men. I thanked them politely and invited Latiana to step outside the barracks with me so I could kill her, but she shook me off and resumed her list of orders for her warriors. As her instructions went on an on, I grew bored and slipped away.

"Audrey?" a voice whispered as I opened the door to my bedchamber.

A dark figure stood near the window. I slipped inside and closed the door.

"Well, did you escape the Queen or did she get a farewell bounce out of you?" I teased.

The shadowy figure moved into a shaft of moonlight from the open window.

"Queen Teriquilla! Oh, crap! Please forgive me, Your Majesty!" I bowed so low I nearly slammed my face against the floor.

She put a finger to her lips. She wore a dark cloak with the hood pulled over her head. "Audrey, come with me. I have something to show you."

Worldhopping 301

The Queen moved quickly down the hall and entered a small chamber used solely to house a collection of hats. There were crowns, battle helmets, bonnets, you name it. There was even a tasselled toque that I recognized from my childhood. I helped the Queen swing a set of shelves away from one wall. Behind the shelves was a wooden panel that she slid aside, revealing a stone stairway.

"Cool," I said, and the Queen shushed me. From under her cloak she produced, to my surprise, a metal flashlight. She clicked the flashlight on and descended the stairs. I followed her through a door that led to a garden enclosed by a tall stone wall.

"Where's Keirt?" I asked.

"He has departed with Prince Nicholas."

"Already?" I meant to sound uninterested, but it came out choked and weepy. As scary and maddening as he and Latiana could be, I had come to rely on their companionship. The thought of going weeks, maybe months, without seeing them put a lonely ache in my chest.

The Queen didn't notice my reaction. She led me into the heart of the garden. We were completely surrounded by tall roses of every colour, their leaves turned silver by the three moons. Overhead the unfamiliar constellations sparkled across Migrara's unpolluted sky. If you're wondering why I'm dwelling on the scenery, it's because this was the last peaceful moment I would experience for quite some time, and I think I can be forgiven for trying to paint a vivid picture of it.

"There," she said, sweeping the flashlight beam across the garden. The light caught a shimmering barrier that stretched the length of the garden. So it was a magic flashlight.

"A fault line." As I approached it, I felt that shivery spider web sliding through my skin, tickling my bones, a sensation I had experienced frequently since arriving at Mount Cauldra.

"Could you open a porthole on a locked fault line?"

"I can try, if you want me to," I said, reluctant to admit I had already done so without royal permission. "Why?"

"Keirt asked me about the gift of the Alphan of Tuoaue. I would like to show it to you."

I pretended to concentrate hard, but the porthole whirled open quite easily. We stepped through the bright circle onto a world of steel and concrete. We stood on the crumbling sidewalk of an empty city street. Many of the buildings, which were cylindrical or pyramid-shaped, suffered broken windows and scorch marks along their glittering walls. Others had collapsed into complete ruin.

I heard a hum, and turned to see an arrow-shaped aircraft bearing down on us. It snorted a blast of light out of its nose and the sidewalk in front of us disintegrated.

The Queen pulled me back through the porthole. I snapped it shut behind us.

"That was Oid," she said calmly while I hyperventilated. "A world at war, as you can see. Come, I will show you another."

The second fault line lay in the opposite end of the garden. This one led to a world whose entire landscape had been blasted flat. Two smutty red suns hung like bloodshot eyes in a sooty sky. A hideously disfigured life form lurched across the wasteland, picked something out of the rubble, and gnawed on it.

"We will stay only a few moments," the Queen said. "Others who lingered on this world returned to Migrara with a fatal sickness."

Hastily I reopened the porthole, and we evacuated the holocaust world. The next fault line lay across an outdoor sculpture exhibit near the edge of the palace grounds. Marble shapes rose out of the ground like bizarre tombstones. A blast of frigid wind whipped the Queen's cloak back as I opened the porthole to a winter world. Suddenly a horde of crystalline beetles poured through it, clicking pincers sharp as glass. I screamed and scrambled onto a sculpture of a giant hand. The ferociously clicking beetles swarmed up after me, paused, and cascaded to the ground, their icy shells melting away in the heat of the Migraran summer night.

I crouched in the palm of the giant hand, shaking. "Queen Teriquilla, what exactly is the point of this horror show?"

She stepped around the puddle of melted beetles and helped me down. "The universe holds thousands of worlds like these, Audrey. Worlds that could wipe out Migrara or your own world in the blink of an eye. We are protected only by their ignorance of our existence. Some must be aware of us, surely, but we are neither threatening nor wealthy enough to warrant their attention. Yet."

"But the dangerous fault lines are locked, right?"

"Against most worldhoppers, but not all, as you have proven. Since the death of my parents at the hands of overlappers, I have been working with the Worldhopping Studies Branch of Mage Hall to permanently seal fault lines. It was not until ten years ago that the Alphan of Tuoaue summoned my husband and me, and gave us Migrara's salvation."

We returned to the secret door that opened into the castle. Instead of climbing back up to the hat room, she descended a stairway into the damp depths of the castle. A winding maze of empty corridors took us to an old dungeon that obviously hadn't been used in a long time. Even the dungeons hadn't escaped the castle's aversion to straight lines. The round doors to the cells were formed of linked rings of iron. The stone walls were laced with iron as well.

The Queen shone the flashlight into a smelly cell, revealing another shimmering fault line. "Open it carefully, Audrey."

I did so. We stepped onto a range of volcanic mountains. Lava oozed out of their crowns. Here and there one would erupt in a more dramatic fashion. I covered my nose and mouth with my tunic to filter the hot, ashy air.

The Queen swept her flashlight over the mountainside, revealing the distant shimmer of another fault line. "Could you open that porthole from here?" she shouted over the booming explosions.

Apparently my range was pretty good. The porthole opened easily.

"That porthole leads to the world of Oid," she said. "Now close Migrara's porthole behind us while keeping Oid's open."

She twisted the flashlight open, and a green stone fell into her hand. It was the gemstone from the battery case of the walkie-talkie.

"The Alphan's gift," she said. "The Eleouss[13] Stone."

As her fingers closed around the stone, Oid's porthole stretched impossibly high and wide, and the world of Oid slid into the world of the volcanoes with the majestic grace of the Titanic bearing down on an iceberg.

"What's happening?" I shouted.

"They're merging. When the process is complete, the two worlds will have merged into one. Each will accommodate

---

[13] El-ay-OH-us.

the other, with the dominant world retaining most of its features."

The worlds themselves weren't actually moving; the port-hole was expanding to encompass both, creating an area of overlap that did not sit well with either planet. Mountains erupted all around us, unable to adjust to the sudden change in the terrain. Skyscrapers collapsed, exploded, were engulfed by the lava that flowed through the city streets. Aircraft zoomed madly through the smoky sky, slamming into moun-tainsides or plunging to the ground as flying debris struck them down. People poured out of the remaining buildings like ants in a flood, only to be boiled by lava or strangled by the ash-choked air.

"Queen Teriquilla, stop it! They'll all be killed!" I screamed.

She nodded. "Neither world will survive. They are too in-compatible to share the same space in time."

I tried to close the porthole that linked the two worlds, but it was like trying to close a submarine hatch with twenty million pounds of water pressure roaring through it.

"Open the porthole to Migrara," the Queen instructed, but I could only stare at the carnage. I had handed two unsus-pecting worlds over to a crazy woman, and now they were dying.

"The porthole, Audrey. Quickly, before the merging reaches us."

The overlapping area swept toward us. Hot wind howled around us like the cry of a wounded animal.

"Audrey!"

I opened the Migraran porthole and stumbled into the cas-tle dungeon with the Queen on my heels. The roar of de-struction and the screams of the dying were replaced by a silence that was somehow even more horrible.

The Queen shook the dust from her cloak. "The merging will accelerate and continue for several days. Using a volcanic world is not as effective as an oceanic or airless one; some inhabitants of the enemy world may survive. But they will be no threat to us."

"How many?" My voice was hoarse with grief and ash. I was bent over, trying not to throw up. "How many worlds have you destroyed?"

"I have lost count, to be honest." There was no grief in her voice. She sounded exhilarated. "I once had in my service a worldhopper with powers as strong as yours. Awnvale Worallan and I visited many worlds and rendered them harmless, beginning with the poachers who had slaughtered my parents. Then Awnvale died in a worldhopping accident, and with him went my access to the fault lines he had locked. A maddening development, when thousands of worlds remain that could wipe us out with a thought!" She paced the small cell fretfully. "Thank goodness you are here now, Audrey. Or rather, thank Keirt. He finally decided to take an interest in my search for powerful worldhoppers."

She smiled sympathetically as I sagged against the stone wall of the cell. "Oh, my dear young Audrey. Did you think his interest in you was personal? You know, the women of Mount Cauldra have a saying about Keirt Prai. 'A face to inspire laughter or lust—'"

"'But certainly not trust,'" I finished bitterly. "Did he know why you were looking for worldhoppers?"

"There is very little Keirt does not know. Do not grieve, Audrey. This is the beginning of an historic partnership. Together, we will make our worlds a safe haven for countless generations to come."

My head was swimming with horror. "You can't seriously expect me to help you kill entire worlds just because they *might* be a threat to us!"

"Oh, no, Audrey, I have a more constructive use for your talent. You see, the merging of two worlds need not destroy them. In fact, if done slowly and with great care, they will not only suffer very little damage, but actually become stronger. The merging combines the best qualities of each world and the inhabitants are the better for it. And that is why I need you. To assist me in the most significant merging of all—that of Migrara with a world that holds all the qualities I admire."

I turned cold. "Oh, no."

"Of all the overlapping worlds I have come to know, yours is the most compatible with my own, in both form and spirit. Never have I seen a world with such a generous array of resources, or with inhabitants so determined and resilient. They rise up and rebuild after even the most devastating disasters. The survivors will recover quickly from the merging. This is why I sent my daughter to your world, to familiarize her with the people she would one day rule. Think of it, Audrey. The combined intelligence, technology and magic of our two worlds—nothing could stand against us!"

"You're crazy," I whispered. How lucky we were in Canada to have a queen who only controlled the weather. This one held the whole freaking universe in her hand.

"Don't you see? There would be no need to neutralize other worlds once our two are merged. By helping me, you would be preventing needless destruction."

"I don't believe you. You're too obsessed to ignore all those other worlds." Jersicke's face flashed through my mind. Jersicke, whose ambition and insecurity had driven her to expel a student over a stupid short story. "You might feel safe for a while, but then paranoia will set in and you'll start going after them again."

"Let me worry about my future, Audrey. Focus on your own. Our partnership would provide you with many benefits. Would you like to marry a prince? Nicholas would not object. Joining with the niece of Lady Ellen Trini would do much to restore his damaged reputation. He has feelings for you; I see it in his eyes when he looks at you."

"You're not only evil, but incredibly tacky," I said. "Setting me up with your old boyfriend? Get real."

"I will give you the night to consider my offer." She backed out of the cell and slammed the door in my face. "If you choose to be stubborn, I will be forced to enlist your aunt's help. You are so much like her—naïve and idealistic. Your grandfather was the same. He thought of worldhopping as a harmless adventure. Your aunt presses her books and her inventive little toys upon us and thinks these will make our world powerful. Still, she has been a good friend. I would regret having to use her to . . . persuade you to help me."

I sucked in my breath. "You leave Aunt Ellen alone!"

"I will return for your decision in the morning." She turned her back on me and walked away, leaving me in the dark.

I yelled for help until I was hoarse. Then I cried. Then I just went quiet and numb. The voices chattered brokenly, trying to calculate how many men, women, children and babies might have died on Oid, and how many more would die if Teriquilla managed to break my resolve. Oh God, how I wished I'd never heard of Migrara, or worldhopping. I wished I could worldhop back in time to when the most serious issue I had to worry about was school.

When a blue light first appeared down the corridor, I just stared at it in a daze. As it drew closer, I threw myself at the iron door of the cell. "Keirt? Keirt, over here!"

The light approached my cell, but the face behind it wasn't Keirt's. I wasn't sure it was even human. It belonged to a tall, orange-skinned man in an elegant robe.

"Professor Shragon Bratch, Headmaster of the Migraran Mage Hall, at your service." He inclined his oddly-shaped head. It looked as if someone had grabbed his bright yellow beard and feathery eyebrows and stretched his face into a triangle.

"Are—are you here to let me out?" I said.

"Actually, I've been sent to torture you. Sorry—*persuade* you, to use Teriquilla's word. Oh yes, I know all about the Eleouss Stone. She took me into her confidence some years ago. But have no fear; your arrival has convinced me to take the Stone from her."

"Thank God," I said, tears of relief squeezing out of my eyes.

"Such a fine tool is wasted in the hands of a woman with so little imagination," he went on. "I mean to say, where is the benefit in damaging a world to the point where none of its assets are salvageable? Wielded properly, it could bring great wealth and power to Migrara, or to any world I choose to claim as my own. And to you as well, Audrey O'Krane. Imagine the power you would hold over your own world's leaders after showing them a brief demonstration of the Stone's capabilities."

I stared dumbly at him. This couldn't be happening. This could not be happening.

"Or perhaps not," he said with a wry smile. "It might be best if the power rests with me. Now that I look at you, I see you are hardly more than a child. So this is what we shall do. You will agree to serve Teriquilla until we find an opportunity to take the Stone from her. Then you will serve me. Is that simple enough for you?"

"Let me tell you what you can do with your fricking Stone," I said, and proceeded to explain. "Is that simple enough for you?"

He flicked his fingers. Impossibly, blue fire shot right through the iron rings of the cell door, ripping into me. I heard myself screaming, and everything went grey. When I opened my eyes, my cheek was pressed to the cold cell floor. My panting breaths stirred up little puffs of ash.

Professor Bratch stepped away from the door. "We will speak again, Audrey O'Krane. If Teriquilla asks, I tortured you mercilessly. In reality, this was nothing compared to what I will do to you if you ever defy me again."

He was gone, and I was back in the dark. I remained on the floor, limp and aching, fighting a sense of unreality. A few hours ago I had been plain old Audrey O'Krane, sipping wine among friends and family. Now I was a weapon of mass destruction and the local superpowers were fighting over who would get to exploit me. And Keirt . . . No, I couldn't stand to think about Keirt. Easier to think about dying worlds than about his betrayal.

There was an obvious solution, I thought. It was right at my fingertips. A flick of my mind, and I could be out of this cell and into the dying world of Oid. I would be out of their reach forever, and all those worlds would be safe.

The voices refused to consider it. The voices wanted to see Aunt Ellen one more time. The voices thought I could hold out against torture indefinitely. Maybe even outsmart Teriquilla and overpower Professor Bratch. The voices were pathetically naïve, but I was too tired to argue with them.

Amazingly, I slept. The scuff of a heel on the flagstones woke me. The flashlight beam was approaching. I scrambled to my feet.

"I'm a bit early," Teriquilla said. "I couldn't sleep, such was my excitement. Do you have an answer for me, Audrey?"

I gave her the same answer I had given Professor Bratch, only with more creativity.

She sighed. "I had hoped Bratch would teach you respect, or at least encourage you to see reason."

"Professor Bratch is almost as psycho as you. He wants to take the Eleouss Stone away from you and use it for himself."

"Ah, well, don't worry about Bratch. He is easily dealt with. Perhaps we will set Keirt up as the new Headmaster. He would like that."

"No, he would not."

Teriquilla flinched. Keirt walked slowly down the dungeon corridor. One look at his face told me the whole Keirt-as-accomplice-to-genocide story had been a lie, and my shattered inner world began to rebuild itself.

His eyes gleamed with tears. "Ah, Teriquilla. What have you done?"

"What I had to, my dear friend," she said gently.

"Release Audrey."

"Release her yourself."

She backed away as Keirt approached the cells. As he drew even with the first of the iron doors, he swayed and nearly fell. He stumbled back a few steps and stretched his hand toward her, but the pale energy that trailed out of his shaking fingers disintegrated against the iron cell door Teriquilla pulled open to shield herself.

Teriquilla laughed. "Oh, my beloved mage. You—" Whatever mocking observation she had composed was cut short as Keirt charged forward and body slammed the cell door. Teriquilla hit the floor and the flashlight in her hand went flying. It popped open and the Eleouss Stone tumbled out. Keirt fell across her and grabbed for the key on her belt. Teriquilla had been stunned by the fall, but the sight of the Stone rolling away from her threw her into a frenzy. She screamed and struck Keirt in the face. A punch from a Migraran woman, even a refined queen, was no joke. Keirt's head snapped back, and he lost his grip on her. She thrust her foot into his chest, pinning him against one of the iron cell doors. He cried out in agony.

Something emerged from beneath the struggling pair and slithered down the corridor, hissing irritably.

"Tist! Get that gem for me, there's a good snake."

I couldn't believe I was talking to a snake. I was even more amazed when Tist actually listened to me. He followed my pointing finger and picked up the gem with his tiny forelegs. Moments later it was in my hands.

"Anyone know where I can find a fault line with a volcano behind it?" I shouted. "Oh, that's right, I'm sitting on one. Say goodbye to your Eleouss Stone, Teriquilla."

"Wait!" She released Keirt and scrambled to her feet as I swooped my arms in a dramatic prelude to opening the porthole. "The merging will have engulfed the porthole. There is no telling what will happen if you open it now."

"Then get your butt over here and let me out."

She did. I took the key from her, shoved her into the cell and closed the door. I threw the gem to the floor and ground it beneath my heel. It grated unpleasantly against the stone, but stayed whole.

"No force in this world can destroy the Eleouss Stone," she said. "The Alphan of Tuoaue made certain of that."

Keirt retrieved Tist and climbed painfully to his feet. He gave her a long, sad look. "Teriquilla, who killed our King?"

She sighed, absently stroking the iron links that separated her from Keirt. "The destructive force of the Eleouss Stone terrified my husband. Like you, his first impulse after witnessing a demonstration of its power was to rid ourselves of it. Awnvale and I had to prevent that."

"Awnvale was the assassin," Keirt whispered. "Awnvale Worallan killed my mother."

"He hadn't planned to, Keirt, I swear to you. During the struggle, Captain Drandima caught his scent behind the mask. He saw the recognition in her eyes, and regretfully . . . It was a terrible sacrifice for you, Keirt, and I'm sorry. Does it ease your pain to know I too have suffered great loss? My husband dead . . . my lover and daughter on another world . . . What lonely years have passed for me in my efforts to keep my world safe. I had only you to stand beside me, my good friend. I could not have accomplished so much without your help."

Keirt staggered back and slumped onto a wooden bench, covering his face with his hands.

"Queen Teriquilla?" I said.

"Yes, Audrey?"

"Duck."

She threw herself to the floor as I opened the porthole. I dodged aside as flames, foul scorching wind and a tornado of ash roared into the dungeon. I opened it for only a moment, but a moment was long enough to hurl the Eleouss Stone through the opening and into a sea of lava.

"Not destroyed, maybe," I said as silence descended once more upon us, "but definitely out of reach."

Teriquilla screamed, lunging forward on her knees to throw herself against the cell door. She clawed at the iron rings, shaking a shower of hot ash down upon herself. "You stupid, selfish child! Do you think this will stop me? I will simply ask Alphan Oureil to produce a new one. He will produce any number of Stones, if I ask it!"

Keirt was back on his feet. He stumbled down the corridor, pulling me with him.

"You cannot prevent this," Teriquilla called, her breath catching on a sob. "You will only slow it down."

"Go to hell!" I yelled, and echoes of *hell* chased us down the corridor and along the abandoned passages of Mount Cauldra.

Flight from Mount Cauldra

Thank God Keirt had been raised in the castle. If not for him, I would still be wandering those secret passages. Once we reached my bedchamber, he locked the door and hugged me tight.

"Oh God, Keirt, I helped her kill two worlds." Brokenly, I told him about Oid and the volcano world, about Teriquilla's madness and Shragon Bratch's treachery.

"I'm sorry I didn't find you sooner, Audrey." He was shaking as badly as I was. "I was stunning megorniths, trying to delay our departure. I knew something was wrong, but I had no idea . . . You're not to blame, Audrey. I am. I handed those worlds over to her. She wouldn't have known about them if not for me. How many worlds did my careless reports doom to death?"

"What are you talking about?"

"I told you the Queen sent spies across our fault lines. I was one of those spies, along with Awnvale, my worldhopping partner. Teriquilla would have us report in great detail our experiences on each world. She showed special interest in the intelligence of the inhabitants, the degree of their technology, and the power of their weaponry. I never questioned why. She arranged for other worldhoppers to accompany me after Awnvale's death, but while they were competent at opening portholes, they were dangerously clumsy spies. When I realized you were not only a powerful worldhopper, but intelligent and courageous, I hoped Teriquilla would recruit you to be my partner." He closed his eyes. "I'm sorry, Audrey, so sorry."

"We should go back down there and kill her," I heard myself say. "Open the porthole and throw her into the worlds she just destroyed."

The voices expressed shock that Audrey O'Krane, rescuer of mice, could so casually propose murder. I was certainly on the slippery slope to becoming a hardened assassin. I assured the voices that I would try to become one of those charming assassins who loves children and small animals and kills only bad people.

"I've thought of that," Keirt muttered. "But I—I can't. And who is to say the Alphan of Tuoaue wouldn't carry on her work?"

"Migrara is absolutely riddled with power mongers, isn't it?" I said, drying my eyes. "I don't know why I expected your world to be any different from mine. I suppose the universe is swarming with corrupt aliens. And they always head straight for Earth, don't they? You know, we're getting freaking tired of everybody trying to exploit our planet's resources!"

Keirt looked surprised. "Such a thing has happened before?"

"Well, no," I admitted. "But we make a lot of movies about it."

A knock came on the door. "Audrey?"

"Aunt Ellen!" I flung open the door and pulled her inside, all bleary-eyed and wild-haired. Kelly nestled in her arms, asleep in her Winnie the Pooh pyjamas.

"What have you two been up to?" she demanded. "I just took a call from Teriquilla. She said Keirt had locked her in the old dungeon and would I please call for help? I sent some of the Cats down to her. I know you have a somewhat playful relationship with the Queen, Keirt, but this sort of prank absolutely crosses the line. Why, Audrey, what's wrong? You look terrible. Have you been crying?"

I grabbed the walkie-talkie from her and groaned. How could we have been so stupid? I told her about my night in the dungeon. She sat down slowly in a stuffed armchair with Kelly still in her arms. Kelly was awake now, but her eyes were unsettlingly blank.

"She always did see things in black and white," Aunt Ellen said finally. "She never took the time to find the middle ground, to compromise. I used to admire her decisiveness. But after Kelly was born, she changed. Her actions became protective rather than progressive. Against my advice, she convinced King Glaem to cut off nearly all contact with our overlap allies. Frankly, it was a relief to retire as their Overlap Advisor. But I never suspected she would go so far."

There came a drumming of running feet in the hall. Keirt lunged for a jar of scented oil on the dresser. He hurled it to the marble floor just as the door crashed open. The Cauldra Cats surged through it like the Riders entering a locker room at halftime. We backed into a corner as the women filled the chamber, Ranarsha at their head. Some were in feline form, some human, but the rest had taken the change halfway. They stalked around the room on shaggy hind legs, sweeping the chamber with their golden eyes and ivory swords. Their gaze passed right over us. Fanged muzzles sniffed the air, but the oil overwhelmed any scent we might have given off.

"He has taken all three of them." Teriquilla's voice held just the right blend of rage and terror. "Oh, Ranarsha, that madman has my daughter."

"We'll get her back, my Queen," Ranarsha promised, "if we have to rip apart that cowardly pixen to do it."

"Try not to harm Audrey. He may have spelled her to do his bidding. Bring her to me so that we may undo his magic."

"I can't believe people are still trotting out that old myth," Aunt Ellen whispered indignantly. "No Migraran, Tuoauean blood or not, has the power to alter the will of another. That's just a racist—" I clapped my hand over her mouth.

The Cauldra Cats cleared out of the room, but we stayed put in case it was a trick. Kelly finally broke the silence. "We'd better go."

I turned around and saw not a frightened six-year-old, but a grim-faced teenager.

"Kelly, do you understand what's going on?" I asked cautiously.

Her eyes were very sad. "I saw my mother use the Stone to destroy two worlds when I was a child. I was frightened, and I didn't understand. When we left Migrara, I forgot what I'd seen. I forgot everything. But now I remember. And I understand." She put her hand on my shoulder. "You have to stop her, Audrey."

First we had to get away from Mount Cauldra. Getting out of the castle was easy, but nerve wracking. It's hard to remember you're invisible when feline people keep barrelling past you, brandishing swords the size of your leg. The gates of the castle grounds were closed and heavily guarded, so we would have to exit via a porthole. Near the stables we passed an open building that held buckets, hoses and other firefighting equipment. Suddenly I felt the shivery tickle of a fault line. I turned around and opened a porthole. Cold salt water exploded through the opening, bowling us off our feet. The porthole collapsed, and the water ceased like a tap shutting off.

"Oops," I spluttered as we floundered in the mud. Something with tentacles tried to wrap itself around my arm.

"Over here!" Ranarsha shouted. The women converged on us, drawn by the flash of light and the sudden flood. Everything exploded into a confusion of swords and claws and spears, with Keirt flickering in and out of sight among the women like a firefly. I scooped up the tentacled thing and hurled it into Ranarsha's furry face. Keirt scattered the rest of the Cats with a handful of sizzling lightning balls, allowing us to slip past them.

"Where are those iron bracelets I called for?" Ranarsha shouted, yanking at the tentacles.

"Mount Cauldra is riddled with fault lines," Aunt Ellen said encouragingly, but we crept nearly to the wall before I encountered another. This one I opened more carefully. The crisp white surface of a vast glacier stretched out before us. The Cauldra Cats saw the flash of light and roared off in pursuit, but we were already on the glacier, the porthole safely closed behind us. We followed the fault line across the glacier until I judged we were well beyond the castle wall. I opened a new porthole, and we stepped back into the warm night air of Migrara. On the other side of the wall, an agitated rumble of voices arose.

"Now where to?" I asked.

"My nephew's vineyard," Aunt Ellen said. "We have to pick up Bernie. Then we will return to our world." I was pleased that she no longer calling it *your* world. "Teriquilla's forces would be quite restricted there. We'll use it as a bridge."

"How much you want to bet they'll be waiting for us at the fault line?" Kelly said.

"Not if we get there first," Keirt said. "Baub won't have left Cauldroot yet, not with the finest taverns on Migrara beckoning him."

Most pilots stayed at the same inn, so we had little trouble finding Baub. Hauling him out of bed was more of a challenge, until Aunt Ellen mentioned our destination was a vineyard. He didn't even question why Keirt wanted to fly three bedraggled women across Migrara to a vineyard in the dead of night. He led us to the Eyrie, where an assortment of megorniths roosted on ledges halfway up the mountain. Dusty saw us coming and heaved a weary sigh.

As Baub worked out how to fit five people on a four-passenger bird—no one wanted to ride in Dusty's chest harness—a crackling voice emerged from Aunt Ellen's shoulder bag.

"Ellen. This is Teriquilla. Please speak to me."

Aunt Ellen pulled out the walkie-talkie and moved away from us. "Excuse me, I have to take this. I'll just be a minute."

As Aunt Ellen disappeared into the deep and stinky cave that had sheltered Dusty, two tall figures came up the path that led to the Eyrie.

"There you are, Prai. Where the hell have you—Kelly? What are you doing here?"

"Oh, good evening, Prince Nicholas," I said weakly. Baub took refuge behind one of Dusty's warty legs. "I thought you'd left Mount Cauldra."

"Good morning, you mean. We've spent the night in search of transportation. Someone," Latiana said, glaring at Keirt, "stunned all the castle megorniths. The Lioness knows when they will be fit to fly again. We came to hire another. Answer the question, Keirt—why is the Princess here?"

"Because my mother is a power mongering psychopath," Kelly said calmly. "Keirt and Audrey are taking me away from her."

Zap—Latiana hit the ground, her sword skidding across the stone to rest at my feet.

"What did you do that for?" I yelled. "She could have helped us!"

"Or arrested us," Keirt said. "We can't take that chance."

Prince Nicholas drew his own steel sword. "What's the deal, Prai? Ransom? Or has the Princess become the object of your pixen lust now that she's finally matured?"

"No, Uncle Nick!" Kelly cried. "You don't understand."

Keirt launched a second lightning bolt as Nicholas came at him, but the Prince seemed to absorb the energy without faltering. He threw his cloak aside, revealing a vest of glittering chain mail.

"Did you think I would consent to travel with you without protection? You've made a mistake, Prai. A fatal mistake."

"Keirt!" I tossed him Latiana's ivory sword.

Nicholas grinned in anticipation. "Come then, young mage. Let's see if you handle a blade as well as your mother did."

Kelly and I shouted a summary of the night's events at the Prince as he launched a vicious attack on Keirt, but he completely disregarded us. He was caught in the past, back when a reckless boy had scarred him for life in a misguided attempt to avenge his mother.

There was no elegant dancing around like in the movies. They charged back and forth across the Eyrie, whacking at each other, at times scuffling dangerously close to the edge of Dusty's ledge. It was obvious Keirt had never seriously used a sword before. Nicholas was all offence and Keirt all defence. He showed no fear; his catlike reflexes easily made up for Nicholas's strength and experience. The chain mail prevented Keirt from getting close enough to do any damage, but he was swiftly wearing the Prince out. Nicholas backed off and swiped an arm across his sweating face.

"Speaking of your mother, I'll tell you something I know from experience, Prai," he panted with a sly grin. "Fighting wasn't the only sport she excelled at."

"Don't listen to him!" I yelled. "Stay cool!"

Keirt did listen, and he did not stay cool. His face darkened as he lunged at the Prince, slashing recklessly. Nicholas neatly sidestepped and parried the ivory sword. Keirt's arm brushed the steel links of the chain mail, and he staggered dizzily.

Kelly screamed as a wicked slice nearly removed Keirt's head. Suddenly she darted between the two men. Keirt grabbed her arm and swung her out of the way, lowering his guard for a moment. A deft flick of the Prince's sword sent Keirt's blade spinning out of his hand. Keirt lunged backward to avoid a sword thrust to the chest and fell hard on his back, nearly skidding off the ledge. Nicholas advanced on him, enraged beyond all good sense, blade levelled at Keirt's throat.

"Gribbet him," Keirt shouted, and Dusty's enormous beak swooped down and clamped shut on Nicholas, encasing the entire upper half of his body. He freed an arm and flailed the sword around, dangerously close to Dusty's one good eye. She dropped him and pinned him to the ground with a clawed foot. This was obviously more excitement than she was accustomed to; she raised her tail and loosed one humongous dropping, splattering the unfortunate Prince. Kelly and I shrieked and scrambled out of range. Baub made hysterical choking sounds.

"What's all the noise?" Aunt Ellen came back to us, stuffing the walkie-talkie back into her shoulder bag. She peered down at the Prince. "Oh, my."

I crouched next to him. "We'll take good care of Kelly, I promise."

"When next I lay hands on you," Nicholas said quietly, "you'll regret the day you set foot on this world."

"You'd be totally intimidating if you weren't covered in bird crap."

"Don't tease, Audrey," Keirt chided. "He's had a difficult night."

I looked at Latiana's limp form. "Should we take her with us? It's not like she's part of the conspiracy. At least, I don't think she is."

"Nor do I, but Dusty wouldn't manage her weight," Keirt said. "She'll have to take her chances."

"Goodbye, Uncle Nick," Kelly said. "Sorry."

When we were all on board, Dusty released the Prince and lurched into the sky. Kelly screamed in delight as we became airborne. I smiled over my shoulder at her, expecting to see the innocent six-year-old she had been for ten years. But we never saw that little girl again.

We flew for three nights, taking refuge during the day in deep canyons and remote wilderness valleys. Aunt Ellen fretted at our slow pace. With all the extra weight, Dusty wasn't making good time.

"It won't take the Queen's forces long to catch up to us," Aunt Ellen warned. "She is determined to get you back, Audrey, despite my best efforts to talk her out of it."

I felt a leap of joy every time I looked at Aunt Ellen. The pallor and weariness had disappeared from her face. She was bursting with energy. Yinkara Belderkin's potion had worked.

As the land below us turned bloody with sunrise at the end of our final night of flight, Aunt Ellen directed Baub to land at her nephew's vineyard to collect Bernie. She also wanted to send messages to various allies across Migrara. She knew of several provinces and islands whose governors weren't happy with the Queen's decision to cut off contact with overlapping worlds. Aunt Ellen hoped they could be convinced to turn against her.

I had pictured a quaint little farm. This vineyard was a full-scale operation spread across the slope of a river valley that branched off from the larger Migraran River. The family produced honey as well. Beehives stood scattered throughout a huge field of blue flowers. Women and men toiled at various vineyard tasks while children romped among the rows of grape vines with furry domesticated life forms barking at their heels. It was the sort of idyllic setting a movie director would arrange to have brutally raided at the earliest opportunity. I was anxious to grab Bernie and be gone.

"Welcome back, Aunt Ellen." A middle-aged man met us in front of the house and gave her a hug. "Did you enjoy your flight? You just missed your friend Bernie. He went down to the river. Who are these young folk?"

When Aunt Ellen introduced me as her niece, a wave of cousins swamped me with backslaps and hugs, the children laughing over how small I was. Overwhelmed, I wiped away a couple of tears. I'd grown up with hardly any family, and now I had all these relatives.

"Look, it's Keirt Prai!" exclaimed a giggling young woman. "I saw him perform a skyplay the year the Queen toured the Rivergreen."

"You cut that out, Fria," Aunt Ellen's nephew Heter scolded. A decade's worth of years dropped away from the giggling young woman's face and figure, revealing she was no more than thirteen. My cousins mobbed Keirt, begging him to put on a performance.

"I'll be on the hill, keeping watch," Keirt said, and made his escape.

"We don't have much time," Aunt Ellen said. "The Queen's forces will be here shortly."

Heter's wife Aildya turned white. "The honey! They must have found out!"

"What about the honey?" I asked.

"The flowers the bees harvest are imported from an overlap world." Heter shot a panicked glance at the beehives. "They produce a honey that is, er, medicinal in a way the Queen might not consider quite lawful. We mix it with the wine."

Oh my God, my relatives were drug lords.

"It's not the honey," Aunt Ellen said, exasperated. "If you invite me in, I'll explain over a quick cup of tea. Audrey, go collect Bernie, would you?"

My drug lord cousins accompanied me across the vineyard, explaining every step of the winemaking and honey harvesting process. I tried to pay attention, but my eyes kept straying upward, alert for invading forces. You shouldn't look at the sky when you're among agricultural people. It inspires them to comment on the weather, and then arguments break out over the accuracy of their predictions, and then everyone has to march off to Old Stoddle to see if his cricky knee thinks it's going to rain that night. Apparently too much rain was a bad thing, as it caused the grapes to mildew.

After they left, I wandered alone through the quiet grapevine rows. Blades of sunlight pierced the tangled vines, soothing me as they slipped over my face. Here I said a silent farewell to Migrara. Until now I had considered it a collection of obstacles that lay between me and my various destinations. Only now, when I was about to leave it, did I realize how much I liked this alien world, despite its psychopath queen.

I reached the end of the row and came up against the reeds that lined the river bank. A wind-powered pump moved river water through pipes that ran along the top of the grapevine fencing. The cousins said they had last seen Bernie down here tinkering with the irrigation system, but I saw no sign of him.

I took the opportunity to do something I'd wanted to try ever since I saw Latiana do it—pee standing up. The attempt ruined my new Migraran boot. Swearing in disgust, I waded into the river in order to ruin both boots equally. I had to duck under one of the irrigation pipes as I returned to shore, and when I straightened up I found myself face to face with Prince Nicholas.

Captured

I have often wished I had a ladylike scream. My scream sounds like a bull that's been stung on the butt by a bee. Prince Nicholas cut off my inelegant outburst by clapping a hand over my mouth. His other hand gripped my hair.

"We have Prai. Take me to Kelly and your aunt will remain free."

I followed his glance. About a dozen Cauldra Cats were visible on one of the hills overlooking the vineyard. I saw a flash of pale hair among them—Keirt.

I wrenched my face away from his hand. "Listen, there is something you have to know. The Queen had this gemstone, and she was using it to merge worlds—"

"I don't give a damn about Teriquilla's worldhopping project. I just want Kelly back."

"Worldhopping *project*? She's destroying worlds! How can you not care?"

"You've been misled by Prai. The man is mad, Audrey. No doubt his ideas sound plausible to you, but he is a pixen, after all. They have the power to weave their thoughts through your mind until you think their ideas are your own."

"Teriquilla's the one who's crazy. She's killed more planets than she can count, she had that worldhopper Awnvale Worallan murder your brother, and she tried to bribe me by offering you as my husband!" God knows why I threw that in. It was hardly the worst of her crimes.

"She did suggest we'd make a good match. I laughed in her face. You are young, crude, reckless, and a bad influence on Kelly."

I could think of nothing to say in my defence. After all, the man had just seen me pee on my own foot.

"However, I can't deny I'm somewhat attracted to you." He loosened his grip on my hair and ran his hand through it slowly. "Not marriage, perhaps, but a briefer and more passionate union would not be intolerable."

When Keirt had described him in his younger years as irresponsible, I thought he meant the Prince attended wild parties and gambled away his allowance. But it was worse than that. He was so caught up in his own needs, nothing else even registered with him. No wonder he had been so easily led by Teriquilla.

"Wow, I'm touched by the romantic proposal, but no thank you. Ignore those smouldering glances back at Cauldra Castle. I was just trying to score off Keirt."

He transferred his grasp suddenly to my arms and yanked me against him. "I did promise that when I next laid hands on you, you would regret it." He kissed me, hard enough to split my lip and put a crick in my neck.

Sex! Hormones chirped happily.

This is the man who tried to hack off Keirt's head, a more sensible voice reminded me.

Impulse Control did nothing to prevent me from jerking my knee up so hard I was surprised the Prince's nuts didn't pop out of his nostrils. Nicholas hit the dirt, writhing and swearing.

"Here! What do you think you're doing to the girl?" Bernie hustled up to us, panting indignantly. He froze as an enormous red lioness bounded up the riverbank, placing herself between him and Prince Nicholas.

Prince Nicholas staggered to his feet and limped in a circle, trying to walk it off. "I ordered you not to follow me."

The lioness rose up on her hind legs and went halfway to human. Ranarsha stood there in all her naked furry glory. Bernie displayed the early warning signs of a heart attack.

"My apologies, Prince Nicholas, but I take my orders from the Queen, not you." Her rough, clawed hands wrenched my arms behind my back. "You've caused us no small amount of grief, overlapper."

I tried one last time to get through to him. "Prince Nicholas, both our worlds are in danger. Teriquilla wants to blend them together and create a super world, like a corporate merger on a universal scale—"

"Audrey, I just want Kelly back," Nicholas said wearily. "Take me to her, and I'll help you escape."

Suddenly Ranarsha's head exploded.

One moment she was gaping in dismay at the Prince; the next I heard a squashy thump and wet chunks exploded from the side of her skull, spattering me and Nicholas. She slumped to the ground and lay motionless, one side of her face smeared with bits of greenish matter. A hideous smell arose.

I dropped to my knees beside her. "Ranarsha! Oh my God, what happened?"

"Audrey!" Kelly was running toward me through the vineyard. A herd of cousins came galloping after her. One of them carried a short wooden tube over his shoulder, one of the pipes from their irrigation system. I knew exactly what it was, because years ago I myself had made one out of a length of PCV pipe and accidentally destroyed a neighbour's window with it. It was a potato cannon. Ranarsha had been shelled by the Migraran version of a potato. A rotten one, by the smell of it. Her eyes were closed, but she was twitching and making little snarling noises.

"Don't move, you!" the cousin with the potato cannon snapped as Nicholas made a move to intercept Kelly.

"Audrey, come quick," Kelly gasped. "It's Granny Ellen."

With the cousins hauling Ranarsha and Prince Nicholas along behind us, we returned to the house at a run and burst through the front door. Aunt Ellen was in Aildya and Heter's bed, unconscious. She had black circles under her eyes and her lips were blue.

"We heard a scream and went to look out the window. When we turned around, she was on the floor," Aildya said. "I think it's her heart."

I knelt by the bed, my own heart pounding painfully. Tears flooded my eyes. "Aunt Ellen?"

Her eyes flickered open. She clutched at my hand and mouthed words at me, but no sound emerged. I tried to read her trembling lips. *Dragon patch?*

"We have nothing to help her," Heter groaned. "There's a pixen healer in Zantallion City, but with that piece of metal in her leg, he wouldn't do her any good."

I still had Yinkara Belderkin's vial of potion. I brought it out and hesitated, looking from Aunt Ellen to Bernie.

"Was that meant for me?" Bernie asked. I nodded. He took it from me and knelt by the bed. "Here, Ellen. Bottom's up." And he emptied the vial into Aunt Ellen's mouth.

My eyes stung with tears. "Oh, Bernie."

"It's working," Aildya whispered. Aunt Ellen's eyes had slipped closed, but her colour was improving. "She won't be travelling, though, not until she's stronger."

"It's all right, Audrey," Kelly said. "I'll look after her. You and Keirt go on to Earth. As soon as you're away, I'll have Baub take us somewhere safe."

"Kelly, I can't just leave you—"

"I want to stay, Audrey. It's my duty. When the Queen fails in her campaign—and she will fail, never doubt that—I'll need to step up and take her place. With Granny Ellen's help, I can gather allies here on Migrara."

She marched out of the bedroom and to the front door. Heter, Aildya and I trailed after her, stunned by this display of power in a teenager who had been a little girl only a few days ago. She called for my cousins to bring Prince Nicholas into the house. Ranarsha had regained consciousness and looked like she was about to start biting people's heads off any second now.

"Time is running out, worldhopper!" she shouted at me. "If we don't return to that hill within 11.847 minutes, my warriors will begin to relieve Keirt of his body parts."

Kelly closed the door and fixed Prince Nicholas with a stern look. "Uncle Nick, you must help us."

He nodded. "So long as you take me with you. But we must tread carefully. *There is more to this situation than meets the eye.*" Prince Nicholas stared meaningfully at me. Was he trying to warn me about something? If so, I wasn't getting it.

Kelly was taken aback by his ready agreement. "Oh. Um, okay. I need you to go back up the hill with Ranarsha and tell them we've agreed to give ourselves up. If Keirt is wearing iron manacles, take them off."

"I'll make a pretence of challenging him to a fair fight. They would believe that." Seeing his smile of grim satisfaction, I wondered how much of a pretence it would be.

Once Ranarsha and Nicholas had gone, I headed off to search the estate for our resident pilot. I had to search a dozen underground wine cellars before we found him. I shook him awake, kicked him up to the surface, and dragged him to where Dusty squatted on the bank of a small lake. The vineyard children had been fishing and feeding her all day.

The Cauldra Cats didn't look up as Dusty soared high over their hilltop camp. Their attention was focused on Keirt and

Nicholas. As I watched, Nicholas lashed out with a fist, striking Keirt to the ground. Dusty went into a dive. The wind from her pumping wings sent the warriors tumbling in all directions as she descended upon the camp. By the time they recovered, Dusty had scooped Keirt into her long beak and swooped back up into the sky. A few arrows whistled past us, but they were just warning shots. No doubt the Queen had given strict orders that I wasn't to be harmed. Dusty deftly flipped her catch over her shoulder. I grabbed him and helped him settle in front of me.

"That was brilliant, Baub," Keirt said.

"Don't thank me, 's her idea," he slurred. "Girl's crazier than you."

"I certainly shall thank her." Keirt twisted around to put his arms around me. He pulled back just in time. "Audrey, why are you smoking a pipe?"

"I'll tell you later. Blech, don't hug me. You smell like decayed fish."

"That comes of having my head halfway down Dusty's throat. Where are Perikelli and your aunt?"

"Hiding in one of the secret illegal wine cellars. They're staying on Migrara for reasons I'll explain later. Prince Nicholas is going to slip away and join them while the Cauldra Cats are chasing us. He's helping us, believe it or not. Baub will come back for them after he drops us off on the fault line. You look awful, Keirt. You're white as a pickerel belly. Oh my God, what happened to your leg?"

"Ranarsha shot me with an iron-headed arrow, and then they put iron manacles on me. I'll be fine, so long as I can avoid further iron poisoning until I heal."

"I thought the Cauldra Cats liked you. Your mother was their captain!"

"Ranarsha once challenged Latiana for command of the Cats, and lost. She has always accused me of using magic to secretly help Latiana win the challenge. It seems she leads the Cauldra Cats now. No one will tell me what's happened to Latiana."

"Heia, lookit here," Baub said.

We had been following the river toward the fault line of my world. Below us lay the hill that overlapped my front yard. A flock of megorniths had lined up along the riverbank. The fault line itself swarmed with an army of young women and men wearing short red robes and tall black boots.

"Veer off, Baub, those are students from the Mage Hall!" Keirt shouted. Baub gave a sharp whistle and Dusty turned on a wingtip, nearly throwing the unharnessed Keirt off her back. A pale lightning ball sizzled past us as Dusty flew back the way we had come. The young mages had spread all along the fault line on both sides of the river.

"What now? Back to the vineyard?" Baub shouted.

"Fly us back across the river and follow the fault line." Dusty made a loop and took us across the river again. "The fault line ends right about there," Keirt said, pointing. The mage students were spread out a few hundred yards beyond that point. "Audrey, I think they have underestimated your power. You could force open a porthole a little beyond the tip of a fault line, couldn't you?"

"I have no idea."

"We'll have to risk it."

I picked up the wooden tube I had tied to Dusty's harness. Warning Keirt to duck down and hold still, I balanced it over his shoulder, sighted on our landing area, and dipped the short fuse into the smouldering contents of the clay pipe Heter had given me.

Whump—the potato cannon erupted, firing not a potato but a small gourd filled with a highly flammable by-product of the Trini vineyard. It struck dead on target, exploding in a most impressive manner. The frightened mage students scattered like chickens in the car chase scene of a cheesy movie. I flung away the cannon, which had caught fire.

"Well done," Keirt said when he had put out his hair. "Land quickly, Baub, before they recover."

The mages were already running toward us as Dusty landed on a smouldering patch of grass. We tumbled off her back and hit the ground running. Dusty launched herself back into the sky.

"When we enter the porthole, we'll be about 2.128 kilometres east and a bit south of your house," Keirt panted. He was limping badly from his wounded leg. "In what sort of area will we emerge in your city?"

I tried to remember what neighbourhood lay east of our house. "Forest Grove, I think. It's a nice neighbourhood."

"A forest is good. The trees will hide our arrival."

In the corner of my eye, I saw red robes converging on us. Lightning balls whizzed around us like wasps. One grazed my hip, and I stumbled as my leg spasmed. Keirt threw an arm around me to hold me up. A porthole snapped open for me, and we lunged through it. Before I could close it behind us, Keirt gave a strangled cry and collapsed, dragging me down into the snow with him.

We weren't in Forest Grove. We were a bit south of it. In the CPR Yard. Completely surrounded by trains and iron rails.

19

A Freaking Invisible Tuoauean

"Close it!" he groaned, writhing away from the train tracks beneath him.

I dragged him off the rails. "Get up, Keirt. We have to go back!"

"Close the porthole!"

"You'll die here!"

"Close it! And lock it!"

Red robes and wild-eyed faces had appeared within the porthole. I snapped it closed. Lock it, he'd said, but I wasn't sure I knew how. What if I opened it again by accident? I slung Keirt's arm over my shoulder and hoisted him vertical. Together we staggered over one set of tracks after another, Keirt growing weaker with every step. By the time we cleared the last of the tracks, he was barely conscious. I laid him down in the snow and looked around for the first time to see if anyone had witnessed our dramatic arrival. It was night and the rail yard was deserted. Rows of freight cars stood on the tracks, unmoving. A trickle of traffic moved along College Avenue.

"We'll have to have to hitchhike, Keirt," I said. In reply, he raised himself to his hands and knees and was violently ill. I hovered uselessly. Sharp snowflakes hurtled from a bitterly cold sky. I clutched the warm cloak Heter had given me more tightly around me. He had given me one for Keirt too. I pulled it out of my backpack and wrapped it around him as he lurched to his feet, shivering.

No one stopped for us no matter how hard I waved and smiled. One car did slow down, but sped away as Keirt suddenly parted with another portion of his breakfast. Finally I threw my arm around him, and we started walking.

With a screech and a hiss, a bus pulled up beside us.

"You're lucky, this is my last run of the night," the driver said as we tottered gratefully into its warmth. Oh my God, it was the driver who had run me down on the day of the mouse.

"We don't have any change," I said, wrestling Keirt around so I could hide my face behind him.

"Don't need any," the man said cheerfully. "No charge to-night."

We stumbled past a handful of passengers who appeared to be in no better condition than Keirt. Falling into a seat at the back, I pulled Keirt down beside me and put my arms around him to hold him upright. He groaned. How much iron was on this bus? I should have thought of that before I dragged him on board.

I glanced at the watch of the half-conscious woman across the aisle. It was nearly three in the morning. Buses in Saska-toon stopped running shortly after midnight. Now I knew what was going on. One of those mage lightning balls had hit us head on, and we had died without realizing it. The bus was some kind of Chariot of Death. The driver was actually the Grim Reaper, cruising the city in search of the recently departed to deliver them to that great Bus Depot in the sky.

The bus made all the usual stops along College and around the university, then crossed the University Bridge. I pulled the cord as we passed Spadina. Would Death let us off?

He would. "Happy New Year!" the Reaper called as I dragged Keirt off the bus. Of course. On New Year's Eve, the buses ran late and free of charge to encourage polluted Saskatonians to stay away from their cars.

Relief swept over me. I'd had a nagging fear that all those apocalypse fanatics were right and my world would end as the year 2001 drew to a close. The Queen and her Stone of Mass Destruction hadn't eased my concerns.

A few blocks later, we were home. Oddly, there were many fresh footprints in the yard. People had been snooping around the house. Why? I let myself in with the spare key. The power was still off and the house was freezing. I dropped Keirt on the couch.

"Oh, Keirt, you look horrible. I'm taking you to the hospital."

"No. No hospital." He rolled over and passed out.

I bandaged the arrow wound in his leg, covered him with a blanket and got a fire going in the fireplace. I flipped the main breaker to get the power back on, then brought in the mail and a stack of newspapers. I skimmed the headlines. There was a brief article about cougar tracks spotted along the riverbank in my neighbourhood. The rest was all Osama Bin Laden, Osama Bin Laden, more Osama Bin Laden—and me.

I stared in astonishment at my most recent school photo on the front page of yesterday's paper. *Christmas Expulsion Leads to Disappearance of Student*, the headline read.

"No way!" I yelled. Keirt flinched in his sleep. I clamped my mouth shut and read the article. Someone, maybe my school guidance counsellor, had gone to the press with the story of my expulsion and the reason behind it. The tone of the article indicated the reporter had taken a dislike to Jersicke, who "couldn't be reached for comment." The journalist had discovered the mysterious disappearance of Aunt Ellen and myself. Everyone he interviewed believed there was a link between the expulsion and our disappearance. My friends feared I might have done away with myself. After all, I had thrown myself in front of a bus when my boyfriend broke up with me. Idiots! Lyle had broken up with me *after* the bus incident.

"We can't stay here," I told Keirt. "Everyone will be looking for me."

Keirt didn't care. Keirt was unconscious, and not going anywhere for a while.

As I poured myself a glass of water, it occurred to me that a drink of our tap water might be fatal to Keirt. I took a plastic mixing bowl outside and filled it with snow that had gathered in the crater where the quinzhee once stood. The frozen slush had been trampled into ragged lumps of ice by the paws of the Cauldra Cats. I could feel the Migraran fault line. Strange to think that just beyond this invisible barrier, hundreds of enemies lay in wait for me.

All at once I opened a porthole, screamed, "Happy New Year!" and hurled a snowball into the startled face of some poor mage student barely old enough to shave. I snapped the porthole shut and rolled around in the snow, laughing hysterically. Okay, Audrey, get a grip.

To my annoyance, my bowl of snow yielded only half a cup of melted water. A film of grey particles floated on the surface. Silently cursing my disgusting polluted world, I ran the water through a coffee filter and carried it into the living room. Keirt remained stubbornly unconscious when I tried to wake him. I could have used some sleep myself, but I was too restless to settle down. I had a hot shower, then checked the bathroom scale to see how much weight I had lost hiking around Migrara. Three pounds! Was that all?

I returned to the living room in my warmest pyjamas and slumped down in front of the fireplace, gazing wearily into the flames. To my surprise, the fire thrust its face forward and snapped at me, singeing my eyebrows with its flaming nose.

I scrambled back and leaped to my feet. "Keirt, that's not funny—What the hell?"

Professor Shragon Bratch sat in Aunt Ellen's armchair. He was reading one of her library books, some goofy mystery where a cat solves the crime.

"How did you get in?" I gasped. Why am I always in nightwear when confronted by alien invaders?

He put the book down and lit Heter's pipe with his fingertip. "You let me in. I've been your constant companion since you left your cousins' house on Migrara. We have unfinished business, Audrey O'Krane."

Great. We thought we were being so clever and evasive, and all that time we had a freaking invisible Tuoauean clinging to us. *That's* what Aunt Ellen had been trying to say back at the vineyard. Prince Nicholas must have known as well, but he never said a word except for that feeble warning about treading carefully.

"You attacked Aunt Ellen, didn't you?"

"Had you dragged her along you most certainly would have been captured, and that did not suit me at all."

"But the train tracks—the bus—"

"Having once succumbed to iron poisoning, I am somewhat immune to it now. I managed to retain my magic during my brief exposure."

Suddenly blue fire engulfed me, making me feel like I was being stung by wasps all over. I screamed and fell to the floor.

"For revealing my plan to the Queen," he said.

Keirt jerked awake and attempted to lunge off the couch. He lunged only as far as the floor. He pushed himself up to a crouch, shaking with the effort. I could see his fingers moving, trying to work up a bit of magic, but not a single spark emerged. He swore helplessly.

Bratch laughed. "The iron rails stripped you of your magic, did they? You're in for a very rough time, my young friend."

In one smooth motion, Keirt pulled a small ivory dagger from his boot and whipped it at the Headmaster. It struck Bratch in the chest. An invisible force grabbed Keirt and hurled him across the room. He slammed against the far wall and crumpled to the floor, knocking over the Christmas tree. Ornaments bounced across the hardwood.

Bratch calmly pulled the dagger from his chest and ripped open his robe. Blood flowed, slowed, trickled to a halt. The wound sealed itself. Bratch gave a gentle cough and turned to Keirt. A tongue of fire leaked out of the fireplace and snaked across the floor toward Keirt. He tried to push himself away from it, but not fast enough. It licked maliciously at his hands.

"Stop it," I cried. "Don't hurt him. I'll do what you want." The firesnake vanished in a puff of smoke. I ran to Keirt and poured my cup of snow water over his hands.

"Keirt Prai." Bratch examined his bloodied robe and shook his head. "You were a most disappointing student. I was staggered when Teriquilla appointed you Court Mage. Everyone knew it should have been me. For year after bloody year, I taught you pixen freaks how to perform tricks for the magicless masses, and she 'rewards' me by making me Headmaster of her pathetic institution. Now I have not even that dubious distinction. She has stripped me of my title and turned my own staff and students against me. Fortunately, I discovered an ally in Prince Nicholas. He promised to deliver you to me if I reunited him with the Princess."

I exchanged an incredulous look with Keirt. Actually he didn't look all that incredulous. He knew Prince Nicholas better than I did.

"She tells me you threw the Eleouss Stone into a volcano. Is that true, or was it a pathetic attempt to discourage me from taking it for myself?"

"It's true," I said. "The Stone no longer exists. Sorry, but you came all this way for nothing."

"Oh, not for nothing. We will be making a trip to Tuoaue, you and I. The Alphan is an old friend of mine. He will certainly grant us a Stone of our own. Now, don't kick up a fuss, my girl, or I will leave Keirt Prai in pieces scattered about your house." He pulled an obsidian blade from his belt. Its edge glowed with blue fire.

Keirt tried to push himself to his feet, but fell back into my arms. "Don't do it, Audrey," he rasped.

"I have to," I said. The voices had gone very quiet. "I have to, Keirt."

Bratch nodded approval. "Fetch some wine, girl, and we'll seal our partnership with a toast."

I went into the kitchen to open a bottle of wine. When I returned, Keirt sat slumped against the wall. He seemed to be whispering to himself. The Tuoauean had moved over to the fireplace to warm his hands. He nodded at the clock on the mantle.

"I see you have clocks on your world too. The folly of the thinking creature. Time is a concept created by limited minds to explain the constant state of change in the universe. By breaking the continuum into minuscule increments, they deceive themselves into believing they have some control over it. In the same way, they imagine the universe is linear, when in actuality it bends in upon itself in infinite loops with an infinite number of connections."

Keirt raised his head. "Professor Bratch, one of my greatest pleasures at leaving the Mage Hall was the knowledge that I would never again have to listen to one of your lectures. Please allow that privilege to continue."

Bratch poured the wine and handed me a glass. "To a long and fruitful partnership." He tipped his glass toward me.

"To your health." I raised mine back. He waited for me to drink. I drank. He drained his glass with a swallow, shuddered, and burst out laughing. "You tried to poison me! How amusingly predictable. Punishment will have to wait. We must be on our way. But first—" He produced an iron collar from beneath his robe and turned to Keirt.

Cold terror rippled through me. "What are you doing?"

"Making certain your young mage doesn't attempt to hinder us."

"No! You'll kill him!" I reached for his arm. The shockwave he launched threw me against the fireplace. I struck my head on the mantle and crashed to the floor, bringing the clock with me. The clock chimed crazily as it smashed on the hearth. Through a haze of pain and dizziness I watched Bratch advance on Keirt, who still sat muttering to himself beside the fallen Christmas tree, head bowed with pain and exhaustion.

Bratch grasped Keirt's hair to tip his head back. He snapped the collar open. Keirt grabbed the Tuoauean's wrist. Bratch laughed at his weak attempt to defend himself, and that's when Tist shot out of Keirt's sleeve and bit Bratch on the thumb.

Bratch withdrew his hand and examined the puncture wounds in disgust. "I can't believe you still carry that creature around with you. How many times did I punish you for setting it loose in my class? An admirable attempt at revenge, but even the venom of a Tuoauean viper is no match for a Tuoauean healer."

"Speaking of health, mine hasn't been so good lately." I raised myself to my hands and knees among the splinters and gears of the clock. Blood trickled behind my ear. "The doctor says it's anemia."

Bratch frowned at his hand. Instead of healing, it had begun to swell. He smacked it a couple of times, like he was trying to get a stopped watch started again. "I'm sad to hear it. Not fatal, I hope?"

"Not at all. The cure's simple. Lots of rest, a balanced diet, and iron."

Bratch went still. "And what?"

"Iron. It comes in liquid form. I mix it with my drinks. Just how immune are you, Professor Bratch?"

Not immune enough, apparently. None of us enjoyed the next few minutes. Shragon Bratch's death was one of the most gruesome events I had ever witnessed. By the time he finally stopped twitching, I had my face pressed so hard against Keirt's shoulder I'm sure I left a dent in his collarbone.

"Why didn't you tell me that thing is venomous? It could have bitten me a thousand times!"

"He only strikes when I talk him into it. Besides," he added with an air of pointing out the obvious, "Tist would never bite you. He likes you."

Lyle Pops In

Shortly after I had disposed of Bratch's body and put Keirt in my bed, a vicious fever gripped him. His muscles twitched uncontrollably. At one point, he jumped up and prowled around the room, muttering to himself, rubbing and slapping at his arms as if they crawled with ants. He pounced on various items that caught his attention. My CDs, my stuffed animal collection, my underwear drawer and anything with Velcro were subjected to intense scrutiny.

As the sun rose he became ravenously hungry and demanded Pop-Tarts. He had never tasted a Pop-Tart in his life, but he had to have them right now. I brought him a box of Pop-Tarts, untoasted, and he scarfed down the whole box and fell into a deep sleep. I watched him and reluctantly faced the fact that I had some decisions to make. Up to this point I had allowed myself to be led around by various people—Aunt Ellen, Keirt, even Kelly. Now, for better or worse, the fate of the universe was in my hands. I started to hyperventilate, but ruthlessly squashed the terror. No more panic attacks, no more being comforted and coddled. It was time to toughen up and take charge. But first, a nap.

At first I confused the knocking with Keirt's heartbeat. I had fallen asleep with my head on his chest. When I finally realized it was the front door and not Keirt having a heart attack, I stumbled into the living room and opened it. Lyle was fishing around behind the mailbox for the spare key.

Lyle and I had grown up in the same neighbourhood. He was two years older than me. I had been thrilled by the attention of this incredibly smart and entertaining guy when I was fifteen and all the guys my age seemed so immature. We had so much fun, and the deep conversations that stretched far into the night convinced me I had found my soul mate. Then he went to university to study psychology, and everything changed. I rarely saw him. My conversation bored him. His playful teasing took on an unpleasant edge. If I rested my hand on the gear shift while I drove, he told me I had "control issues." When I tried to pet a stray cat and it scratched me, he told me I was "attracted to things that hurt me." After we broke up, he became one of the voices in my head, the one that told me I couldn't do anything right.

"Audrey?" he said, as if there was a possibility I might be someone else. "You . . . look . . . wow."

It was not a wow of admiration. I had a bruise on my forehead and little purple blisters all over my skin, courtesy of Professor Bratch. My hair was madly off in all directions.

I scrubbed at my puffy eyes. "What are you doing here, Lyle?"

"You called me, remember? You left a message saying you needed a ride."

"Oh, right." Aunt Ellen had told me there was a fault line at Wanuskewin[14] Heritage Park, but it was outside the city. The batteries had died in Aunt Ellen's car and in my old beater because the power to the block heaters had been off for so long. We needed a chauffeur, and I didn't want to put any of my friends in danger. Enter the ex-boyfriend.

He stepped inside. "Where the hell have you been? The police questioned me, can you believe that? They tried to get me to admit I had something to do with you disappearing.

---

[14] Wanna-SKAY-win. It's Cree for "Seeking Peace of Mind."

Hey, you have a tan." He rubbed my cheek with his thumb. I smacked his hand away.

"Aunt Ellen and I just got back from a holiday in, um, Miami. We left the morning after I got expelled. I guess we forgot to tell anyone."

"Miami? Man, it must have been crazy down there with that guy with the shoes."

"What guy, what shoes?"

He stared at me incredulously. "The terrorist who tried to set off explosives hidden in his shoes. He was on a flight from Paris to Miami. If the flight attendants and passengers hadn't jumped him, he would have blown up the plane. It happened the morning you left."

"Geez." I wondered if this would affect airport security regulations. Probably not. I didn't see how they could get any more strict than they already were.

Lyle was shaking his head. "I know you have the attention span of a hummingbird, but how could you have missed *that?*"

I took a deep breath. "So can you give us a ride, or not?"

"Don't get upset. God, I'd forgotten how over reactive you are. A ride to where?"

"Wanuskewin."

I expected him to interrogate me about why I wanted to visit a closed park on New Year's Day, but he had just noticed the ravaged living room. "What happened here?"

"New Year's Eve party. Things got a little out of hand."

"Are those my fins?" He focused on some of the diving equipment Keirt and I had tossed aside while preparing for our kayak ride. "That reminds me, while I'm here I should pick up my kayak and stuff."

"You can't. I sold them to pay for our flight to . . . Florida. I'm sorry, Lyle. When I get a chance, I'll pay you back. Right now I've just got too much to deal with."

His face filled with sorrow, and I gritted my teeth. Ever since he broke up with me he had been treating me like some pathetic Dickens character whose life had been ruined by unrequited love, like that creepy old woman in *Great Expectations* who never took off her wedding dress.

"Listen, Audrey, I want to apologize for the way I ran out on you back when . . . when you had all those issues. I left so you could concentrate on getting your life back together," he explained earnestly. "I know you only tried to kill yourself because you found out I was seeing someone else—"

"You were cheating on me?" I shrieked. No wonder he'd kept trying to convince me I was damaged. He wanted to keep me busy doubting my sanity so I wouldn't notice what he was up to.

"Well, yeah. Sorry." He stood there, jingling his keys in his pockets, and I stood there, sucking deep breaths and reminding myself that the fate of the universe depended upon him giving us a ride, and Lyle suddenly shot his face forward to kiss me, and that's when Keirt entered the room in his underwear.

Keirt looked like he had just stepped out of the deepest pit of Hell. His body was splotched with bruises and burns. He glared at Lyle with eyes sunk into black rings in a chalky face. His pale hair stood on end as if it had absorbed all the electromagnetic energy the CPR Yard had driven out of him.

"She'll never give up, will she?" He lurched toward us, clawing at the wall for support. "The Queen will just send one minion after another, and no matter how many we outrun or kill there will always be more of you. Don't think we will make it easy for you. The lightning is gone from my hands, but there are many weapons on this world."

Lyle's eyes bulged. I stepped between the two men. "It's all right, Keirt. He's a friend. Sort of. Well, not really. Actually I kind of hate his guts right now. But I don't think we should kill him."

Keirt pushed me aside and grasped Lyle's coat collar with shaking hands. "Queen's servant or not, stay away from Audrey. I grow tired of watching people try to use her."

"Sure, buddy. Audrey, could I talk to you? Outside?"

"In a minute, Lyle. I have to put him back to bed. Come on, Keirt." I pried his hands loose from Lyle's coat and steered him back to my bedroom.

"I ache, Audrey," he murmured as I pushed him down on the bed and hastily flung a quilt over him. Migraran underwear doesn't cover a lot of territory.

"You still have a fever. I'll get you an ice pack. What's that in your hand?"

"I don't know. It eases my pain."

"It's the magnetic headband Irene gave me for my birthday. It's supposed to cure headaches. Here, I'll wrap it around your head."

"Was that the imbecile, Lyle?" he asked as I fastened the straps.

"Unfortunately. I'm hoping he'll give us a ride."

Keirt abruptly fell asleep. Shoot. He was in no shape for a car ride. I'd have to convince Lyle to come back later. I fussed with the quilt, reluctant to go back out there. I heard the front door open. Lyle was leaving. Good. No, not the front door, the back door, oh no, *the back door.*

I ran down the hall and into the kitchen. Lyle stood in the back porch, staring at the long, sheet-wrapped bundle on the floor. Even as I drew a breath to cry out in protest, he peeled back the frosted sheet.

"Audrey, what is this?" he said, only with more profanity.

I came and looked over his shoulder. "Dead body."

"I can see that, my God, look at that face—what happened to him?"

"I killed him. He was cheating on me. It pissed me off."

Lyle gave a strangled squeak and lunged past me, sprinting for the front door. I ran after him and tackled him before he reached it. The impact as we hit the floor jarred Tist out of one of my slippers. He slithered across Lyle's hand and took refuge under the couch.

"Ignore the snake; it's just something we brought back from Florida. Calm down, Lyle, would you stop flopping around and listen? It's not a dead body. I was just joking, all right?"

Lyle stopped trying to break free of my grip on his legs and just lay there, panting. "If it isn't a dead body, what is it?"

"A sculpture, a wax sculpture. Aunt Ellen's taking a class. This is her final project. She kept it in the porch while we were away so it wouldn't melt."

The mention of Aunt Ellen sent a wave of grief over me. Oh, God, she must be crazy with worry. She would have no way of knowing we were no longer in danger from Bratch.

I made a decision. "Lyle, could you do me a huge favour and help me carry it up to the attic? That's where she works on it. Keirt is too weak to lift it."

Lyle sat up. "Keirt. Who *is* that guy?"

"An exchange student from Switzerland. Aunt Ellen is hosting him."

"Crackhead, by the look of him. I'll bet your aunt thinks she can rehabilitate him." His expression turned solemn, and I sighed, knowing what was coming. "She's a chronic rescuer, Audrey, and so are you. Remember that game we played when we were kids, Frozen Tag? While the other kids tried to get away, you'd duck under the arms of the 'frozen' ones to free them, even if it meant getting caught yourself. Rescuers have issues with low self-esteem. You blame yourself for your mother's death, and you try to build yourself up by—"

"*Lyle.*" I felt my fingernails cutting into my palms, and forced my fists to uncurl. "Please, Lyle, the sculpture? It will only take a couple of minutes."

I tried not to shudder as I grabbed Bratch's sheet-wrapped legs. Lyle took his shoulders, and we stumbled through the kitchen and up the steep stairway to the attic. A fold of the sheet fell away as I fumbled for the light switch, revealing for a second time the Tuoauean's contorted face. His clouded eyes seemed to glare at me.

"This is a pretty gruesome piece of work for a woman your aunt's age. I wonder what was going on in her head. Maybe she should go for counselling." Lyle looked around the cluttered attic. "How does she find room to work up here?"

"Lay him—it—on the floor. No, farther this way. That's good."

Lyle bent down to get closer look at Bratch's face. "It's so lifelike. You know, issues or not, your aunt is a talented lady."

"You have no idea. Stand back, Lyle, I have to do something."

"She could get some serious cash for a work like this. Does she have any other sculptures? My father knows the curator of the Mendel Art Gallery. If she wanted to do an exhibit—"

The attic exploded with swirling light as I opened a porthole in the floor next to Bratch's body. I stepped forward to look down at the Queen's army scattered along the fault line. Ranarsha had probably ordered them to stay there on the off chance that I would decide to turn myself in. Mages and warriors, most of them in the process of setting up tents for the night, gaped up at me in astonishment. The porthole illuminated their faces like a floodlight.

"Tell the Queen to leave us alone," I shouted. "Anyone who follows us will meet the same fate as Shragon Bratch."

I kicked Bratch's body through the porthole and as he plummeted into their midst I let the porthole close. With any luck, word of his death would reach Aunt Ellen, and she would know we were safe.

"That takes care of the evidence," I said briskly. "Going somewhere?"

Lyle was already down the stairs and halfway to the front door. He didn't even stop for his boots. He clawed the door open and shot outside, flapping his arms wildly to keep his balance on the icy front walk.

"What's the matter, Lyle?" I yelled from the doorway as he bolted to his car. "You got issues or something?"

We'd lost our ride, but oh, it was worth it.

Keirt was awake again when I checked on him. The magnetic headband seemed to be helping, physically. Emotionally, he was scaring me. He sat on the edge of the bed, staring with wide empty eyes at the wall as he rocked slowly back and forth.

"Audrey, we can't stay here," he said. "You must worldhop us away from your world. We will travel from world to world until there is no chance of the Queen tracking us down."

I shook my head. "I'll go one or two worlds over, but no more. The more worlds we worldhop to, the farther behind we leave Aunt Ellen and Kelly. Prince Nicholas certainly can't be trusted to look after them. Once we've lost Teriquilla's army, we can return to Migrara and talk to the Alphan of Tuoaue before Teriquilla shows up to ask him for another Eleouss Stone."

"No. I delivered you into Teriquilla's hands once. I will not do it again!"

He was shouting. I stepped back, staring at him. He had aged, literally overnight. He looked ten years older than me. It was sad, and unnerving. My playful companion was gone. I didn't know what to do with this grim, grown up Keirt.

"Don't worry about your aunt," he said, more softly. "She is a resourceful woman with many friends. We will gather allies of our own in our travels, and return with an army to help her and the Princess defeat Teriquilla."

"But that would mean declaring war against her," I said. "Against Latiana and the Cauldra Cats, the mage students, and who knows how many other innocent people."

The expression on his face seemed to add even more years to his age. "They will have to choose a side."

Arguing with him in this fierce mood would get me no-where. I sat beside him on the bed. "We won't be gathering any armies today. You're still too sick to travel. Do you want something to eat? More Pop-Tarts?" I was turning into Aunt Ellen. When in doubt, feed people.

"Maybe later." He touched my lip. "Did Lyle do that?"

I touched my tongue to the healing cut. "No, Prince Nicholas. He won't be trying that again anytime soon."

"I know. I was watching from the hill. Poor Nicholas. He may never father children."

"Why did you kiss me when we first met?" I blurted. "That night by the river, I mean."

"Because you were so courageous, and lovely, and . . . and you made me nervous," he admitted.

"I made *you* nervous?" I said incredulously. "The guy who dated *Latiana?*"

He took me by the shoulders and kissed me, very gently, on the uncut part of my lips. I kissed him back, not so gently. I lost all good sense and pushed him down on the bed, but he sat up and turned away.

"I can't, Audrey."

"Right. I wasn't thinking. I don't have any birth control."

"That's not a worry. Pixens can't breed. Only full-blooded Tuoaueans produce offspring. The problem is . . . well, the iron rails have taken more out of me than just my magic."

It took me a moment to figure out what he was talking about. "Oh," I said, trying to hide my disappointment. "Um . . . do you think it will come back?"

"I don't know," he sighed. "I must have slept through the class where my professors discussed this aspect of iron poisoning."

I thought of Thamb Opi, his chains and his sad eyes. "Keirt, this isn't permanent, is it? The loss of your magic, I mean."

"I've seen others of Tuoauean blood recover from iron poisoning. Some have regained the use of their magic. Most have not."

I tried to think of something encouraging to say, but my mind was blank. I'm always having these conversations in my head where I say wise, insightful things that leave a deep impression on people and turn their lives around. Outside of my head I hardly ever say anything insightful, and the few times I do, no one's listening.

He lay back and pulled me down to join him under the covers. I curled up beside him. It was nearly midnight back on Migrara, and we were suffering from jetlag, or maybe I should call it worldhoppinglag.

The day slipped away while we slept. A short screech of brakes and a loud bang woke me. I sprang out of bed, stood swaying for a moment trying to remember where I was, and staggered into the living room. I pulled aside the curtain and looked out the front window. It looked like one car had rear ended another right in front of my house. The drivers had just gotten out of their cars, but instead of inspecting the damage, they were staring at the seething mass of Cauldra Cats and Migraran mages in my front yard.

21

Wanuskewin

Several neighbours had come out of their houses to check out the accident. The mages were putting on some kind of magic show in an attempt to pass themselves off as performers. The neighbours stood entranced by the fireworks and illusions, not to mention the shapely female warriors who stalked around the edges of the performance, scanning the neighbourhood with their sharp feline eyes.

Keirt put a hand on my shoulder, and I nearly let loose one of my bull-stung-on-the-butt screams.

"Ranarsha must have had the worldhoppers among them combine their powers to open a porthole," he whispered.

"If Teriquilla can use a team of worldhoppers this way, what does she need me for?"

"Would Teriquilla display the destructive power of the Eleouss Stone in front of so many witnesses? And as I said, it's dangerous. The greater the number, the greater the risk. Should one member of the circle lose concentration, the porthole's rimfire would flare out of control, lashing out at those gathered around it." He handed me my cloak and backpack. "Out the back. We'll cross the iron rails. They will at least prevent the mages from following us, if not the Cats."

"Won't the rails make you sicker?"

"I'm past the point where any amount of iron will affect me, Audrey."

Cautiously, we navigated the dark alley that led to the tall embankment at the foot of the train bridge. We climbed across the CPR rail line and slid down the other side. Our progress slowed as we floundered toward Thirty-third Street. The ground was all snowdrifts and shadows here. My foot sank into a gopher hole, and I sprawled forward, banging my knee on a sharp ridge of ice.

Keirt crouched next to me. "Are you all right?"

I forgot about toughening up and just bawled my head off. Keirt pulled me up and held me close, wrapping his cloak around me. I was so tired of all this running. I had run away from Jersicke. I had run away from my world. I had run away from Teriquilla and her minions. Worst of all, I had run away from numerous opportunities to bounce Keirt, and now it was too late.

A thought came to me. If the Alphan of Tuoaue was as powerful as everyone said, he might have the power to give Keirt back his magic, or at least cure him of his . . . other problem.

My courage returned with a rush.

"Come on, we have to find a ride." I grabbed Keirt's hand and hauled him to the drugstore down the street. He stood guard while I used the pay phone out front.

"Hey, Lyle," I said when he answered. "You never got back to me about that ride."

"You have got to be kidding me," Lyle said. "Why would I expose myself to more of your twisted pranks?"

"Because if you don't, I'll pull the next 'prank' at your house," I said. "And don't think a locked door can stop me."

Lyle promised to be there in ten minutes.

The cashiers gave us wary glances as we entered the drug store to warm up. Keirt and I looked like we'd been in a gang fight. I took the opportunity to do a little shopping. I grabbed some food and bottled water, then sidled casually over to the aisle where they kept all the embarrassing stuff. I stood between the shelves, overwhelmed by the different options, positive everyone in the store was staring at me. I believed Keirt when he said pixens were infertile, but suppose the rules had changed now that he had no magic? I loved babies, but they did produce mass quantities of snot and poo, and I wasn't ready for that on a fulltime basis.

"What are those?" Keirt asked, appearing at my elbow. My hand shot into my cloak pocket, carrying a package of condoms with it.

"Nothing," I said. "You're supposed to be watching for Lyle."

"I wanted to remind you to purchase some dressings for our journey." He took a package of Kotex off a shelf and pointed to the picture on the front. Now people were definitely staring at us.

I handed him some cash. "Here. Take them up to the front and pay for them."

He was back moments later.

"Now what?"

"Get down," he said softly, pushing me into a crouch. He pointed at the round security mirror that hung from the ceiling.

Ranarsha and several other Cauldra Cats stood inside the front door. They sniffed the air fiercely, glared at the woman at the perfume counter, and split up to search the aisles.

As Ranarsha rounded the corner of our aisle, Keirt snatched a can of Metamucil from an elderly man's hands and fired it at the warrior's head. She ducked, her sword whipping around to split the can in midair. Orange powder exploded all over Aisle 3. Ranarsha charged forward, flailing blindly with her sword while scrubbing gummy powder from her eyes. Pharmacy products ricocheted around us as we fled the other way and doubled back down the next aisle. We made a dash for the door, only to skid to a halt as the store manager threw himself in our path.

"Would you empty your pockets please, miss?" he said coldly.

He and the other staff formed a wall between us and the door. Throwing a frantic glance over my shoulder at Ranarsha's approach, I jerked my cloak pockets inside out. A package of condoms tumbled to the floor. I decided to spare my pursuers the trouble of capturing me and just die of embarrassment right here.

The manager put his hand on my arm. "Would you come with me to the back of the store, please?"

Ranarsha grabbed my other arm, and the remaining Cauldra Cats seized Keirt.

"These prisoners are mine," Ranarsha told the manager, who looked her up and down and tightened his grip on me.

"I don't know what gang you freaks belong to, but you're about to learn a new concept. It's called taking responsibility for your actions."

"Ranarsha, listen to me," Keirt said as she and the man played tug-of-war with me. "The Queen can't be trusted. She—"

"Watch your tongue, traitor!" one of the Cats snarled, cuffing him so hard he fell to his knees.

Something had been nagging at my subconscious since we entered the store. Now it popped into my conscious. I summoned a mental map and drew a line from the weir to my house, and beyond.

"The man is right, Keirt," I said loudly. "The *fault* is mine. I crossed the *line*. I mustn't *escape* the consequences. I—"

"No!" Ranarsha shouted. "She means to open a porthole!" Claws sprang out of her fingertips and her powerful arm swung toward me, intending to maim me to the point where I would be unable to even think of worldhopping.

The manager leaped back with a squawk of alarm, and luckily for me he was still holding onto my arm. I fell against him, breaking free of Ranarsha's grasp. The lethal claws swept harmlessly over my head and ripped off the bottom half of the man's tie. Keirt, still on his knees, snatched his small knife from his boot and stabbed one of the Cauldra Cats in the foot. She gave a roar of pain, and for a moment he was free. I untangled myself from the store manager and opened a porthole. Keirt and I shot out of the store and into the morning sunlight of Migrara. We ran straight into a cook fire. Pots and sparks flew everywhere. Screams and curses rose from the group of mage students seated around the fire. Keirt tripped over one of them and in a burst of unfairness called him a nasty name. I jerked him to his feet and we ran, but not far. Hoping our short dash had at least carried us outside the store, I opened the porthole to my world. We jumped through it, ducking as spears and bolts of energy whizzed past us. I snapped it shut behind us and ran headfirst into a brick wall.

"He's here!" Keirt said, picking me up off the sidewalk and dragging me across the parking lot toward the car that had just pulled up. "The Imbecile Lyle. Hurry, Audrey!"

Lyle had arrived in his pride and joy, a cherry red Corvette convertible paid for by his father back when his parents were newly divorced and competing for their son's love. Lyle was obsessed with that car. Twice he had taken it back to the dealership and insisted they redo the entire paint job because of some microscopic flaw only he could see.

"Thanks, Lyle," I panted as we crammed ourselves into the front seat, me sitting on Keirt's lap. "Step on it, would you?"

"I drove past your house," he said, putting the Corvette in gear. "What the hell is going on over there? Where's your aunt?"

"She's fine. Everything's fine," I said a moment before a massive red lioness slammed onto the hood of the Corvette.

"Holy Mother of God!" Lyle bellowed, suddenly converting to Catholicism as Ranarsha pressed her face against the windshield and glared at us with wild yellow eyes. He stood on the brake and Ranarsha skidded to the ground, leaving a matching set of claw marks across the hood.

"Drive, drive!" I stomped my foot on top of Lyle's. The Corvette shot out of the parking lot, narrowly missing the cheetah who tried to cut us off. Our relief lasted about five seconds. A heavy thump rocked the Corvette, nearly sending it into a parked car. Claws stabbed through the vinyl top and ripped it down the center. Lyle cranked the steering wheel and pumped the gas and brake, but he couldn't shake her loose.

Keirt had thrown his arms around me to keep me from being flung through the windshield. I wriggled my arms loose and punched the cigarette lighter.

"No smoking in the car!" Lyle shouted automatically.

A furry red tail hung over the side of the Corvette, snaking around the windows as Ranarsha struggled to keep her balance. As a powerful foreleg thrust through the rent in the top and clawed the toque from Lyle's head, I plucked the red hot cigarette lighter, opened the passenger window and reached for the tail. A piercing scream made my ears ring. The paw withdrew and the Corvette stopped rocking. Looking out the back, we saw Ranarsha, human now, race naked across the street and sit in a snow bank.

Lyle sent the Corvette flying down Warman Road. We left the city limits and sped through prairie landscape glowing with snow and moonlight. The gate to Wanuskewin Heritage Park was locked, so he dropped us off there.

"Thanks, Lyle," I said. "Sorry about the car."

Lyle roared away, sobbing something about insurance.

We walked the short road to the interpretative centre. While Keirt paused to catch his breath, I climbed one of the buffalo hunt sculptures in front of the building, and painfully discovered the folly of sitting on a bronze bison on a January night. We set off across one of the winding trails that crossed the prairie. I pointed out the outdoor amphitheatre where, on a rare warm day in April, Prince Charles had received a star blanket and an incredibly long and elegant Cree name.[15] He had spent most of the ceremony battling the prairie wind for control of his hair. Aunt Ellen and I had followed the royal entourage there after Charles viewed the weir. Is it my imagination, or does the heir to the throne seem drawn to fault lines? Hmm.

"It's called a medicine wheel," I said as we approached the edge of the circle, or rather, where I sensed the circle to be, since it was buried beneath the snow. It was about twenty meters across. "This one's around fifteen hundred years old. Lyle tried to tell me these medicine wheels are just naturally occurring phenomena, something to do with soil chemicals, but I've always sensed there was something special—"

"Who cares? Just open it," Keirt said rudely, shivering and stamping his feet. He had lost his tolerance for our Saskatchewan winter when his magic left him.

"Hey, do I interrupt you when you go on and on about the history of your Six Spinning Islands?"

"Circling Islands."

"Whatever. Strange—this fault line runs in a circle, not a straight line."

"That means it was created by design, not by accident."

"Created? By whom? And what kind of accident could cause a—"

---

[15] Kisikawpisim Kamiyowahpahmikoot, which means "The Sun Watches Over Him In a Good Way."

"Audrey, my testicles just froze off and rolled into my boots. Get us out of this sunforsaken wasteland."

As we reached the center of the medicine wheel, I gasped. "Keirt, there is more than one fault line here. In fact, this spot is surrounded by them. Rings and rings of fault lines."

We stared at each other, and slowly smiled. Even if the Cauldra Cats tracked us to Wanuskewin, it would take them forever to figure out which world we'd gone to.

I spun around, laughing, my arms thrown wide. A ring of portholes opened around us, their bright colours flickering across the snow. "Pick a world, any world!"

Hand in hand, we stepped out of the Saskatchewan winter and into the universe.

Worldhopping 401

After leaving Earth, we crossed from world to world to world; Keirt searching for a safe haven, and me secretly searching for fault lines to Migrara. I had decided there was no point in arguing with a man stubborn enough to spend ten years of his life chasing down an assassin. Keirt had a new obsession: Keep Audrey O'Krane safe. So I didn't bring up the idea of confronting the Alphan of Tuoaue again, but I didn't give up on it, either.

Keirt, determined to compensate for my grim worldhopping experiences, turned the universe into our own personal amusement park. We sledded down a mountain. We skated across candy-striped glaciers. We rafted down a river so wide we couldn't see the far bank. We swam in a warm purple sea. We explored high-tech cities and remote jungles. We bummed rides in vehicles that travelled over land, under the sea and through the air. We met life forms strange beyond anything I had ever imagined. Every day was a fascinating adventure, and I didn't want it to end. Most of the time.

"You seem troubled, Audrey," Keirt observed as we attended a concert one night. The musicians used their own tree-like bodies to create a woodwind and strings ensemble. "Do you miss your world?"

"Not really," I said. "It's just that—well, at first I was blown away. I couldn't wait to see all these worlds. Anything seemed possible. Now—I don't know. It's stupid, but I feel let down."

"Because there are no elves, dwarves or hobbits?" He put an arm around my shoulder. "You'll never find them, you know. These worlds you keep looking for—Pern, Shannarah, Central Earth—exist only in the minds of your world's storytellers."

"*Middle* Earth. Is it so hard to believe that at least one of my favourite authors might be a worldhopper?"

"Put your expectations aside, Audrey. Then you'll find you can enjoy these worlds for their own sake, despite the lack of hobbits."

There was another reason for my uneasiness, but I wasn't ready to share it with him. I felt like I was running away not only from my enemies, but from my responsibilities. I had left some serious problems behind, and instead of dealing with them I was gallivanting around the universe like a kid in a giant playground.

I guess I wasn't so good at keeping my thoughts hidden, because Keirt suddenly said, "Let it go, Audrey. You've earned some fun."

With all this practice, my worldhopping power increased by the day. I could detect fault lines from many miles away. I developed the ability to sense details about the terrain and atmosphere on the other side of a fault line. This cut down on the number of unpleasant surprises that greeted us upon opening a porthole. Sometimes I could tell if the world was inhabited or not.

"Isn't it strange that we see so many humanoid life forms on the worlds we've been to?" I said to Keirt as we floated across a dusty sunset sky. We were on an unnamed world with almost no gravity. With a steady wind and our cloaks tied to our wrists and ankles, we could sail through the air like flying squirrels.

Keirt swooped playfully past me. "Most worlds that support life have 'humanoids,'" he said. "In the years since worldhopping was discovered, our kind have spread across the universe. But no one knows from which world our species originated."

"It would have to be Earth," I said. "We've always been there. We evolved from apes."

"Don't be too sure. Why do you think your apes suddenly evolved?"

A flock of feathery life forms resembling dandelion fluff twirled past us, seemingly at the mercy of the wind but all moving in the same direction. I wanted to spend the rest of my life here, just flying around and watching these airy, hairy creatures whirl and tumble on the wind.

According to Migraran law, we were supposed to avoid revealing ourselves to any species of an overlapping world, a law we cheerfully ignored. Keirt searched among them for allies who might join us in a war against Teriquilla. He wasn't successful. Half of them refused to believe our story, and the other half didn't care. Never mind that their world could be wiped out at any moment if Teriquilla took a dislike to it.

The very few that did believe us, and cared, requested immediate access to Migrara in order to launch their own invasion. The request usually came with an attempt to imprison us. I had to scramble to worldhop us out of those situations.

On one world, we got careless. The humanoids we were negotiating with got between us and the fault line that had brought us there. It was here that I discovered a new talent. We were sprinting across a field, pursued by hysterical four-armed farmers shouting something about demons come from Khahkar to steal their souls and piss on their crops. In an effort to lose them, Keirt pulled me into a crop of tall stalks topped with clouds of fuzzy little flowers. We took ten steps and fell to the ground, choking. The pollen from the pretty little flowers was poisoning us. It was either exit this world or die, so, although we were nowhere near a fault line, I ripped open a porthole. We fell into a hot swamp, sucking grateful breaths of steamy oxygen. When we staggered to our feet, wiping green slime off our clothes, I felt the familiar shiver of a spider web passing through me. I had created a fault line.

I guess I should have been happy to discover another dimension to my talent, but all I could think was, why hadn't I discovered this sooner? We could have escaped Migrara anywhere, anytime, and Keirt would still have his magic.

If Keirt thought the same thing, he gave no sign. "Well, Audrey, this officially makes you the most powerful world-hopper I know," he said, grinning.

"It also means we can go back to Migrara anytime we want," I said. "And I do want to. Now."

He shook his head. "We've not yet raised an army."

"No. No army." I turned to face him. My knees trembled even worse than when I had faced down Teriquilla and Shragon Bratch. Why is it so much harder to challenge someone you care about? "No army, no battles, no war. Keirt, half my planet is ready to go to war because a handful of crazies attacked one of our countries. It just makes no sense."

"War seldom does, but our particular 'crazy' is extremely powerful," Keirt pointed out.

"I know that. But throwing an army at Teriquilla isn't going to help."

"Then what will?"

I swallowed. "I'm going to ask the Alphan of Tuoaue to shut her down."

Keirt stared at me for a long moment. "Alphan Oureil is the most dangerous creature on Migrara, Audrey. Do you think I would allow you to march up to him and try to turn him against his strongest ally?"

"How are you going to stop me?" I flicked open a porthole behind me. I didn't have to look to know the Migraran landscape was at my back.

"The Alphan would make a terrible enemy." I could see he was making an effort to speak calmly instead of attempting a quarterback sack. "He might lash out at you without even hearing you out. And I have no way to defend you." His last words were so anguished, I wavered and nearly gave in.

The steady whoosh of my porthole's rimfire strengthened my resolve. "We can make him listen, and I can defend us both. My portholes will dump a world of hurt on anyone who challenges me." His eyes widened, and I blushed. From absolute power to absolute corruption in under a minute. That had to be some kind of record. "Sorry. That sounded a lot like Teriquilla, didn't it?"

"I'm not accusing you of abusing your talent. I'm just coming to terms with your potential."

Encouraged by his thoughtful expression, I said, "Maybe I don't need your protection, but I could sure use your help. You'll come with me, won't you?"

To my huge relief, he smiled. "Lead on, worldhopper. I ask only that you allow me to instruct you. I may not understand the subtleties of worldhopping, but I can describe the ways Awnvale defended us when we ran into trouble."

"Agreed." I didn't like the idea of following the example of a truly corrupt worldhopper, but I trusted Keirt not to teach me anything too vile.

We stepped into a forest of trees that reminded me of the giant cedars on Vancouver Island. "I wonder if this *is* Migrara," I said, suddenly doubtful. "It looks like half a dozen other worlds we've been to."

"It's Migrara. See the runes?"

I noticed intricate symbols carved on the green bark of several trees. I ran my fingertips over the graceful curls and swoops of the runes, wondering if they might set off some mysterious Migraran magic. "They're beautiful. What do they say?"

"'Wiplar loves Mayra.' 'Thash loves Ozyra.' And that one is too rude for your young ears. I think we're in the Shale Forest. I recognize the flowers." He picked a bouquet of pink blossoms and handed them to me.

Keirt and I were falling in love. We were too chicken to admit it, so we found sneaky ways to tell each other.

"I love seeing the universe through your eyes," he'd say as I laughed in delight at the antics of some adorable fuzzy life form.

"I love seeing you smile again," I'd say as we watched the sun set over a stretch of rainbow sand dunes.

Every day I watched, with fading hope, for signs of his magic returning. He had informed me that in all recorded cases of iron poisoning, those who recovered their magic did so within a few days of exposure. It had been over two weeks now.

It had also been over two weeks since we'd tried to make out, although there had been some spectacular kissing. There were moonlit desert kisses, icy mountaintop kisses, flying through the air kisses, and acrobatic underwater kisses. I was content to leave it at that. For now.

The Migraran coast was a two day hike. There we would find transportation to Tuoaue. We reached the coast at sunset. We could just make out an ominous grey mass on the horizon. It was the Tuoauean Cloud Wall, a layer of fog that never left the island. Keirt folded his arms across his chest and glowered at the fog as if engaged in a silent argument with it.

I cleared my throat. "There's something you should know."

"Yes?"

"I told you I had disposed of Bratch's body. I didn't tell you how I disposed of it." I shifted uncomfortably under that sharp, green-eyed gaze. "I opened a porthole and chucked him at the mage students."

He slumped onto a rock and stared at me in shock. "Thus presenting the Mage Hall with undeniable evidence of the murder of the Alphan's closest friend?"

"I guess." I scuffed my toe into the dirt.

He buried his head in his hands. "Well, that settles it. I will be travelling alone to Tuoaue. I couldn't possibly keep you alive long enough to present our case to the Alphan."

"Oh, don't be such a drama queen. If they give us trouble, I'll just pop us onto another world."

"Can you pop faster than an enraged Tuoauean can shred you with a spell?"

"No problem," I gulped, and changed the subject. "Will your father be there?"

He raised his head wearily. "Probably."

"Are you excited about meeting him?"

He shrugged. "Not particularly. I don't think he's aware of my existence—and if he was, I doubt it would please him."

"Liar. You *are* excited about meeting him. And I'll bet he'll be happy to see you too."

He gave me a pitying look usually reserved for naïve children. I stuck my tongue out at him and wrapped myself in my cloak. As I drifted off to sleep, he was still on his rock, watching the cloud wall fade into the night.

"Audrey."

I startled awake. Keirt's hand was on my shoulder, his hair a silver halo in the dazzling light of the three full moons.

"What is it? What's wrong?" I rolled onto my stomach and peered through the trees that sheltered us. Nothing moved there. I could hear no sound above the pounding waves at the foot of the cliff where we had made our camp.

Keirt wasn't looking at the trees or the ocean. He was looking at me. "Audrey," he said again, very softly, and kissed me.

"Oh," I said, and pulled him down on top of me.

Tuoaue

When I woke up, all the voices were humming happily, even Impulse Control. I jumped up and did the touchdown victory dance. My euphoric mood lasted until I discovered its source had disappeared.

I called Keirt's name. No reply. As I stood at the edge of the cliff, I noticed what I had overlooked in the darkness last night. Down the coast a community of huts clustered on the shoreline. A small wooden cargo ship stood at anchor in a narrow bay. It must have arrived overnight. A small knot of passengers gathered at the rail, watching the crew load boxes and barrels onto the deck. No doubt the passenger knot contained one Keirt Prai, determined to leave one Audrey O'Krane safely behind.

Swearing, I threw my stuff together and tore along the path that dipped down to the seashore. As I drew closer, I saw the sailors were loading not from the docks but from the cliff itself. A long, heavy plank extended from a wide ledge on the cliff face to the deck of the ship. The sailors were using the natural platform as a loading dock. Men and women on the platform cranked a giant wheel, raising the plank free of the deck. The ship's sails swelled.

"I'm going to kill you, Keirt Prai! Wait, wait!" I raced down a stone stairway hacked into a cut in the cliff, scattering the startled plank crankers on the ledge. I galloped up the rising gangway and leaped off the end. Barely clearing the railing of the slowly moving ship, I hit the deck hard and sprawled at the feet of the astonished crew.

"Where is he?" I demanded when I got my breath back and wobbled upright. "Where is Keirt Prai?"

"Keirt Prai? The Court Mage of Cauldra Castle?" a young woman asked.

"Yes, he just boarded. White hair, green eyes, he was carrying a snake—"

"No man outside of the crew boarded the *Queen Teriquilla*."

"Is that him?" one bent old sailor asked, pointing.

Keirt stood on the loading dock, which had fallen far behind us as we sailed out of the bay. I could just barely make out his expression of incredulous dismay.

"Oops," I said. "Go back. Turn around and take me back."

"Can't," a sailor barked, running across the deck to grab a rope. The ship had given a mighty lurch, nearly throwing me off my feet. "We've caught the current. No ship sails against the Clockwise Current."

Women and men hurried around the ship, climbing ropes, swinging booms, and spinning wheels and gears; a ballet of organized chaos. A woman with long steps and sharp eyes approached me. "I am Captain Sierri. If you want to leave my ship, you'll have to wait until we dock at the next port—unless you want to swim."

"We—I—I need to go to the Island of Tuoaue."[16]

Her head hitched back in surprise. "Do you have the price of passage?"

Keirt had earned a small fortune by collecting odds and ends from each world we visited and selling them on other worlds. However, most of our assets lay in his backpack;

---

[16] Too-WOE-ah-way. Yes, I know I've already given the pronunciation, but it's a tricky one and worth repeating.

mine held only travel supplies. I checked my pockets and produced a pretty seashell, a fossil stone, and a purple feather, none of which impressed the Captain.

"How about an exchange of favours?" I said. "Watch me find you a strong wind."

I focused hard on the space behind the ship and opened the biggest porthole I had ever attempted. Gale force winds hurtled out of a tornado world and nearly ripped the sails off the mast. The ship slewed to one side, almost throwing several crew members overboard. I snapped the porthole shut.

"Sorry about that," I said as we picked ourselves up off the deck.

Captain Sierri was certainly impressed now, but not favourably. "A most effective threat, worldhopper. We will take you to the island."

"No, no, it wasn't a threat! I just—"

"You realize we can't pull ashore. We'll have to put you off the ship on a raft. The current and the Nyshuans will take you to the island." She spoke about Nyshuans as if I should know who they were, and I didn't want to look like a tourist so I didn't ask. "How you get off the island is your own problem. We'll not linger in those dangerous waters, waiting for you to finish whatever business you have there."

It occurred to me that I had the power to turn the ship around, blow it back to the coast, and pick up Keirt. I opened my mouth to share this with the Captain, then hesitated. Maybe it was better this way. I loved Keirt for wanting to protect me, but sometimes it made him lose sight of the big picture. And this was a mighty big picture. There was too much at stake to risk him sabotaging our mission just to keep me safe.

Captain Sierra watched my internal struggle and waited to see if I would confide in her. When I stayed silent, she shrugged and went back to running the ship.

I watched the coastline drop away behind us. When I could no longer see Keirt, I turned toward Tuoaue and rehearsed what I would say to the most dangerous man on Migrara.

Several hours later I was cursing Captain Freaking Sierri. The raft they had put me on was hardly more than a few wooden planks strung together. Did they honestly expect it to survive the breakers crashing against the island? I couldn't see them because of the thick fog of the cloud wall, but I could hear them.

The raft gained velocity, and I shrieked in alarm. This was a heck of a current. Then I realized the current had help. A pair of white dolphins were pushing the raft along. A baby dolphin raced alongside, a rainbow sheen dancing across its glossy skin as it arced playfully in and out of the water. We ploughed right through the cloud wall and the breakers, which weren't as bad as I had expected. Maybe it was because the island was on the move. It was a Circling Island, after all. The pearly dolphins—Nyshuans?—escorted me nearly to the shore and then went on their way without waiting for a tip.

The raft washed up on a beach bordering a thick jungle. The sand was black, and it glittered weirdly. I walked down the dark beach, searching for civilization. The only sign of life was a tall figure hunched over a driftwood fire, frying what looked like an eel on a flat rock. I approached warily. The figure turned and jumped to her feet.

"Latiana! What are you doing here?" I raced across the sand and hugged her, so happy to see a familiar face that my eyes leaked a couple tears.

"By my sword, you are naïve, Audrey," she exclaimed, half laughing, half exasperated as she pushed me away. "What do you think I'm here for? To return you to the Queen. She sent me to Tuoaue shortly after you fled Mount Cauldra. She said you would eventually come to the island, though she did not say why. You took your bloody time about it. I've been here most of a cycle. I'm missing the tumbleball tournament. I don't suppose you've heard whom they found to play my position? I was forward charger."

"Um, no."

"Have you at least heard the early scores? No? Oh well. Where is Keirt?"

"I don't know. We got separated, and I had to come alone."

"It's incredible you made it this far. You two are the most hunted people on Migrara! Why *are* you here, Audrey? Only a madwoman would land on Tuoaue."

"So what does that make you?"

"The beach is safe, more or less, and I haven't left it since I arrived." She suddenly drew her sword and slaughtered a harmless piece of driftwood. "I've been banished," she said savagely. "My punishment for allowing you to escape. If I do not return with you, I will not be allowed to return at all. The Queen no longer trusts me, and my own trust in her is much diminished. It is not a warrior's place to question her queen, but lately she smells of lies and betrayal."

"Your nose is right, Latiana. The Alphan gave her a stone that destroys worlds. She's gone all psycho paranoid and is killing any civilization she sees as a threat."

"Ranarsha has taken charge of my Cats," Latiana growled, obviously seeing this as more of an atrocity than genocide. "Ranarsha! The warriors will chafe under her leadership. She dominates rather than inspires. I will have to battle her for command when I return."

"Aunt Ellen—" I hesitated, wanting to ask if she'd heard anything, but not sure it was safe to let her know Aunt Ellen, Kelly and Bernie were on Migrara.

"Lady Trini, Princess Perikelli, Prince Nicholas and Bernie Bahtcracke have found a secure refuge. The Queen gave me her own Wakitaki when she sent me away. She thought I might have more success than she at talking sense into them, but it is they who have persuaded me. What we must do, Audrey, is join them and decide together the best course of action."

"I already know the best course of action. I'm going to convince the Alphan to help us depose Teriquilla. Is that the word I'm looking for? Or is it dispose?"

She bent down, wrapped her arms around my legs and slung me over her shoulder.

"What are you doing? Put me down!"

"I'm saving you from your own insanity, Audrey." She said carried me toward a boat just down the shore. "I'm no sailor, but hopefully the Nyshuans will take pity on us and guide us back to the mainland. Making demands of the Alphan of Tuoaue! I could kill that pixen for putting such thoughts in your head."

She looked down in astonishment, suddenly finding herself sinking through a porthole into the ooze of a swamp. When I closed the porthole moments later, she stood buried to the hips in the black Migraran sand. Struggling free of her grip, I jumped up and popped her right between the eyes. Cradling my bruised knuckles against my chest, I made a dash for the trees.

If the jungle contained dangerous, frightening life forms to beware of, I ran too fast to see them. Even so, it didn't take long before I heard behind me the pounding feet of Ironskull Latiana. She tackled me at the crest of a steep hill. I skidded through the undergrowth and lay there, panting, as Latiana crouched over me cursing every aspect of my existence. Strange sounds came to the ear I had pressed against the ground. Rumbles, thuds—voices?

The noises stopped, and then the hill split in two, me on one half, Latiana on the other. A huge figure heaved out of the crevice, avalanching soil all over us. Fingers the size of logs dug me out of the dirt and picked me up, then retrieved Latiana. I had thought Thamb Opi was big—this guy made him look like an infant. I took one look and snapped my eyes closed. Not out of fear, but because he was absolutely bare-butt naked.

Without so much as an introduction, the giant stepped out of the hill and lumbered through the jungle, raining soil and leaves from his skin, hair, and beard. Latiana and I tried to strike up a conversation with him—I even opened my eyes after a while—but he ignored us.

The landscape grew unruly as we travelled deeper into the jungle. Poorly behaved trees wrapped their roots around the giant's ankles or slapped their branches against him. He just slapped them back and kept going. Life forms with too many heads and impossibly long fangs stalked us, slashing at his legs. He kicked them out of the way. A species of monkey with a dozen limbs fell shrieking upon his arm and reached for me with spidery claws. The giant tucked Latiana under his reeking armpit and flicked the monkey into the trees with one dirt-crusted finger. Winged fairy-like life forms buzzed angrily around his head. He swatted them away like flies.

The giant stopped. We stood at the edge of a small village paved with tiny glittering stones. Their colours formed designs that twisted the eye like an Escher drawing. In the center of the village, a leafy throne protruded like a fungus out of the base of a massive, white-barked tree.

On the throne sat the Alphan of Tuoaue.

The Alphan

The giant—I never did catch his name—set us down on the ground and lumbered back into the jungle without even a "Well, here you are." I barely noticed his departure. Among the Tuoaueans gathered around us I had spotted a familiar face.

"Keirt!" I ran toward him, not even stopping to wonder why he had disguised himself with long blue hair and red skin. With one wild, startled look at me, he burst into flames and vanished in a puff of smoke. That thud you just heard was my jaw hitting the ground.

Latiana grabbed my arm, wheeled me around to face the throne, and shoved my head toward the ground. "Alphan Oureil, we are deeply honoured to be in your presence," she said, bowing low herself. "Please forgive our intrusion."

The Alphan of Tuoaue was taller than Latiana, unusual in a Migraran male. His limbs were long and slender. Feathery eyebrows perched on sharply defined ridges. With his sage green skin and glowing orange eyes the size of tennis balls, he reminded me of a praying mantis.

"I might be more inclined toward forgiveness were I to receive an explanation," he said with an imperious air that suggested "Seize them!" would be his next words.

"Alphan Oureil, I've come to speak to you about the Eleouss Stone," I said.

He rose from his throne. "Bring them into the White Circle," he said, and left the clearing.

The motley crew of Tuoaueans herded us after him. They seemed compelled to touch us, which freaked me out more than a little. Some of the Alphan's people were breathtakingly beautiful, but some not so much. One creepy guy with sharp teeth and bugs in his hair slouched along beside us, leering and plucking at our clothes with filthy hands. I walked as close to Latiana as I could without actually clinging to her.

"That man who looked like Keirt," I muttered. "Do you think he was—"

"Keirt's father? Most likely," she said. "He's a pyrogin. They're incredibly shy. I've often wondered how Drandima managed to seduce one. Suppose he burst into flames during the proceedings?"

"Ouch."

The Alphan led us to a ring of white trees connected by shimmering curtains of tiny stars. The sparkling motes thinned to let us through, then became opaque, shutting out the curious eyes of the Tuoaueans. Oureil beckoned us to seat ourselves on delicate wooden chairs that grew out of the ground. Sweet-smelling blossoms opened all around their frames as we sat down. I sank into the soft cushions and relaxed. This was more like it. Obviously the stories about the Alphan were greatly exaggerated.

"You are Lady Audrey Oak," he said, taking a seat himself and wrapping his long fingers around his knee. "Niece of Lady Ellen Trini."

"Yes, and this is Latiana, Captain of the Cauldra Cats of Migrara."

He ignored her. "I have a question for you, Lady Oak. Why did you slay Shragon Bratch?"

The glittering walls grew dark. The blossoms snapped shut. Rough roots and tendrils wrapped around our ankles and wrists, binding us to our chairs. The ground collapsed beneath our feet, revealing a deep and smelly pit whose sides writhed with creatures out of a nightmare.

"To save the life of one of your people," I said, trying to keep a frightened quiver out of my voice. Latiana snarled wordlessly, her chair creaking with the force of her struggles.

Oureil's winged eyebrows lifted, giving his nose the appearance of a bird about to take flight. "Keirt Prai? He is not of my people."

"No? He's done a pretty good imitation of Tuoauean magic."

The eyebrow wings flapped down in disgust. "The fact that you magicless women invade our island and steal our men's seed does not give your half-breed offspring the right to claim Tuoaue as their own."

At the words "steal our men's seed" I burst into hysterical giggles. Latiana's exasperated hiss and the Alphan's cold mantis eyes reminded me I was on trial for murder here, so I struggled to get a grip on myself.

The darkened walls around us rippled, and a slender, feather-haired woman drifted into the White Circle. She glided straight over to me, leaned over the open pit, and placed her palm on my forehead, the heel of her hand pressing against the bridge of my nose.

"My mate, Eleouss," Oureil said, and the walls brightened again.

"Pleased to meet you," I said, trying not to go cross-eyed. How romantic, to name a weapon of mass destruction after your sweetie.

Eleouss removed her hand and touched Oureil's shoulder. "Husband."

Grudgingly, the Alphan nodded. The pit at our feet closed and the chairs' roots and tendrils released their grip on us.

"Tell us how you came to know of the Stone, Audrey," Oureil said as Eleouss took a seat beside him, her feather-trimmed gown puddling gracefully around her feet.

I told him what Teriquilla had done, omitting only the parts with Shragon Bratch. "I know there are many dangerous worlds out there," I concluded. "Some might be a threat to Migrara, I don't know. But I do know it's insane to slaughter something just because it frightens you, because it's different. It's a lesson the people of my own world are still learning. The Queen says she wants to merge Migrara with my world to make a stronger world, but cramming two civilizations together is not the way to strengthen them. They have to come together on their own."

"Yes," he said after a long pause. "Yes, she did say you would spin such a tale."

"It's no tale!" As usual, I had actually said something in-sightful and no one was listening.

"If what you say is true, what exactly do you expect me to do about it? Give you a Stone of your own?" His mouth gave a cynical twist.

"Oh hell no. Just don't give Teriquilla any more."

"But I have already sent one to Teriquilla upon her request, and there are many more in existence. I have sent them to worldhoppers on worlds all across the universe."

Everything went grey for a while. When my vision finally cleared, all I could see was the underside of my chair.

"Deep breaths, Audrey," Latiana said. She was holding my head down between my knees.

I flailed my arms. "Let me up!" She let go. I sat up slowly, gripping the arms of my chair as the room spun around me. "Could you turn off the walls, please?"

The brightly shimmering walls dimmed once more. Eleouss leaned forward and put her hand over mine. "Lady Oak, there is nothing destructive about the Eleouss Stones. I designed them to be a healing power. Our worldhoppers use them to mend the weaknesses in the barriers between worlds, both here on Migrara and on worlds where they may safely travel. Without fault lines, there will be no invasions of hostile overlappers, no contamination from poisonous worlds. These fault lines are an aberration of nature. No one knows where they came from, but we do know, finally, how to correct them."

I know where they came from, I thought, feeling sick. People like me. Careless worldhoppers ripping portholes open all over the universe.

"Eleouss, Queen Teriquilla is not repairing fault lines. She's tearing them wide open to let these worlds smash into each other. What do you think will happen to you Tuoaueans when she merges Migrara and Earth? There will be iron everywhere. Maybe she's counting on that. Maybe she wants you weak and powerless."

The Alphan gave an impatient sigh. "You have gone mad, Audrey. This happens on occasion with powerful worldhoppers. I will return you to Teriquilla and allow her to deal with you. There will be no punishment for you or the Cat for violating our island. You meant well, I suppose. As for Shragon Bratch, I will leave that up to the Queen as well, as it was she who employed him."

I stood.

"On your feet, Alphan Oureil." My voice sounded strange to my ears, cold as the heart of a Saskatchewan winter. "We're going on a tour."

"Audrey. Don't." Latiana, staring at my face, looked frightened for the first time since I had met her.

The Alphan of Tuoaue rose and hammered me with a glare. "My patience for your malady is rapidly disappearing."

"When I was at Mount Cauldra, the Queen showed me a world she thought might be a threat to Migrara. Here is the healing power of your Stones." I turned and ripped open a porthole to the dying world of Oid.

The two overlapping worlds had finally merged into a single vision of destruction. We looked across a wide valley where once there might have been farms or towns. The valley had become a lake of lava with the odd building poking out of it. In the distance, shattered mountains sputtered and rumbled. There were no signs of life across the devastated landscape. Near the porthole lay a scorched body.

Eleouss collapsed to her knees, sobbing. The Alphan staggered back, waving away the ash that blew into his pristine White Circle. "Take it away, close it, close it, what have you done?"

"I opened the porthole for her, Alphan, but it was Teriquilla who used her Eleouss Stone to merge the world of Oid with a world of fire."

I closed the porthole and the Alphan knelt beside his mate, his hands on her bowed back. "I cannot believe she would do this. The woman is mad."

"She's not the only one," I said. "Your friend, Shragon Bratch, caught up to me on my world. He tried to force me to use the Stone so he could loot the broken worlds."

Eleouss moaned. Oureil continued to stroke her slender shoulders soothingly.

"The power of these Stones is too tempting for some people, Alphan Oureil. They have to be destroyed."

The shimmering walls disappeared, leaving us exposed to the Tuoaueans who had remained gathered around the ring of trees.

"Tend them," the Alphan snapped. "I will return."

As he led Eleouss away, the Tuoaueans took Latiana and me to a lovely grove filled with explosions of the wildest flowers I had ever seen. They brought us water, wine, and a wonderful array of Tuoauean delicacies. We ate and drank and then sat around sleepily, waiting for the Alphan to return.

"Wake up, Audrey." Latiana shook me awake for the third time. "You'd think a girl whose fate hangs upon a Tuoauean's whim would be more alert."

"I didn't get much sleep last night." I yawned so widely my tonsils squeaked, then blushed fiercely.

Latiana beamed her approval. "He's very good, isn't he? Those nimble hands are good for more than just juggling."

Oh, in case you're wondering, yes, we did use protection. Keirt had grabbed them off the floor as we were escaping the drug store, guessing they must be important. Only he didn't know what they were, and I was too embarrassed to tell him, so he blew them up and made some lovely balloon animals. Luckily, I managed to sneak a few before he traded them all away for supplies.

Latiana appeared to be about to launch into a description of Keirt's other talents, so I quickly changed the subject. "Oh, look! Acorns!"

Latiana watched me scrounge a handful of acorns off the ground. "What do you plan to do with all those seeds?"

"If we ever return to Earth, Aunt Ellen will have the most exotic garden in the province." I added the acorns to my already bulging pockets. The Alphan had given me the idea with his remark about stealing seed. "I just hope they can survive our Saskatchewan weather."

"It's you who might not survive, if you're around when the Phoenix tree reaches maturity."

"Why, what happens then?"

"It bursts into flame. And are you aware that when coern seedlings are exposed to water, they give off a poisonous gas? That reminds me. As you were worldhopping with Keirt, I assume you inspected your clothing for seeds and insects of an invasive species that might overrun an entire world?"

I hastily dumped my seed collection out of my pockets. "Um, sure."

"Did you really slay Professor Bratch, Audrey?"

"Well, Tist did, but I helped."

"The foul old sack of wind," Latiana muttered. "I for one won't miss him."

A touch on my elbow startled me. Tuoaueans had been doing that all through our meal; sneaking up invisibly on us, flickering into sight to pat us or peer into our faces, and then disappearing. This one didn't disappear. It was the pyrogin, Keirt's father. He looked distressed.

"Come," he said, politely not bursting into flames. We followed him back to the clearing where the giant had dropped us off. The other Tuoaueans had gathered around a stone altar near the throne. They parted as we approached. A man—pale, battered, and unmoving—lay stretched across the altar.

"Keirt!" I cried.

Shards

I ran to him. His clothes were damp; his face cold. A bloodstained cloth was wrapped around his leg. The invincible Tist lounged on his chest, looking bored.

"Oh my God, what happened to him?"

"We found him on the beach," one of the Tuoaueans said. "What is wrong with him? No son of Tuoaue would fall prey so easily to the small perils of the ocean. The magic in his blood should have protected him."

"He has no magic in his blood. Iron poisoning." I shoved Tist out of the way, put my head down on Keirt's chest, and was relieved to hear a weak heartbeat. Later I learned he had hijacked a fishing vessel, but when the crew discovered he had no magic, they threw him overboard. The Nyshuans had rescued him.

The pyrogin flickered into sight at my side, lightly touched Keirt's face, and vanished, leaving a wisp of smoke behind. Keirt's eyes fluttered open, focused on my face, and slowly closed. A faint smile touched his mouth.

"Audrey," Latiana murmured, jerking her head toward the trees on the far side of the clearing. Eleouss stood in shadow. She motioned for me to follow her.

"Go on," Latiana urged as I hesitated. "He'll be all right. The Tuoaueans will tend him." Latiana glared at the circle of Tuoaueans, daring them to argue.

I kissed Keirt's forehead and reluctantly left him to follow Eleouss. She led me back to the White Circle. The glimmering curtains were gone, leaving only the ring of white trees. I could sense the fault line I had created by tearing open a porthole to Oid.

Eleouss turned to face me. Her face was white as the bark of the trees around us.

"Is it true?" she said without preliminaries. "That woman destroys worlds? Inhabited worlds?"

"She does," I confirmed. "Eleouss, about my friend Keirt—he lost his magic from iron poisoning while we were escaping Migrara. Do you think you could . . . ?"

I trailed off. She had turned away and was staring blankly into space. After what felt like an hour she took my hands in hers and gazed intently down at me.

"I have a gift for you, Audrey." She withdrew her hands, leaving a purple Stone on a chain cupped in my own hands. "This is the first Eleouss Stone ever created. Return to Mount Cauldra and use it against Queen Teriquilla."

My head spun and my fingers turned icy, as if the Stone drew the warmth out of them. "How am I supposed to do that?"

"I do not know. The Stones were never meant to be used as weapons."

"Well, thanks for nothing. I don't even know if I have the power to control this thing. What if I accidentally destroy worlds myself? This is all wrong. You should be the one to confront Teriquilla and her minions." I was becoming more comfortable using words like "minion."

"It must be you, Audrey. You have a warrior's spirit, and companions to help you. Your worldhopping powers are greater than any I have ever known, greater even than my own. I sensed it when I laid my hand upon you."

"Does the Alphan know you're giving me the Stone?"

"The responsibility, and the decision, are mine."

For a creature who appeared to be composed of feathers and air, she had quite the steely look to her. Reluctantly, I slipped the necklace over my head.

"Test the Stone, Audrey. Remove the fault line you created earlier."

I clutched the Stone in a sweaty hand, terrified I would lose control of it and send Migrara crashing into the ruined world of Oid. But when I turned my attention to the Oid fault line, I felt it waver, shrink and disappear. All I'd had to do was think *Go away*. It was easy. I threw a triumphant grin at Eleouss.

She did not smile back. "The Stones are your responsibility now, Audrey."

She turned away from me and opened a new porthole to Oid. I backed away and closed my eyes against the hot, polluted wind that gusted over us. When I opened them, Eleouss had stepped through, and, without looking around, walked toward the lake of sluggish lava. Her gown trailed through a thick layer of ash.

"Eleouss? Where are you going?"

She turned to face me, balancing on the rim of the lava lake. The heavy clouds of ash had turned her a ghostly grey. Her downy hair floated on the hot wind, curling and singeing.

"How many beings were slain by my creation? How many billions of deaths am I responsible for? I can't bear it, Audrey. I can't live with this burden."

"No!" My cry startled birds into flight. "Eleouss! No!"

"Goodbye, Audrey."

The porthole closed in my face. I stared at the empty space where it had been. I tried to open it, but nothing happened. I put my hand over the Stone on my chest. I had felt only a subtle flicker when I erased the fault line, but now

I felt a powerful force at work, an energy like a living thing. I sensed its connection to worlds across the universe. I fell deeper into its magic, tempted by its destructive force, awed by its healing power.

The Eleouss Stone exploded.

"Oh, God," I cried, staggering back. A searing pain pierced my chest, and I fell into darkness.

The first time I opened my eyes, Keirt was kissing my face, and crying.

The second time I opened my eyes, a ring of Tuoaueans stood over me, outlined by a steady red glow. They frowned down at me like neighbours hovering over a barbecue, wondering if the burgers have been cooked long enough.

The third time I opened my eyes, Keirt was running through the moonlit jungle, carrying me in his arms.

"What the hell . . . Where . . . Put me down!"

"Quiet," he gasped. "The Alphan has banished us from the island."

He kicked open the door of a twiggy little hut that had been woven together in the middle of a dense thicket. His father was inside, speaking with two elderly Tuoaueans who had the reddish skin and blue hair of the younger. At our abrupt entrance, the trio simultaneously burst into flames. A moment later they were gone. I sneezed as smoke curled into my nostrils.

"What's going on?" I asked as he placed me on a wooden cot and hastily extinguished the fire the disappearing pyrogins had ignited along one wall. "Eleouss! Is she dead?"

"Don't get up! You're freshly mended and likely to unravel yourself if you don't take care. Yes, Eleouss never returned from the ruined world. The manner of her death was not known at first, but in your delirium you spoke the truth. Those who healed you have informed the Alphan. They say he's maddened with grief."

I too grieved for Eleouss, but I didn't blame myself for her death. It had been her choice to die rather than use her power against the woman who had defiled it. She could just as easily have said, "That bitch! Let's kick her ass."

"We must not allow you to fall into Oureil's hands. As soon as Latiana joins us, we'll leave the island."

"Where *is* Latiana?" I asked.

Keirt paced restlessly around the little hut. "That's what I'd like to know. Earlier tonight she said something about 'stealing seed,' and I haven't seen her since."

I smiled, and pulled him down to sit beside me on the cot. I gave him a kiss, which he returned only briefly. He was tense as a cat. "What about your magic? Did the Tuoaueans give it back to you when they healed you?"

He shook his head. "Don't grieve, Audrey. I've accepted it."

"Then why do you look so . . ." Haunted was the word I was looking for, but you can't go around accusing people of looking haunted, it sounds goofy. "Angry," I said instead. "Are you mad because I left you behind? I'm sorry, it was an accident. I thought you were on the ship."

He pulled me into his arms and held me so tight I could hardly breathe. "It nearly killed you, you know," he said, finally releasing me. "The Eleouss Stone. When it shattered, a shard pierced your heart. The healers couldn't remove it without killing you, so there it will stay until the end of your days. They've spelled it so it will do no damage."

"Oh," I said uneasily, peeking into my shirt at the pattern of faint purple scars between my frontal protrusions. "Well, I guess I can live with a bit of magic shrapnel. But it really sucks about the Stone. I was supposed to use it against Teriquilla."

"Latiana said there are others scattered among overlap worlds. We'll just find another."

The thought of taking on yet another quest made me feel weary. I sighed and leaned against him. "I see you've met your father."

"Yes," he said, but maddeningly, didn't elaborate.

"Does he have a name?"

"Prai Naeryl. The other two pyrogins were my grandparents, Naeryl Vionou and Wrylla Alsamae. They've taught me my name."

"Had you forgotten it?"

"In a formal introduction, a Tuoauean recites the names of his forefathers—or foremothers, for women—to the seventh generation."

"It must take forever to get a meeting started."

"My full name is Keirt Prai Naeryl Vionou Loemicau Ukeoan[17]—oh turtle turds, I've forgotten the last one."

I remembered him telling me pixens couldn't have kids of their own. I took his hand, saddened by the thought that the future would bring no little Keirts.

"You could always adopt," I said.

One of Keirt's many talents was the ability to follow my thought processes without hurting himself. "I've been asked to foster Latiana's child. The Cauldra Cats often rely on foster parents during periods of heavy duty."

I nearly fell off the cot. "Latiana has a kid?"

---

[17] They whipped by too fast for me to catch the pronunciation. All I heard was one long vowel with a few consonants thrown in.

"Not yet. But she vigorously pursues conception whenever the Queen sends her away from the castle."

"I've noticed. She can't find anyone closer to home?"

"The men of Mount Cauldra fear Latiana."

All this talk of reproductive activity was giving me ideas, so I kissed him. He pushed my wandering hands away. "You're in no shape for this sort of thing."

"I'm the perfect shape for this sort of thing." I placed his hands where they could get a better indication of my shape.

The rickety door flew open, and Latiana shouldered her way into the little hut.

"We must depart," she said. "The Alphan hunts the island for us. I have convinced one of the Tuoaueans to coax the giant cliff bats to carry us to the mainland. Will your father provide us safe passage to the beach?"

"Never mind the bats," I said. "I'll just worldhop us to an overlap world."

Latiana looked at Keirt. "You didn't tell her?"

"She was too weak for such a shock," Keirt said, not meeting my eyes.

"Tell me what?" I demanded.

Latiana handed me the walkie-talkie the Queen had given her. Frightened by the look on her face, I hailed Aunt Ellen. "Breaker one-nine, this is Little Ant calling the Big Ant. What's your twenty?"

"Hello, Audrey," Teriquilla said. "Your aunt is currently unavailable. Perhaps you should return to Mount Cauldra and speak to her in person."

Final Exam

As we followed Keirt's father to the beach, I ran rescue scenarios for Aunt Ellen, Kelly, and Bernie through my head. (Prince Nicholas was on his own. It was probably his fault they had been caught. The Cauldra Cats could eat him, for all I cared.) I had yet to find a scenario that didn't result in multiple deaths and endless torment.

"Audrey? What do you think?" Keirt put his hand on my shoulder as we reached the glittering black beach. He and Latiana had been talking to me for several minutes, but I had been in a daze of despair and hadn't heard them.

"Sorry," I said. "I was in a daze of despair. What do I think about what?"

Latiana huffed in annoyance. "About our plan for getting you to Mount Cauldra. We might have the means to travel more swiftly and safely than by wing, wheel, or water."

"*Safely* might be an exaggeration," Keirt said. "But if it works, it's possible we can free Teriquilla's prisoners without having to face her at all."

"As a worldhopper opens a porthole, she instinctively aligns the ground she stands on with the terrain of the over-lapping world," Latiana explained. "In a similar way, a strong worldhopper could shift a fault line *sideways*, allowing her to enter at any point upon the overlapping world."

"It's near to what happened on Delene," Keirt elaborated. "Remember the porthole you opened to the desert? Though the island was slipping away from the fault line, you held the porthole steady. That's a rare talent. If we worldhop to another world, you may be able to align our current location with Mount Cauldra. We could slip into the castle unseen, long before the Queen expects us to arrive."

"Okay, I think I get it," I said, growing excited as their plan took shape in my head. "Let's give it a try."

Keirt's father had been listening quietly to our conversation. He now came forward and showed Keirt a steely blue collar.

"It will deflect the attacks of Tuoaueans," he said.

"This belongs to the Alphan," Keirt said, touching it in wonder. "I can't believe he gave it to you!"

"He did not," the pyrogin admitted, snapping it around his son's neck. Keirt's thieving skills were inherited, it seemed. "Farewell, Lady Oak. Thank you for bringing my son to me."

He and Keirt touched each other's faces with their fingertips; the Tuoauean version of a hug. Then the pyrogin vanished with a flash and a puff of smoke.

I looked at Keirt and Latiana. They stood eagerly awaiting my worldhopping magic, trusting me not to lead us all to our deaths.

"Why these tears?" Latiana demanded. "By the Lioness, I've never seen such a girl for weeping."

"I can't help it," I said, weeping even harder. "I'm no warrior. I'm scared out of my wits."

"What nonsense is this? You need not be fearless to be a warrior. You need only to care enough to do what must be done. And I've never seen such a girl for caring." Latiana gripped my shoulder and gave it a shake; the Quampuish version of a hug.

Keirt said nothing, but gave me a proper version of a hug. I had myself a good cry all over him, then blew my nose and settled down to work.

First we needed an overlapping world to use as a base of operations. I opened a porthole to Earth, forgetting to take a sense of what might be on the other side, and found myself facing an oncoming taxi. It swerved to one side, provoking a riot of squealing tires, honking horns and screaming pedestrians. Judging by the skyscrapers and the chill rain, we had nearly stepped into downtown Vancouver or Seattle. Hastily I snapped the porthole closed.

Keirt and Latiana were staring at me with a peculiar expression on their faces.

"What is it? Is it in my hair? Kill it!" I scrubbed my hands vigorously through my hair to rid it of gruesome Tuoauean pests.

Keirt grabbed my wrists. "It's not your hair. It's your eyes. When you opened the porthole, your eyes glowed. They blazed with many colours. It's the rimfire, the light that swirls around the edge of a porthole."

I didn't know what to think about that, so I decided not to think about it at all, focusing instead on choosing a different overlap world. I picked an uninhabited world with a lush forest filled with fruit trees so we would have snacks for the journey.

"Take it slowly, Audrey," Keirt cautioned as we stepped through and turned to face Migrara through the open porthole. "This technique is not without its dangers."

I tried to remember what I had done to anchor the porthole on Delene. I would have to do the opposite now, I would have to move it.

The porthole shot sideways. Oops, I was moving the wrong side.

"That's interesting," I said. "When the porthole moves, it extends the fault line."

"Yes, provoking earthquakes, if it reaches a great enough length," Latiana snapped, rubbing her arm where the swirling rimfire had stung her as it whipped past. "I told you this was a bad idea, pixen."

"It was your idea, Latiana. She can do it," Keirt said calmly.

I wasn't so calm. Earthquakes? Almost without thinking, I reached out and erased the fault line I had just created. Had I somehow retained that aspect of the shattered Eleouss Stone, or had I held the ability all along without knowing it? I concentrated again on the porthole. The Tuoauean beach on the other side of the porthole slid toward us.

"I'm doing it!" I whooped. "I'm moving Migrara!" This wasn't entirely accurate. I was just shifting the fault line between the two worlds. But my eyes told me I was moving an entire planet.

"A little faster, perhaps?" Latiana said. "At this rate it would be swifter to walk."

The porthole skimmed over the sparkling black sand, through the cloud wall, and across the water. When it reached the mainland about an hour later, we realized this wasn't going to work. It attracted too much attention, a porthole flashing by like that. Also we kept scooping up Migrarans unlucky enough to step in front of the porthole as it whizzed by. The third time a startled Migraran shot through the porthole, only to be thrown back like an under-sized trout by an irritated Latiana, it occurred to me to raise the porthole into the sky and tip it over it so we could see the ground. Not only did we stop collecting Migrarans, we had a much better view of the terrain and could move faster.

As we hurtled across Migrara, I had to throw my concentration behind us as well to mend the breach we were tearing across the world. My head ached from the strain of focusing on two jobs at once. I didn't slow down, even when Keirt begged me to take a break. Our flying porthole was taking us to Aunt Ellen and Kelly. The sooner we arrived, the easier it would be to take Teriquilla by surprise.

"Audrey. *Audrey.*" Keirt hands were on my shoulders. "You can stop now. We're nearly there."

I blinked at him. As the hours passed, I'd fallen into an exhausted trance, barely aware of their directions guiding me to Mount Cauldra.

"Return the porthole to the ground, Audrey," Latiana said. "And reduce its size, if you can. It blazes like a shooting star."

I looked down. I was seated on the ground of the overlap world with the porthole at my feet, a magic pool through which the dark Migraran landscape could be seen slipping away beneath us. In the distance, I could see the lights of the city Cauldroot and Cauldra Castle above it. I lowered the porthole. As we neared ground level, the rimfire flickered and dimmed, becoming lost in the specks that swirled in front of my eyes.

"Quickly, bring her through!" Latiana's voice sounded far away. "If she passes out, the porthole will collapse, and she may not be able to open it again."

I felt Keirt lift me in his arms. When my vision cleared, the porthole was gone, and we were at the side of an empty Migraran road, about an hour's walk from Mount Cauldra.

"You'll have to carry her, Latiana."

Latiana stiffened. "The Cauldra Cats are *not* beasts of burden."

"Oh, don't take yourself so bloody seriously. You used to romp around with the Princess on your back all the time when she was a toddler."

Muttering Migraran obscenities, Latiana handed her sword to Keirt, her clothing to me, and shifted into cat form. With a toss of her head, she invited me onto her back. I had barely taken hold of the thick fur of her neck when she shot forward, her powerful legs launching us into the trees that lined the road. With Keirt running silently behind, we slid from shadow to shadow until we reached the outskirts of Cauldroot. We took refuge in a small barn. The life forms inside voiced complaints at finding a large cat in their midst.

"We'll leave you here, Audrey," Keirt said. "Latiana and I will find Lady Trini and the others. You rest and regain your strength. You'll need it to help us escape."

"No," I said. Now that we were actually here, I realized it wasn't enough to just rescue them and escape. "Bring me with you. I have to get that Stone from Teriquilla. No, I have to do more than that. I have to make sure she never uses it or any other Stone again."

Latiana shifted into human form. "And how will you manage that?"

I threw her clothes at her. Did she *have* to keep appearing naked in front of my boyfriend?

"By letting people know what's going on," I said. "You can go to the Cauldra Cats, and Keirt and I will go to the Mage Hall. Surely some of the mages and worldhoppers will listen to us."

"Yes, and covet the power of the Stone for themselves," Keirt said. "I know of at least a few who would follow Bratch's example. It's a noble plan, Audrey, but it must wait until we remove the Stone from Teriquilla and destroy it."

"And *that* must wait until we find Aunt Ellen, Kelly, and Bernie," I said. "I'm not making any moves until I know they're safe."

"If they're on the castle grounds, I will find them by scent," Latiana said. "But I don't know how we'll travel through Cauldroot and up the mountain unseen. We'd have to fly."

"We *can* fly!" I grabbed their hands as a plan popped into my head. I opened a porthole to the weightless world of the airy hairy life forms and dragged Keirt and Latiana through with me. The light wind immediately swept us off our feet and into the air, where we drifted along the currents.

"We rise, but we do not rise toward Mount Cauldra," Latiana snarled, clawing at the air like a cat dangled over a tub of water. "We have no way of controlling our direction."

"Oh yeah? Watch this." I opened a small porthole to the world that had nearly sunk Captain Sierri's ship. I angled the porthole behind us, and a strong gust of wind sent us sailing across the sky like arrows from a bow. "See? The next time I open a porthole to Migrara, we should be close to the summit of the mountain!"

Keirt was laughing at Latiana's expression. "You're brilliant, Audrey. But how do we know we're approaching Mount Cauldra without opening a porthole and alerting them of our presence?"

"We . . . um . . ." I closed the windy porthole, and we drifted once more.

"Try opening a very small porthole," Keirt suggested. "Enough for a quick look."

My attempt rewarded us with a tiny peek at a wall of dark stone.

"Wonderful," Latiana said. "You'd put us *inside* the mountain."

"No, this is perfect," I said. "The dungeons, remember?"

It took a good hour of trial and error, and at one point I accidentally dumped a load of soil on us, but at last I drifted us into an area that overlapped the underground tunnels of Mount Cauldra. We stepped into a dank corridor, lit only by the rimfire of my porthole. Keirt automatically raised a hand to summon a ball of electric light, then lowered it with a grunt of annoyance at having forgotten his loss.

"Bring the porthole with us." Latiana crouched low, her shoulders tense. She enjoyed confined spaces even less than flying. "To provide light—and escape—should we require it."

"Do either of you know where we are?" I asked as we explored the corridors, the porthole trailing after us. "Are we close to the dungeons?"

"We are close to them," Latiana said, her nostrils flaring, "and they are not occupied. But I do scent your aunt, faintly."

Latiana's nose led us to a stone stairway. The stairway itself didn't smell of Aunt Ellen, but the door at the top did. Judging by the fresh breeze and the light around it, the door led outside. I closed the porthole that had lit our way and raced up the last few steps.

"Audrey, wait!" Latiana cried.

"It's okay," I said breathlessly. "If anyone's with her, I'll just scoop her up into a porthole before they can blink, and then we'll jump through one ourselves."

I flung open the door. It led to the secluded garden where the Queen had first revealed the world of Oid to me. Aunt Ellen sat on the edge of a bubbling fountain, irritably tearing petals off the roses and tossing them into the water. Tiny ducks paddled up to snap at them, then spat them out in disgust. A feisty drake yakked at her in rebuke.

"Aunt Ellen!" I rushed over to her.

She rose to her feet and smiled at me. Her face shimmered. Suddenly it was not Aunt Ellen, but Queen Teriquilla who stood before me.

27

Rimfire

I didn't even stop to think. I flicked open a porthole and cold salt water blasted her ass over teakettle into the fountain. The ducks laughed hysterically.

A wave of pain struck me to the ground, and the porthole to the ocean world collapsed. A ring of Mage Hall professors closed in on me, stern and menacing in their long red robes and tall black boots. One of them, no doubt, had the power to disguise faces. The Cauldra Cats rose from their concealment among the roses. Ranarsha stalked toward me, snarling, and yanked me to my feet.

Teriquilla stepped out of the fountain and regarded me with a scary calm. "You've grown in power since I last saw you. Sadly, you have not grown in wisdom. These are the most powerful mages on Migrara, Audrey, and I would advise you to tread carefully in their presence."

"You don't look surprised to see me," I said bitterly. I couldn't believe all that sophisticated worldhopping had been for nothing.

She shrugged. "I assumed you would board one of the flying craft of your own world and travel swiftly to a city that overlaps Mount Cauldra." Obviously she hadn't been through airport security lately. "Ah, Captain Latiana. Thank you for returning them to me."

Latiana and Keirt came up behind me. While I had been stupidly blundering around getting captured and drawing mage fire, Latiana had slipped a rope through the collar Keirt's father had given him. He groaned and staggered as if in agony, playing the iron-stricken pixen. I wanted to smack them. Why hadn't they run back into the dungeons while they had the chance? I was the one Teriquilla wanted.

Latiana handed the leash to Teriquilla and stepped back with a respectful nod. Keirt stumbled to his knees at the Queen's feet. Teriquilla bent down to stroke his head and opened her mouth, no doubt to offer some mocking comment. I picked this inopportune moment to break into a sneezing fit brought on by the roses. The Queen jumped back. Half the mages whipped toward me, hands outstretched, their eyes wide. The rest, determined not to fall for such an obvious distraction, aimed their lethal fingers at Keirt. The Cats drew their swords. I sneezed and sneezed, and finally the sneezes subsided into sniffles. Satisfied that I wasn't about to shoot a secret weapon out of my nostrils, everyone relaxed.

"Where are Aunt Ellen and the others?" I snuffled. One thing was clear now; the Queen's minions were scared to death of me. This didn't inspire confidence. If anything, I felt even more terrified.

"You will see them when you have proven your dedication to my campaign." Teriquilla gestured to one of the mages, who stepped forward and frowned in concentration. A fine mist rose from the Queen's damp clothes. Within moments, they were dry. "We must find a temporary refuge while the merging of our two worlds takes place. I have selected several overlapping worlds that might prove satisfactory. You will accompany me on a brief tour of these worlds to decide which would best serve as a sanctuary for our people."

The first fault line she led us to lay across the castle's huge outdoor arena. To my astonishment, the arena was packed with spectators. They roared with enthusiasm as the Queen led the mages, the Cauldra Cats, and us onto the field.

"They have come for the tumbleball tournament," Teriquilla explained. "They assume this is part of the games. Open the porthole, Audrey."

I closed my eyes and obeyed. *Ooh, aah,* went the audience. I didn't dare look. According to Keirt and Latiana, my eyes flashed colours each time I used my worldhopping powers.

Teriquilla mistook my closed eyes for emotion. "Try not to dwell on the destruction, Audrey. You should be aware that your world has one fatal flaw—you have allowed your population to swell out of control. At the rate your people are reproducing, they will be wiped out by disease, starvation, or wars over scarce resources. A brief swath of deaths by merging could very well save your world." She held up a hand as Latiana moved toward the porthole. "Latiana, you will remain here until we return."

"My Queen—"

"My dear Cat, I know the look of betrayal when I see it. Captain Ranarsha, I trust you to deal with her appropriately."

Leaving Latiana and the Cauldra Cats in the Migraran arena, Keirt and I followed Teriquilla into an eerily empty city made mostly of glass. At Teriquilla's command I closed the porthole behind us. The mages stayed close, never taking their eyes off us. Keirt moved slowly, his head bowed as if overcome by weakness, but he winked reassuringly at me. I wasn't reassured. Our plans had fallen apart, and now we'd lost Latiana as well. The Cauldra Cats were probably tearing her apart.

The Queen waved a hand at the empty city. "Plague. It killed an entire population of sentient beings. That was many years ago; no traces of the disease remain. Fiuron would make an excellent refuge."

"I'll tell you right now," I said. "I'll go no further with this until you show me my aunt and the others alive and well."

"Very well. If you open a porthole to Migrara, you will find them directly below our feet."

I opened a porthole in the ground, revealing a small chamber of stone laced with iron. The ground below the arena must be riddled with tunnels and prisons leftover from a more barbaric period of Migrara's history. Aunt Ellen, Kelly, Prince Nicholas and Bernie looked up and shielded their eyes against the sudden light. Bernie looked terrible. The Queen had obviously done nothing to treat his cancer.

Their elation at the sight of me turned to dismay when they saw the Queen standing beside me. The mages helped Kelly and Nicholas climb out of the porthole, but Aunt Ellen and Bernie didn't move. Aunt Ellen had a chain around her ankle. The royal bitch had actually chained her to the wall. Oh, crap, that meant I couldn't worldhop her to safety. I fell to my knees and reached down to clasp her hand, my eyes filling with tears.

"I'm sorry, Audrey," she said. "They found us on Jring. I was once on good terms with the director of the Worldhopping Technology Facility. However, old friends aren't what they used to be, especially when a reward is offered."

"You have your aunt, Audrey," the Queen said. "Now you must keep your part of the bargain."

"Teriquilla, enough," Aunt Ellen said. "You can't possibly mean to go forward with this ridiculous scheme."

"Ellen, anyone can see Audrey's world is moving toward war. The merging will put an end to that. Her world's population will unite against what they see as a catastrophe. Surely you agree that a minor degree of geographical upheaval is a small price to pay for world peace."

"They might unite against *us*," Nicholas said. "Have you thought of that?"

"Turn against those who offer them shelter, food and comfort? They will have no way of knowing we were responsible for the merging. They will see us as fellow victims, rising above our own turmoil to lend a helping hand to our new kin."

A wave of weariness swept over me, and I staggered a bit. "How many other worlds do we have to look at?" I asked.

"None. I had already decided on Fiuron." Teriquilla produced an amber Eleouss Stone. "The merging will commence immediately."

"What about the evacuation?" I cried.

"I'm afraid I was not quite truthful about that. It would be impossible to carry out a widespread evacuation without arousing suspicion. Beyond our little circle of friends and family here, there will be no evacuation. Do not fear for the Migrarans gathered in the arena. I've found the heart of a merging suffers the least damage. The islands are at the highest risk, but perhaps that is for the best. Many of their governors have become openly critical of my efforts to minimize contact with overlap worlds."

Teriquilla," Nicholas gasped. "Our people will kill you."

She shook her head. "Once the merging is well under way, I will leave Migrara. Audrey and I will travel from world to world, neutralizing those we find perilous. You were right about that, Audrey. As long as they pose a threat to our people, I can't ignore them. It may take a lifetime, but one day we will return and see our blended civilizations thriving on the powerful new world we have created for them." Her eyes shone with tears. "Until then, you, Perikelli, will rule them. These mages who have proven loyal to me will form your advisory council."

"She will be the daughter of a traitor and a killer," Nicholas said hoarsely. "They will turn against her."

"No, my dear Nicholas. They will turn on *you*. Our people will find it easy to believe you were the source of the destruction." He staggered back from her expression of contempt. "Why do you think I've kept you alive all this time, despite your efforts to turn my own daughter against me?"

"I'll tell them the truth," Kelly shouted. "I don't care if they turn against me."

"Do you care about the wellbeing of Lady Trini and Keirt Prai? I have charged your advisory council with their caretaking. Should you disregard my wishes, they will suffer for it."

An elderly mage stepped forward. "My Queen, my loyalty has limits. I can't allow this."

"You have no choice, Mage Tamrif. Stop trying to interfere, Audrey. Step into Migrara, and open the porthole to your world."

I had been fighting to close the Migraran porthole where Aunt Ellen and Bernie still stood imprisoned. Teriquilla was already using the power of the Stone to hold it open.

"No," I said.

"Mage Flagghin." The Queen nodded at Keirt. The mage who had zapped me earlier raised his hands. Keirt abandoned the stricken pixen act and launched himself at the mage. His look of fierce anticipation turned to shock as a roiling wave of light slammed into him, throwing him to the ground. The Tuoauean collar flared white around his neck. Keirt thrashed and screamed. Instead of deflecting magic, the collar seemed to magnify it.

"Stop!" I screamed. "Okay, I'll do it."

The mage lowered his hands. I ran to Keirt, who lay on the ground, staring blankly at the sky. Tist's head dangled lifelessly out of his shirt collar. A sparkling layer of electricity played over his skin. I tried to brush it away, but to no effect. I thought about opening a porthole and worldhopping him somewhere safe. Mage Flagghin, reading my mind, aimed a warning hand at me. I pulled Keirt's limp, sparkling body against me, trembling. I couldn't, *couldn't* let Teriquilla hurt him again. But I couldn't let her kill all those people either.

"At least bring Aunt Ellen and Bernie out of Migrara first," I said, stalling for time. "Those walls might collapse."

Teriquilla fished a key out of her belt and dropped it into the stone chamber. Bernie helped Aunt Ellen remove the shackle from her leg, then allowed himself to be hauled out of their prison. Kelly and I helped Aunt Ellen climb out. I tried to embrace her, but she grabbed my arms and thrust me away.

"Worldhop, Audrey," she said urgently. "Now! Get as far away as you can. You mustn't concern yourself with us. There is too much at stake."

"I warned you about this, Ellen," Teriquilla sighed, and nodded once more at the mages. Mage Flagghin, with about as much emotion as a man wielding a flyswatter, launched a jagged sphere of energy at Bernie, surely enough to stop his weakened heart.

Quick as thought, I whipped open a porthole between Mage Flagghin and Bernie. The ball of energy whooshed harmlessly into the desert world I had seen on Delene. A second porthole opened beneath the mage. He plummeted out of sight and the porthole swirled shut. I think I'd dropped him onto the world of the grouchy demon-hunting farmers, but I would never be sure, because no one ever saw him again.

There was a moment of stunned silence. "Her eyes!" someone gasped. "She holds rimfire in her eyes!"

"Attack her!" Teriquilla screamed at the mages. "Strike them all down, even the Princess! Quickly, before the girl opens another porthole!"

Lightning burst from their hands. I managed to snap a porthole open to protect me, Aunt Ellen, and Bernie, but

Prince Nicholas and Kelly were too far away. Nicholas flung himself in front of Kelly and was hurled senseless to the ground. The mages circled around me in an effort to clear my porthole shield, while others prepared to blast the defenceless Kelly. The elderly Mage Tamrif was shouting, trying to stop them, but they ignored him. I covered my head with my arms as a swarm of lightning balls converged upon me.

Light blazed all around me, but there was no pain. I was still on my feet. The mages' mouths were hanging open in shock. Bewildered, I looked around. Keirt stood at my side, eyes closed, arms outstretched, absorbing the energy the mages were hurling at us. The sparkling layer of electricity that had been dancing over his skin since Mage Flagghin's attack had intensified to a fierce glow. The mages about to attack Kelly turned on him instead. Keirt glowed even brighter with the strength of the power flowing into him. Then, he opened his eyes and turned it against them.

White light shot in all directions. I felt a shockwave that blew my hair back. The light hurtled into the mages, scattering them across the ground like bowling pins.

"This is impossible," Teriquilla cried. "You should be half dead of iron poisoning! That collar should have shredded your magic!"

"Well, it's not actually an iron collar. It's a rare Tuoauean gift. I misunderstood its purpose. It doesn't deflect magic *away*, it deflects it into the wearer." He smiled at the mages. "You've just made me the most powerful pixen on Migrara."

Teriquilla's grip on the Migraran porthole slipped for just a moment. I seized control of it, tipping it upright, expanding and moving it toward us. The rainbow of rimfire swept over us and suddenly we were all back on Migrara with the Cauldra Cats. A collective gasp arose from the spectators in the arena as they tried to make sense of what they were seeing. An enormous, moving porthole. Prince Nicholas unconscious. Mages struggling to rise from the ground. Keirt still glowing from the force of their attacks.

"How dare you raise your hands against Lady Oak!" he shouted. Tist reared up on his shoulder, hissing. Keirt exuded power and rage, and the mages shrank away from him. "She has risked everything to save your world from the Queen's madness. You should be kneeling at her feet in gratitude. If you have one mote of courage, or intelligence, you will turn against Teriquilla and swear your fealty to Princess Perikelli."

"Our loyalty lies with our Queen," one of the younger mages said.

Kelly had been kneeling beside Prince Nicholas. Now she rose to her feet. "I'm your Queen now," she said, her voice carrying across the arena.

"Stop this, Perikelli," Teriquilla ordered. "I am your mother."

"You had my father killed," Kelly said coldly. "You tortured my friends. You banished me to another world for *ten freaking years*. Do you really think you have the right to call yourself my mother?" And she called Teriquilla a name that drew another gasp from the spectators. Prince Nicholas was right; I *was* a bad influence on her.

"Captain?" Ranarsha looked humbly toward Latiana. Both women were bruised, bleeding and dishevelled. We had missed a major battle. I was pleased to see Ranarsha had gotten the worst of it. The Cauldra Cats stood behind Latiana, awaiting her command.

"What they say is true." Latiana shouted her words for all to hear. "Teriquilla is a traitor to the throne."

The spectators were roiling in their seats, trying to take it all in. I heard someone ask, "Who is that actress playing the Queen? She doesn't even resemble her."

Keirt thrust his hands skyward. Bands of lightning arced across the sky, forming images of Queen Teriquilla, King

Glaem, Prince Nicholas, Captain Drandima, and the world-hopper assassin, Awnvale Worallan. The Migrarans fell silent as Keirt replayed the night of the King's assassination. He did Prince Nicholas the kindness of omitting the reason he had been in the Queen's bedchamber, instead coming into the story at the point where the two brothers were arguing.

"Lies!" Teriquilla shouted. "Someone seize them!"

"No! No seizing," Kelly yelled.

"Audrey!" Keirt whispered. "The Stone!"

I had been staring up at the skyplay in fascination along with the rest of the audience, nearly forgetting the psychopath power monger among us. I whirled toward Teriquilla, opened a porthole, and swept it over her, then over myself. I snapped it closed, and now it was just the two of us, alone on a mountaintop in the heart of the Rocky Mountains. God, my planet was so beautiful. It was hard to believe I had ever considered it a waste of space.

"Look around you," I said. "This is what you would have destroyed. Give me the Stone, Teriquilla."

She didn't even look. "Enhanced, Audrey, not destroyed."

"Come on, Teriquilla. You have no power here, no allies, no hostages. Just give me the Stone, and I'll worldhop you to where you can't do any more harm. I recently sent a whole crowd of Migrarans to a very nice world. I think you'd fit right in with them."

"Do you think my plans have changed because you have revealed them to my people? I care little for what they think of me. I care only for their wellbeing. I will sacrifice anything for them, anything."

I sighed impatiently, shivering. A mountaintop made a nice dramatic setting for a confrontation, but it was fricking cold and hard to breathe. What I would do, I decided, was drop her onto an airless world. Once she was unconscious, I would bring her back to Migrara, take the Stone from her and—

Her arm whipped forward. There was a high-pitched crack. I staggered back, feeling as if someone had whacked me in the chest with a baseball bat. I fell to my knees, staring in disbelief at the blood on the front of my Migraran tunic. Teriquilla stalked toward me, a small, gleaming weapon in her hand. Are you kidding me? A gun? After everything I had been through, she just up and shoots me with a gun? But that's not *fair*.

She thrust the amber Eleouss Stone into my hand as I crumpled onto my side. She gripped my hand in hers, so that we were both clasping the Stone. I felt its power flare, and an answering throb in the shard of Stone lodged in my heart.

"It was foolish of you to bring me to your world," she said. "Open the porthole to Migrara, and we will initiate the merging."

I shook my head and coughed up some blood.

"You have no choice. You will die, Audrey, unless you return to Migrara for healing."

I wanted nothing more than to return to Migrara, to see once more the people I loved. Instead, I opened a porthole beneath us, and we dropped into the ocean world. I thought the shock would make her release me, but she only tightened her grip.

"Very well," she shouted, flinging wet hair out of her face as we surfaced. "If I can't have your world, neither can you."

The porthole above us stretched wide, and wider still, until it expanded into the ocean around us. Cold salt water roared over the mountain top, washing away my blood, the snow, everything. She was going to drown my world. And I was helping her do it, helpless to prevent the flow of power the Eleouss Stone was drawing through me. In moments, the merging would advance beyond our power to stop it.

The frigid water and the wound in my chest drained me of the strength to swim. We sank beneath the surface, and still Teriquilla would not let go. I looked away from her and up through the water, beams of light from the bright winter sky of my world flickering across my face. I stopped trying to pull away from the Eleouss Stone, and instead threw my concentration into it, as I had done on Tuoaue. For once in my life, I experienced no fear, no anger or uncertainty, just pure, sweet focus. There was a surge of power against my hand, and within my heart.

The Eleouss Stone shattered, throwing our clasped hands apart. The smooth swirling motion of the porthole turned erratic. Spikes of rimfire pierced the water, striking all around me but leaving me untouched. Faintly I could hear Teriquilla screaming. The light dimmed as I closed the enormous porthole using the fresh new power surging through me. The merging ceased; the water calmed. With the last of my fading consciousness, I opened one final porthole. A wave of ocean water swept me onto the field of the Migraran arena, into the arms of family and friends.

Practicum

"I can't believe we pulled it off," I said to Kelly. "I can't believe we managed to cram all these people into my little house for Easter dinner."

Prince Nicholas had provided an unspecified roast beast, my cousins Heter and Aildya brought fresh baking, veggies and several bottles of their best Silver Rosé, Aunt Ellen had baked a pie, and I had run out to Safeway to buy Stove Top Stuffing. Our small kitchen was a happy chaos of cooks. Kelly, Aunt Ellen, Heter and Aildya competed for counter space, while I supervised and sampled the pie. Aunt Ellen had gone all weepy, having learned England's Queen Mum had died yesterday at the age of one hundred and one. I found Aunt Ellen's attachment to her suspicious. I'll bet the Queen Mum was a worldhopper too. I could just see her sneaking off to check out the pubs on other worlds. I wonder how many fault lines cross Buckingham Palace?

"So, Your Majesty, should we have ice cream or whipped cream on the pie?"

"Both. And none of this 'Your Majesty' stuff when we're away from the castle, okay?" Kelly said. "Only a year ago you were teaching me to tie my shoelaces."

She smiled with an easy, grown-up grace that often disconcerted me. She had become an intelligent young woman, literally overnight.

"Are you going to miss the house?" she asked. Aunt Ellen had decided to sell our Spadina Crescent house to Bernie, who had moved back to Saskatoon after Keirt healed him of his cancer. Hence the farewell supper.

"Sure, I will. I grew up here, you know. But Migrara is my home now." Specifically, the student residence at the Mage Hall. Some Migrarans thought it a shame that an international hero should live in such humble accommodations, but I had no complaints. I was at school learning an exciting new career, and that was more than I had ever hoped for the day I first left my world.

There was a loud hum, and the lights went off with a bang. We rushed into the living room. Keirt sat on the floor with a dazed look on his face. Across the room, a scorched power outlet spat a few feeble sparks and subsided, smouldering. Latiana and Kelly's personal guard, Sarline, collapsed onto the couch, laughing hysterically. Baub and Bernie, who had been watching a hockey game on TV, glared at Keirt.

"Keirt Prai!" Aunt Ellen scolded. "How many times do I have to tell you to stay away from those outlets?"

"How are we supposed to finish cooking the turkey or whatever it is without power?" I wailed.

"I could cook it." Keirt lit the logs in the fireplace with a flick of his fingers.

"No way. The last time you tried to 'cook' supper, you blew it up."

"I'll check the circuit breaker." Bernie headed for the basement with an air of relief. Being around the two Cauldra Cats made him nervous.

"Where's Uncle Nick?" Kelly asked, and I realized we hadn't seen him for a while.

"Prince Nicholas is behind the house," said Latiana.

"Sneaking a smoke, I'll bet," Kelly said.

She was right. Nicholas stood on our small deck, puffing on a Migraran pipe and sending smoke rings into the frosty March evening. I went out and joined him. He had been one sad and quiet prince since Teriquilla's death. At least, we assumed she was dead, drowned on the ocean world. I had tried to feel bad about that, without much success.

"I told Kelly she ought to invite some of her friends over, and she reminded me that her Earthish friends are in grade one," I told him. "It must feel strange to return to Earth as an adult, and a queen."

"She seems comfortable with both, and we have you to thank for that," he said. "You've made the transition much easier for her."

"You're not doing so bad yourself as Ambassador to the Circling Islands. Thanks to you, their leaders have finally acknowledged Kelly as their ruler. Even the Alphan of Tuo-aue has stopped threatening to secede from Migrara."

"It wasn't difficult. She has earned their respect with her wisdom and compassion."

I thought that was pretty cool. I knew parents who got all freaked out when their teenagers showed signs of maturity and independence. They would practically sit on them in an attempt to squash them back into childhood. To step back and not only watch your sixteen-year-old take over the running of an entire planet, but admire her for it, must take a lot of courage.

Behind us, the lights came on in the house. Cheers arose. The turkey was saved.

"I want to apologize to you, Audrey," Nicholas said suddenly. "For trying to stand in your way while you fought to save my world. For not doing more to help you. I lie awake at night, cursing myself for allowing you to fall into the hands of Shragon Bratch."

"Oh, well, don't worry about it," I said, shivering at the memory of the Bratch's death. Absentmindedly, I opened a porthole to the desert world and let a wave of hot air wash over us. Then, remembering where I was, I hastily closed it, looking around to see if the neighbours had noticed.

Nicholas grinned. "Showing off?"

"My worldhopping instructors would kill me if they saw me do that. The number one rule for worldhopping is 'Thou shalt not attract attention.' In fact, I'm not even supposed to open portholes without supervision."

Not that I had much time to visit overlapping worlds. My first year of Worldhopping Studies included courses in Ecology, Astronomy, Biology, Anatomy, Psychology, and Universal History. In my second year, I would take Self-Defence, Navigation, Cartography, Orienteering, and Wilderness Survival.

Speaking of school, Aunt Ellen and I had come back to Saskatoon shortly after Kelly's coronation to file an appeal of my expulsion. I was finished with high school, of course, but I felt it was important to fight this one last battle. We were pleasantly surprised to find the battle had already been fought. Apparently my expulsion was not only illegal, but also the most recent entry in a long list of school policy violations by Jersicke. She had already been fired.

The director of Migrara's Worldhopping Technology Facility had also lost his job. This was the butthole who had turned Aunt Ellen and the others over to Teriquilla's minions. One of Kelly's first acts upon becoming Queen had been to fire his ass and replace him with Aunt Ellen. I missed her, but once in a while I would use my porthole moving trick and skim across Migrara in the middle of the night, dropping out of the sky to visit her on the island of Jring. She would scold me for violating school rules, but she was always pleased to see me.

"With all you've experienced, one would think you've had all the training you need," Nicholas observed. "*You* should be teaching *them.*"

"Actually, they've asked me to be an instructing assistant." Me, the high school failure!

"The Mage Hall is lucky to have you. Anyone would be lucky to have you." Prince Nicholas turned to me, his expression serious. "I proposed an alliance to you once out of anger, Audrey. Would you accept a second proposal based on respect, and affection?"

My mouth fell open. He gently pushed it closed and kissed it.

"Take it under consideration," he said, and went back into the house.

In a daze, I followed him. Aunt Ellen intercepted me as I entered the kitchen, and shoved something into my hands.

"Bernie brought over our mail today," she said. "This is for you."

It was an envelope addressed to me at our Spadina Avenue address. The return address was St. Andrew's University in Scotland. Who did I know in Scotland? I tore it open. It was a single page with a few handwritten lines.

To Audrey O'Krane:

Well done, and thank you!

Sincerely,
William

I stared at the signature. "Aunt Ellen, when is Prince William's birthday?"

"Twenty-first of June," she said promptly.

I waved the letter in Kelly's face. "I just got a thank you note from the world's most eligible worldhopping bachelor!"

She grabbed the letter, and we jumped up and down, screaming.

"Don't get your hopes up, girls," Aunt Ellen said, scanning a letter of her own. "Charles says Wills is seeing an art history student named Kate."

Keirt had entered the kitchen. He did not seem to share our celebratory mood. "Audrey, may I speak to you *outside?*"

The emphasis on "outside" meant outside of Earth. Uh-oh. I followed him into the back yard and opened a porthole onto a world with a pale lavender sky. Mountains slathered with thick green forest rose around sparkling, clear lakes. Keirt and I called it Heaven, and it was our favourite place to make out. As far as we knew, this world contained no humanoid life forms—not that all non-humanoids lacked the intelligence to embarrass us. I recall one pretty little world we used to visit frequently because of the soft grass in its flowery meadows. We paid no attention to the herds of bovine life forms that grazed the meadow until the day one of them ambled over to us and asked if we could please keep the noise down; she was afraid we might attract predators.

Keirt waited until I closed the porthole behind us before he spoke. "Prince Nicholas claims he respects you, but what he respects is your power and your high status. As does this Prince William of yours, no doubt."

"What high status? I'm just a student!"

Keirt was a student too. Headmaster Tamrif had agreed to teach him how to use his newly enhanced power to its full potential. He could heal people now, and help plants grow, and all kinds of cool stuff. Best of all, he had regained his invisibility ability. This made it easy to sneak him into the women's wing of the student residence after hours. The downside was he had to travel a lot, and I didn't get to spend nearly as much time with him as I would like.

"You helped return Perikelli to Migrara," he went on. "You risked your life to keep our world safe and whole. You hold the hearts of the people, and that means much to Prince Nicholas, who is still trying to find his place at court."

"I promised you we'd sneak away and go worldhopping together during summer break. Do you think I'd be planning a trip with you if I was hot for Prince Nicholas?"

"I know you don't care for him in that way. I'm only warning you against trusting him. As for our journey, I think we should wait until you finish your training. You don't even have your worldhopping license yet."

"That never stopped us before."

"You still have much to learn, Audrey O'Krane."

"All the more reason to get out there and practice." He just folded his arms stubbornly, so I made an appeal to his social conscience. "What about all those fault lines between incompatible worlds that I could be mending?"

"How do we know some of those worlds haven't developed friendships with one another?" he countered. "What about worlds who want to share their knowledge and skills? I don't think it's our place to force peace upon the universe. Let the universe make its own peace."

"Maybe you're right, but don't forget all those damaged worlds out there. You and I could do a lot to help them. My own, for a start."

To be honest, my motives had less to do with repairing the universe and more to do with getting away from our responsibilities and having him all to myself.

"Your world doesn't need help," he said.

"Like hell it doesn't."

"Do you really believe that?"

I thought it over. Earth was still wracked by violence and environmental carnage, but I wouldn't go so far as to say it was a hopeless ruin. The world had undergone a lot of healing since the day we had watched the World Trade Center towers crumple into rubble.

"Maybe you're right," I said, "but—"

Suddenly his arms were around me. "Do you realize how long it's been since we've had a moment alone? Nearly 84.609 hours."

His attempt to distract me was quite obvious and entirely successful.

"Mm," I said. "We're going to miss supper."

"They'll wait for us," he said. "After all, they can't get back to Migrara without you."

"So this is where you and Keirt have been when you come back to Migrara with weeds stuck in your hair," a voice said.

It was Kelly. We'd been so busy distracting each other we hadn't noticed the porthole open.

"Geez, Kelly, how about a little privacy? And how did you follow us? I'm the only worldhopper around here who can open a porthole on an off-solstice day."

"It wasn't me." She stepped aside to let someone else come through.

"Hello, Audrey," Eleouss said.

The last time I'd seen Eleouss, she'd been ashy and singed, and on the verge of flinging herself into a pool of lava. Her appearance had improved considerably since then.

"Oh, hey, hello," I said, hastily repairing my own dishevelled appearance. "This is a nice surprise. I thought you were dead."

"On the brink of hurling myself to my death, I recognized it for the empty gesture it was." Her air of cold sorrow had been replaced by grim determination. "I then travelled from world to ruined world, striving to heal what I could. I felt I must do that much, at least, to make amends for the havoc my creations have unleashed."

"What an excellent idea," I said, shooting Keirt a smug glance. But he wasn't looking at me. He was staring at Eleouss with an expression of dread. He reached out and gripped my hand, as if he thought she might snatch me away.

"When I felt I had earned at least some degree of forgiveness, I returned to Tuoaue," Eleouss went on. "There I learned the Eleouss Stones scattered across the universe have not returned to our world, despite my husband's efforts to retrieve them. This is the new task I have set for myself, to find and destroy the remaining Eleouss Stones. And that is what brings me to you, Lady Audrey Oak. I would ask that you join me in this."

"What, now? But I have classes," I stammered. A brief stint of worldhopping with Keirt was one thing. Dropping everything to run around the universe with an unstable Tuoauean was another.

"I will provide your training. I doubt your instructors even comprehend your potential. I have heard of your accomplishments since we parted. You didn't destroy the power of my Stones, Audrey. You drew it into yourself. With great power comes—"

"Great responsibility," I finished, resigned to the inevitable.

"Eleouss, great power also brings great enemies," Keirt said. "And we speak of a girl who hurls herself into horrendous danger at the drop of a hat. I will help you find the Stones, but Audrey must remain at Mount Cauldra, where she is surrounded by protectors."

"Hang on a minute," I protested. "This is my choice, not yours!"

"Order her to stay, my Queen," Keirt said, appealing to Kelly. "You need her. She has been one of your greatest advisors."

"No, Keirt," Kelly said firmly. "I admit I was scared to death at first, but it's time for me to stand on my own. I've been making my own plans for Audrey, and now I can set them in motion. We know so little of the overlapping worlds. Traditionally, the leaders of Migrara have suppressed that knowledge. Mother was fanatical about it. I, however, think it's time to change the rules. I want to see the Mount Cauldra Library overflowing with books about every world we can set foot on. I want to learn what I can from these worlds to make Migrara a richer place to live. You and Audrey can do that for me."

"You mean . . . you want us to be interstellar spies?" My enthusiasm for Eleouss' quest rose a few notches as the James Bond theme music started up in my head.

"Researchers," she corrected. "I want you and Keirt to explore the universe. Come back when you've learned all there is to know about it."

Tears stung my eyes, and I couldn't speak. If only Teriquilla had been half as wise as her daughter.

Keirt wasn't nearly as impressed. He looked betrayed, and desperate. "Audrey, three months ago you lay dying in my arms. If I hadn't absorbed healing power from one of the mages, we could not have saved you."

"I don't need to be safe; I need to be useful. I can't just sit on this power and let it go to waste. Neither can you, and you know it."

Eleouss looked from me to Keirt. "I will return to Tuoaue to prepare for the journey. When you are ready, join me there."

"You'll stay for supper, won't you?" Kelly said. "We have tons of food, and some great wine from the Trini vineyard. The legal kind, not the stuff with the magic honey."

The porthole closed behind them. Keirt and I turned to face one another.

"At least I'll be far away from Prince Nicholas," I said, trying a different approach. "You never know, that smouldering sexual tension could—what are you doing?"

He had lowered himself to one knee and offered me the hilt of his dagger. "I'm pledging myself to you, as the Cauldra Cats pledge to the Queen of Migrara. You must take my weapon and lay the blade across my head to indicate your acceptance. Stop laughing, please. I'm serious. If we're to undertake this task, I want to know that you don't take it lightly."

I took the dagger from him and slapped it across his head, accidentally slicing off a chunk of his hair. "You know I don't. Just because I might want to have a little fun along the way doesn't mean—"

"I pledge myself to you, Lady Audrey Oak of Migrara." He looked up at me with an intensity that stunned me. "I offer you my protection, my allegiance, and my loyalty. I will serve you with my body, heart and soul until the day I die." He bowed his head and waited.

I felt the usual panic that strong emotions inspire in me, but this time I didn't try to chase it away with a joke. I dropped to one knee so we were eye to eye and said, "But I don't want all that stuff, Keirt. Well, the loyalty, yeah, that would be good. But all I really want is . . . is just you." I shrugged lamely as I handed back the dagger. It wasn't much of a declaration, compared to his eloquent vow.

He took the blade and my hand along with it, pulling me to my feet and into his arms for an eloquent kiss. "Too late," he said. "You already accepted 'all that stuff.'"

"You jerk! I suppose you think you can use this pledge crap to manipulate me. Well, think again, buddy."

He kissed me again without responding. Oh well, what the hell. For the sake of our quest, I could put up with being escorted by the most aggravating, impossible, amazing guy I had ever met.

We lingered a while to take part in our own private little celebration, then hurried back to Earth. We had turkey to eat and worlds to infiltrate.

Acknowledgements

The author would like to thank the following people for their assistance in introducing Audrey O'Krane to the universe: Beverley Slopen, Shangeetha Jeyamanohar, Sheena Koops, Darlene Clarke, and the members of the Bert Fox Community High School Book Club; Daisy, Kelsey, Marina, Chanelle, Victoria and Ciara. Your enthusiasm and hard work carried me a long way. A big hug of gratitude also to family and friends who not only put up with my creative mental absences, but nodded understandingly at my explanation—"Sorry, I was in Migrara."

About the Author

Glenda Goertzen lives in Prince Albert, Saskatchewan. She spent many hours of her youth exploring the Great Outdoors and writing stories about it. As a grown up, however, she pursued a career in video production and broadcasting. After a decade of working a wide variety of multi-media positions, she was suddenly overwhelmed by a desire to be surrounded by books rather than TV screens. Shortly after launching into a new career in libraries, her bestselling children's novel, *The Prairie Dogs*, was published. Glenda now spends her days surrounded by books in various stages of completion.

www.glendagoertzen.ca